KILLING SHADOWS

A DCI JAMES HARDY THRILLER

JAY GILL

To Rita Hopkins

CHAPTER ONE

I was giddy with excitement. I opened the car door for Monica and grabbed a kiss. 'I love you.'

Monica chuckled, 'Love you too.' She lowered herself into the car seat.

After helping her with the seatbelt I closed the door, walked around the car and climbed in beside her.

'Good news,' I said while putting on my seatbelt.

We'd just come from an antenatal check with our midwife, Sally. She'd told us Monica's blood pressure was a little high and that was most likely the reason she'd been getting headaches. She'd keep monitoring her blood pressure, but at this stage it was nothing to worry about.

Monica looked relieved. 'You know, in just a few weeks we're going to be up to our armpits in dirty nappies and bleary eyed from sleepless nights. This is *really* happening.'

I looked down at the bump. Our baby. Then back up at Monica. Glowing. So beautiful. We looked into each other's eyes for a moment then burst out laughing. 'We must be crazy,' said Monica. 'Are we really doing this?'

'We are, and I'm pretty sure it's too late to change our minds now,' I joked.

Monica placed her hands over the bump and caressed it as the baby moved. She spoke softly to our baby. 'Did we wake you up? Your mummy and daddy are having an hysterical moment. We love you, baby. You have two big sisters who cannot wait to meet you. And grandparents who are going to spoil you rotten.'

I started the car. We were going to have lunch at Oriel on the Quay. Just the two of us. Their excellent Mediterranean cuisine has quickly made it a favourite of ours. With hand-painted murals on the walls and views overlooking Poole Harbour and Brownsea Island it's a place we need little excuse to go to when we want to spoil ourselves. I checked my jacket pocket and my heart sank. With all the madness that goes with simply trying to get out of the front door these days I'd forgotten something. Knowing it would be just the two of us and assuming we'd be on cloud nine there was something very important I had meant to bring with me. Trying to hide my disappointment I pretended nothing was amiss. 'Every time I speak to your mum and dad I can tell they can't believe it. I think they'd given up on ever having a grandchild,' I said.

'They know everything has worked out for the best. They never warmed to Scott; I suppose they could sense something I couldn't. When I finally admitted to them how he was they insisted I use any means necessary to get away from him. They were heartbroken to think I was in an abusive relationship. They were scared for me. As much as I've always wanted children I'm so glad Scott and I didn't have any. Children with him was the last thing on my mind.' She sighed. 'Those final years with him and the divorce feel like a lifetime ago. It's as though it happened to someone else, not me. Does that make sense?'

'It makes perfect sense.' I could feel the atmosphere darken. Monica's mood changed when she thought about her time with Scott, his drinking and violent outbursts. I didn't want to lose the joy of the moment and moved the subject back to our baby. I said, 'Baby names. If it's a boy I was thinking Odysseus, Thor or Hercules. I don't mind which.'

Monica chuckled and joined in. 'That's fine. But if it's a girl we're going with Barbarella or Glitter.'

I laughed and nodded in agreement. 'Barbarella Hardy does have a certain ring to it. I like it.'

'So does Odysseus Hardy. That could work.' We both howled with laughter. We chatted excitedly for the rest of the drive and all through lunch about what our new life would be like. It was a wonderful day. Life felt good.

CHAPTER TWO

Detective Inspector Gabriel Rayner pushed the wheelchair up the path to the front door. He found the key and unlocked it. The smell of new carpet greeted him as he pushed the door wide open.

'I can walk from here,' insisted Jenny. 'Don't give me that look. I'm going to walk.' She passed Rayner her bag of medication; antibiotics, painkillers and more. He tucked it under his arm.

'Okay, honey.' Rayner crooked his elbow and Jenny used it to pull herself upright. She stepped carefully over the front step. They moved slowly through the bungalow, peering into each room.

'You're doing great.' As she winced Rayner could see the pain in her eyes. 'This is the living room. There's a seat here by the patio doors. I thought you'd like it. You can watch the birds in the garden. There's a lamp so you can read. A coffee table for the TV remote, magazines. It has a drawer for your painkillers. Behind the chair I had a plug point put in so you can keep your mobile phone and your Kindle charged. There's also a small heater I bought for when the days are a bit nippy.'

Jenny eased herself into the armchair. Rayner grabbed a soft grey throw from the footstool beside Jenny's armchair and placed it over her bandaged legs.

'You've thought of everything,' said Jenny. 'It all looks nice.'

Rayner put the bag of medication on the coffee table.

'You like the place? I know it's not home, not yet, but we'll make it ours. We can rent out the west London house until we're ready to move back. It won't be long – as soon as your burns are healed properly and there's no danger of infection. The physiotherapy is going to help too. You'll be back to running rings around me in no time.'

A tear ran down Jenny's cheek, she swiped it away but it was quickly followed by an uncontrollable flood.

'Hey, Jen. What's wrong?' Rayner knelt down, and put his huge arms around her. He pulled her to him. Kissed the top of her head and dabbed the tears away. 'What is it, baby?'

'It's everything. Our life as we knew it is over. We had it all. A baby on the way.' She shoved the bag of medicine off the coffee table. 'Who knows what these are doing to the baby.'

'It's okay,' said Rayner.

'It's not okay. We've lost everything. We had great jobs. A lovely house. Wonderful friends. I should have known it wouldn't last. Nothing good ever does.' She rubbed her eyes with the grey throw then pulled it up to reveal her bandaged legs. 'Look at me. I can barely stand on my own two feet. I can't sleep without nightmares. How am I going to look after the baby when it comes? And how can you love me like this? I can't even look at my own body any more. How can you stand to look at me? Everything we dreamed of is gone. I'm not the same woman you married. I'm not me any more. When James and Monica's house burned to the ground the life we dreamed of went up in smoke, and me with it. None of this is okay. Can't you see that? It's all over.'

Rayner stroked Jen's hair, soothed her and let her cry it out. He fought back his own heartache as he held her. After a while he said, 'I love you. That hasn't changed. I'm sorry this happened to you. Not a day goes by when I don't wish I'd got back to the house sooner or fought harder to get you out, or better still, never left you alone in the house in the first place. There are so many things I would change if I could but I can't. If I could have the scars and pain instead of you I would, without hesitation. You have to understand you're still my Jen. I love you more today than ever. You're the strongest, bravest and most beautiful woman I've ever known. When I look at you I don't see those scars. They mean nothing to me. I see you. You, my Jen. The whole person. Your loving and generous heart, your amazing laugh when I tell a bad joke, the fact that you scare me when you're cross.' Jen cracked a grin. 'You're a part of me Jenny Hot Lips. I'm nothing without you. You're my girl.' Rayner gently held her chin and kissed her again, this time on the lips. He could taste the tears. He looked into her eyes, chuckled and winked.

Jenny smiled back. 'You big softy. I don't deserve you!'

'Everything is going to be fine. You'll see. The burns hospital here is one of the best in the country. The most important thing right now is to get the best treatment, continue the physiotherapy and keep a positive mind-set. When you're up to it, we'll move back to London. So no more tears. You look after yourself. And this baby of ours.' Rayner put a hand on Jen's tummy. 'That bump is getting bigger.'

'It sure is,' said Jen. She put a hand to Rayner's cheek. 'I love you Gabriel Rayner. You're a good man. You've been amazing. I don't know how I can ever repay you for everything you've done.'

Rayner began to chuckle his naughty laugh. He raised an eyebrow up and down a few times. 'I can think of a few ways.'

Jenny pushed him away with a giggle. 'Get out of here, you great fool.'

'I'm joking,' said Rayner. He raised his hands in protest. He was relieved to see her laughing again. 'I'm just kidding. You can't blame me for trying. You do make a very sexy patient. How about I carry you to the bedroom and give you a bed bath?'

Rayner's mobile phone started to ring.

Jenny took another playful swipe at him and he jumped back to avoid it. 'Maybe another time. Right now you'd better get your phone. I'll give you one guess who it is.'

Rayner pretended to look disappointed. He took the call and at the same time mouthed, 'Tea?' Jen nodded and he headed to the kitchen to put the kettle on.

The caller was Hardy. 'I'm sorry to bother you today of all days,' he said.

'That's okay. What's up?'

'Another family has been targeted. A family with twins. We need to get over there. I'll text you the address. I'm not asking you to come right away. Get there when you can.'

He felt his fist tighten. 'Two boys?'

'Afraid so.'

'Parents?'

'Whole family. Just like the others.'

'Okay. It's no problem. I'll make sure Jen's settled in and set off as soon as I can.'

'Sorry. Give Jenny my love.'

'Will do.' Rayner hung up and waited for the address to

come through. When he looked around Jen was standing at the kitchen door. She held onto the frame to steady herself. 'If you need to get going, leave the tea. I can make my own. I need to be able to look after myself. You have a job to do.'

Rayner took a cup from the cupboard and dropped in a teabag. 'You're what's most important.' He waited for the kettle then poured hot water into the cup.

'You've also got to keep working,' said Jenny.

'It's another family with twins. It could be the same guy. James must think it's likely, to have called me today when he knows you're just out of hospital.'

Jenny winced as she moved; she held onto the fridge freezer to steady herself.

'How can I leave you like this? What if you fall?'

'I'm not going to fall. And I'm not asking. I'm telling you to go. Now shoo!' Jenny flapped her hand to get Rayner out of her way and out of the small kitchen. 'Go on, get out, you great lummox.'

Rayner moved behind her, his huge frame filling the doorway as he watched.

She opened the fridge and took out the milk. Sliding the container along as she went she gripped the worktop with her free hand and inched along, carefully putting one foot in front of another. She placed the milk next to the teacup. Reaching the drawers she opened them in turn until she found the cutlery drawer and took out a teaspoon.

'Will you go? I'll be fine. Go!'

Jenny took over making the tea as Rayner hunted around the lounge area wondering where he'd left his car keys. 'They're here, on top of the microwave, Detective Inspector.' She dangled the keys.

Rayner reappeared. He held out his hand. 'Thank you. I'll see you later.' He gave Jenny a peck on the cheek. 'Are you sure you don't need a bed bath before I go?' He ducked in case she took another swing at him.

'Goodbye,' said Jenny. She called after him as he headed for the door. 'And I don't need you calling me every five minutes. Go do your job.'

CHAPTER THREE

Detective Inspector Emma Cotton zipped up her tracksuit top. She opened the back door of her red Ford Focus and dropped her gym bag onto the seat. She climbed into the driver's seat and put the key in the ignition. As she closed the car door she noticed the red envelope.

Her heart sank and a sick feeling returned to the pit of her stomach. Leaning she snatched the envelope tucked under the windscreen wiper. Looking around the car park for someone watching, she closed the car door and flicked the central-locking button on the console.

The colour, shape, size, weight and style of envelope, as well as the way her name was handwritten with a heart at the end, were all familiar. Without reading the card inside she opened the glove box and tossed the envelope inside with the other two. 'Fuck,' she mumbled. She thumped the steering wheel with the side of her fist.

During the drive home questions circulated in her mind. The break-up with Alex had happened nearly a month ago and she knew she'd been clear it was over. Hadn't she?

He had seemed accepting when they'd had the conversation. He appeared to agree they weren't completely compatible, and they'd be better off if the relationship ended now rather than dragging on. Yet he was still in her life.

It was when she realised she had been reluctant to go home of an evening because he'd be there that she knew they were no longer suited. He was attractive, great in bed and financially successful but he was hard work to be around.

He could be jealous and petulant. At first she'd wondered whether she had been silly to end it. In so many ways he was perfect, but he caused her anxiety. He'd make a compliment and lace it with a criticism or disapproval. Be moody if she was late for a date. It sounded like a pathetic reason to end a relationship with someone perfect in so many other ways. She realised she wasn't getting any younger and could be a real bitch herself. Who was she holding out for? Mr Right? Surely he was a girlish fantasy.

Why was she questioning her decision?

It seemed Alex didn't want to let go. She'd have to call him. Make it clear they were over. Yet she was reluctant to do so. Not because she felt wrong about ending the relationship but because she really didn't want to speak to him. He didn't make her feel good about herself.

Emma left the sports-centre car park and headed home. She switched on the car stereo and tried to clear her mind by singing along. As she reached a set of traffic lights the song changed to one she recognised. She thought it might be Gary Barlow. She cranked up the music even louder and moved her body to the beat, swaying from side to side.

The traffic lights turned green and the car in front, a learner driver, the car emblazoned with driving school branding, started moving slowly before it juddered to a halt and stalled. Recalling her own early driving efforts Emma smiled to herself in sympathy and put her handbrake on. *No rush*, she thought. *We've all got to learn.*

A car horn blared. Twice. Emma checked her rear-view mirror then turned in her seat to look out the back window to see which idiot had tooted.

Only her lane wasn't moving. The cars in the lane to her left moved freely and came to a stop as the lights changed from green to red. As she turned back to see how the learner was getting on, her eyes fell upon the driver in the car beside her, a white sporty looking Jaguar XF. It looked familiar.

Emma stiffened and looked forward. With only the slightest movement of her head she moved her eyes left. It was him. Alex. It seemed he hadn't noticed her. Then, his head turned and his eyes fixed on hers, he smiled and waved.

Emma felt the back of her neck prickle. She forced a smile, waved politely. *He's probably got a day off. This is a coincidence; his dental practice is the other side of town.* Then she remembered the card on the windscreen.

She looked at the learner driver in front her. 'Move,' she murmured. 'Get out of the way.'

The lights changed to green. The learner started moving. Emma kept close behind as they turned right. She shot a look back at Alex as she pulled away. He was watching her. He turned his hand into a phone using his thumb and pinky finger and mouthed *Call Me*.

Emma turned onto the straight road. She accelerated and pulled out to pass the learner. Crossing into the lane of oncoming traffic, she caused an oncoming car to swerve. She kept her foot down all the way home.

By the time she arrived she had calmed down but was in a bad mood. She burst into the house and threw her gym bag onto the kitchen worktop which startled Watson, her cat. Tail in the air he ran to the back door where he watched her from a safe distance.

A knock at the front door made her jump. She went to the window and, pulling the curtain aside, peered out. To her relief it wasn't him.

'What now?' she muttered to herself as she opened the front door. She forced a smile. 'Declan, how are you? How's your mum? Is she recovering okay? I keep meaning to pop around and say hello.' Despite her mood, his own happy disposition couldn't help but put a smile back on her face. She couldn't ask for nicer neighbours. His mum baked for her and Declan was always offering to mow the lawn or do any number of odd jobs.

'Mum's okay, Emma, thank you for asking. Are you okay?'

Emma nodded, she realised she must look flustered. 'Are you here for the plate? Come in for a second, I'll grab it.' She disappeared into the kitchen.

Declan took a step over the threshold but remained at the front door, as it seemed the polite thing to do.

She called from the kitchen as she grabbed the plate off the worktop. 'The banana loaf was delicious but really, there was no need.' She was being polite; she'd be happy if the cakes arrived twice daily. Emma passed him the plate.

'Thank you. The other reason I popped around is because I'm having a birthday party at the house and there'll be some music. It won't be too loud, my friends and I aren't that sort, but I wanted to let you know.' He looked at her apologetically. 'I hope you don't mind?'

'That's no problem. If you can't let your hair down on your birthday when can you?' She noticed for the first time how Declan was no longer the lanky teenager she'd always seen him as, but a man. He'd grown up and matured. He was handsome too. His chest and shoulders were broad and filled his shirt nicely. He held himself with confidence. His eyes shone and his smile was warm and inviting. He looked great. She shook the thought away.

'It's this Friday night. I'll make sure it doesn't go on too late. I know you work odd hours.' He turned to leave but turned back. 'In fact you're very welcome, if you'd like to come. If you're not working, that is? Some food, drink and music, nothing crazy, I promise. It's just a few close mates. Mum's away with a friend. I bought her a Spa weekend.'

Emma was caught off guard. She hesitated and fumbled her words.

'I'm sure you're busy,' said Declan.

'You know. I'd love to. If I'm free that is. Just a quick drink.'

Declan's face lit up and Emma found herself smiling along with him.

Behind her Emma's phone rang. 'Duty calls,' she said. It sounded like a lame cliché.

'Okay,' said Declan. 'If I don't see you before, perhaps Friday.'

'Perhaps Friday.'

Emma closed the front door and ran to her gym bag. She realised she was still smiling as she rooted around and pulled out her phone. It was Hardy.

'Yeah, I'm fine. Little out of breath? Yes, I've been for a run,' she lied. 'Oh, my God. Yeah, okay. Give me the address. I'll be there.'

CHAPTER FOUR

Too loudly, the gravel of the long driveway crunched under the wheels of the car. Like soulless eyes the upstairs windows of the Poulson family home watched over me as I approached. On the front lawn the skeletal shape of soccer goals stood empty, nets hanging like monstrous spider webs. Two bikes lay abandoned behind the net nearest the house.

On any other day a casual observer might say the modernised white-walled thatched farmhouse, adorned with rambling roses, wisteria and hanging baskets looked like the essence of an idyllic country home. Today, the police and forensic activity suggested something far more sinister. It was now somewhere evil had laid its bony hand and cast a shadow of murderous barbarity.

My legs shifted reluctantly as I opened the car door and stepped out. Visiting crime scenes of this nature never got any easier. Dead children. Butchered for reasons no sane mind could ever comprehend.

I stretched my neck and heard it click, my body felt stiff. Due to heavy rain on and off, the journey to Burley in the New Forest had been a grim, arduous drive. Gathering my thoughts and getting my bearings I stood by the car and looked around. As clouds parted and sunshine broke through it offered a moment's respite from the crisp breeze of the late afternoon that felt sharp on my skin. In the distance, darker clouds loomed and I anticipated we'd soon receive the rain that had pursued my journey.

In a large paddock beside an outbuilding, a bay horse watched the forensic team. Two family cars, a dark blue VW Passat estate and white Range Rover Vogue were undergoing forensic examination.

I grabbed my suit jacket from the back seat. The cackle of a crow hunched on a low wooden fence sent a shiver down my spine. Its rattling call was like grotesque laughter, seemingly mocking the dead. I slammed the car door, expecting the bird to skulk away. Instead, it opened its wings and dropped closer, its head tilting as an inquisitive black eye followed me. I ignored it and made my way to the house.

On seeing me, my good friend, the man-mountain, Detective Inspector Gabriel Rayner, broke away from an officer he was talking to outside the front door. I'd meant to arrive before him but had pulled over on receiving a call from my boss Chief Superintendent Webster at New Scotland Yard.

Stepping over a low boxwood hedge Rayner strode across the lawn towards me. He waved a thick arm above his six-foot, five-inch frame to get my attention. Realising he was getting his shoes wet on the grass, he did a little side-stepping dance to get back onto the path. He reminded me of a grizzly bear doing a cha-cha.

'What took you so long?' said Rayner. 'You drive like an old man these days.'

'The chief super, he called; they're sending a team from the Yard. They'll be here soon.'

We started walking back to the house.

'How's Jenny?'

'A few tears, unsurprisingly. But she's pleased to be out of the hospital,' said Rayner, unable to hide his delight. 'Nurses and doctors were brilliant, but you know how it is. It gets to a point where you want to get out of the place.'

'That's brilliant.' I rested my hand on my friend's shoulder and squeezed it. 'That's the best news. As soon as you're settled in Monica would like to visit, if that's okay?'

Rayner's eyes brimmed. He cleared his throat and said, 'Yeah. Of course.' He spoke as though he was emptying his mind of his concerns. 'As we were leaving the doctor repeated that her burns were healing better than he could have hoped for. But it's difficult. It's going to be tough for a while yet. You know all this; I don't know why I'm going on.'

'What did she think of the bungalow? Got everything you need?'

'She likes it, I think. We've got the essentials. I still can't believe how much cheaper renting down on the coast is compared with London. I'm happy with the place.'

Standing in front of the farmhouse we paused for a moment, then Rayner turned his attention to the crime scene. 'Inside. It's bad. Even worse on the lawn at the back of the house. A family of four. Mum and dad, Elizabeth and Ryan Poulson and their twin boys, eleven years old; Jake and Gregory. The boys are of similar age to those of the other three families. It's brutal.'

'What's it been, four months since the last family?'

'Yes, four months. Ten months between one and two, the time between each family is getting shorter.'

Rayner put his mouth close to my ear. 'Watch out. Incoming. He's been keen to speak to you.'

A short grey-haired man was making a beeline for us. He carried quite a bit of weight around the middle, and his ill-fitting suit hung off him as though he were shedding it like a skin. I guessed he must be in his early sixties, but his grey, haggard face with deep furrows and exhausted eyes, suggested he could easily be mistaken for a man in his late seventies. 'This the lead detective?' I said.

'Uh-huh. He's old-school. Serious crimes,' said Rayner out the corner of his mouth. 'He took a call from the chief super and I don't think he was best pleased. His name is Swann, with a double en.'

I put out a hand to Detective Chief Inspector David Swann, his firm grip sending a message. 'You must be DCI Hardy?'

'DCI Swann, pleased to meet you. I'm sorry to be intruding in this way.'

'I've spoken with your Super; I want you to know you have my full support. Chief Superintendent Webster explained the role of your team and your experience dealing with cases of this nature. Excuse me, end of cold.' He took a handkerchief from his trouser pocket and blew his nose. 'I know we all agree catching this bastard is the priority. There'll be no dick-measuring from me, if you get my meaning. Your woman, Hampton or Hampshire.' He wriggled his nose and sniffed.

'Heidi Hamilton,' I corrected him. 'She's my forensic officer.'

'When she first arrived, I hadn't been made aware of your team, and your unusual situation. I'll admit we did exchange words.'

Hamilton is all about the victim and I know for sure if Swann had stood in her way and there was a disagreement, she would have given as good as she got, regardless of his rank. 'I appreciate that. What can you tell us?'

'Not a lot at this point.' Swann rubbed the back of his

neck. He was sweaty and looked like he still had a temperature.

'The boy's dismembered bodies were discovered by a couple of their friends. They found the boys about ten-fifteen this morning. They called around to play, seems they all play football together on the front lawn. The two friends are being looked after and treated for shock. We'll get statements from them when they're up to it.' Swann's hand moved to his tie which he loosened, stroked and patted. 'They should never have seen something like that. It's a blood bath. Each child cut into six pieces.' His voice wavered as he spoke. He shrugged his shoulders. 'What can I say? I've been in this job a long time. I've seen terrible things. Never anything like this. Not with kids. Nothing so vile.' He rolled his neck and thumped his chest with his fist. He huffed and puffed. He unbuttoned his top button, loosened his collar. 'Indigestion. Feeling a bit light-headed. I'm five months off retirement. Not sure why this one's got to me the way it has.'

'It happens, sir,' said Rayner. 'Some cases push our buttons more than others.'

'We've all been there,' I agreed. 'Take a step back for an hour, give yourself some distance. Walk it off or go for a drive.' I made a mental note to speak to Swann later about counselling. A lot of the old-school officers refused to talk, even confidentially, about their feelings. Bottling it up isn't good.

'Either of you smoke? I could really do with one right now,' said Swann.

We both shook our head.

'Would you mind if I take a look at the bodies?' I asked.

'Be my guest,' said Swann, absently. 'Parents are in the house. Kids around the back.' He turned to Rayner. 'I'm going to take a walk. See if the forensic team have come up with anything useful. I think this bloody cold is coming back, I'm feeling pretty lousy.'

Over Swann's shoulder I saw Heidi Hamilton; she'd seen us and was beckoning me over. I excused myself and left Rayner and Swann to speak to the forensic team.

CHAPTER FIVE

Heidi Hamilton's big brown eyes shone as we greeted each other for the first time in what felt like decades. Her long brown curls were in a bun. 'It's good to see you again, Heidi,' I said. 'Thank you for taking a look.'

Heidi ignored the hand I'd offered to shake; she put her arms around me and hugged me. Once she released me, she could see the concern on my face. 'Never mind them,' she said, not bothering to look around. 'When have I ever cared what other people think?' Looking me up and down, she said, 'You look different. Healthier. Younger. You must be happy. I'm pleased.'

I looked towards the scene. 'Now we're working together again, we need to find time for a proper catch-up.'

'Okay, got it, enough chit-chat.' Feeling a few spots of rain we both looked up at the clouds that were almost overhead. Hamilton put on the knee-length rain jacket she had slung over her arm. 'The poor babies are this way.'

We walked towards the scene and the forensic tent. Inside the tent the grass was heavily blood-stained, most of the initial blood loss had soaked into the lawn or been washed away by overnight rain. Body parts were carefully collected, bagged and labelled ready for the lab.

'Cause of death?'

'Signs of blunt force trauma to the back of the head.' Hamilton touched the top of her head to indicate where. 'One small blessing is that they were very likely dead before he went to work on them.'

Through a clear biohazard evidence bag containing a leg, I pointed to grass cuttings on the top of a foot and lower leg. The sole of the foot was dirty and grass stained. 'You think he walked them out of the house?'

'Probably. Other than the parents', I saw no blood inside the house to indicate the attack on them took place indoors. It would make sense to walk them out. Much more so than carrying them. The question is why outside? He never did this outside before.'

'My thoughts exactly. Any ideas?'

She shook her head. 'I'll let you figure that out.'

'You feel sure it's the same killer?'

'I'd say so. Family with twins. Parents bludgeoned to death while they slept. The twins cut into six parts with a hacksaw: head and limbs separated from torso.'

We stepped outside the tent. I lowered my voice. 'And the other thing? Did he leave it?'

'Yes. Dice in the right hand of each boy. And just like before the sides of the dice scratched out except for number six. Yeah, it's your killer's signature.'

My neck prickled when Hamilton said *your killer*.

'I'll be attending the post-mortem,' continued Hamilton. 'As agreed with Webster, you'll receive my report alongside the official one. We'll arrange a sit-down, go over what I have once it's complete. It'll be easier if I come to you. I'll call you when I'm ready.'

'I'd appreciate that. Since the house fire Rayner and I

are working out of a secure home office at my mother's place. I also have a fresh recruit, DI Emma Cotton. She's transferred to the team from Dorset Police.'

As we spoke Cotton came bounding around the side of the house. Hamilton looked at me and chuckled. 'This her?'

I nodded.

'She's young,' said Hamilton. 'Or am I getting old?'

'She's young.'

'You always know how to say the right thing,' said Hamilton with a wry smile.

'She's tenacious and talented. Just don't tell her I said so.'

'Your secret is safe with me. Look, I've got to go. Introduce me to Cotton another time. I'll get your report to you quicker than is humanly possible, as usual. And any questions, call my mobile.'

As Hamilton left me. I was joined by Cotton, and Rayner shortly after.

'That was a hell of a drive. What have I missed?' said Cotton.

I nodded towards the twins. Cotton took a peek inside the forensic tent. The colour had drained from her face when she returned.

'Rayner, see what you can learn here. Cotton and I will go to the house. I've a feeling that just like the other scenes we won't find much that'll help.'

Cotton looked puzzled.

Rayner said, 'When a killer has mastered their craft the chance of catching them through traditional means is slim. No forensics or witnesses. They don't make mistakes. It means we either wait to get lucky, and that's not much of a plan, or we look at the victims and examine what links them to each other and how they all link to the killer.'

'It means we have a lot of work to do,' I said. 'And not much time to do it.'

'How long do you think we've got?' said Rayner.

'He's satisfied for now. Whatever motivates this sick bastard will soon begin filling every waking moment until he has no choice but to do it again. We don't have long.'

'That's fine. We go over everything we have so far,' said Cotton. 'We'll start with what ties this family to the other families. If the answer is there, we'll find it.'

Rayner grinned.

'What?' said Cotton.

'Nothing. I couldn't have said it better myself. That's what happens when you hang around this fella.' Rayner pointed at me with his thumb. 'It's Hardy-osmosis.'

'Enough. Let's get on with it,' I said. 'Assume nothing. Look at everything with fresh eyes. Don't accept what anyone else tells you as fact. Look for yourself then look again. Don't miss something because you made an assumption. All we know right now is he's focused and his need is controlling him. He's already fighting and losing to the urge to do this again; that fact might make him sloppy. If we're lucky.'

Behind us there were raised voices and shouting. The three of us ran towards the commotion. A crowd had gathered close to the front lawn. An officer who had been administering chest compressions stood back as another began with a defibrillator retrieved from their vehicle. A voice in the crowd whispered to another, 'It's Swann. Cardiac arrest. It's too late. He's gone.'

CHAPTER SIX

Back at the makeshift office in the converted garage of my mother's home the black pen squeaked, its fumes filling my nostrils, as I wrote the names Ryan, Elizabeth, Jake and Gregory Poulson on the whiteboard on the back wall of my office. Below the names I taped a family photo, the four of them full of smiles in front of Cinderella Castle at Disney's Magic Kingdom. I turned to look at Rayner and Cotton who were talking and sipping their morning tea and coffee.

'What a shit way to go. Five months off retirement,' said Cotton.

'Front lawn. Scene of a quadruple murder. Poor bugger,' said Rayner.

'Only young.'

'Yep. Not even sixty.'

'Christ.'

'Had plans to go on cruises. See the world with his missus.'

'Poor woman. She must be in bits. Heard anything about the funeral?'

'No. You?'

I waited as long as I could for an appropriate moment to

interject. 'Mrs Swann wants a small, private, strictly-family-only funeral. Word is, she'd predicted the job would kill him, and she feels it did.'

'More likely it was years of smoking and full English breakfasts,' said Rayner. 'I reckon the only greens he ever ate was the lettuce in a BLT.'

Cotton looked at him open-mouthed. I shook my head. Rayner's sensitivity filter was way off these days. I assumed it was caused by the pressure he was under at home; saying things he never used to.

'Don't look at me like that you two; I'm only saying what everyone else is thinking.' He realised he'd overstepped the mark and I let it slide.

I went back to the whiteboard and drew lines from the pictures of each murdered family that surrounded the edge of the board to a huge question mark in the centre. 'Rayner knows this case better than anyone. Until recently he was part of the Scotland Yard team heading up the investigation of the first murder in Croydon.'

Rayner took over. 'Since then there have been murders in Dorset and the neighbouring counties of Hampshire, Wiltshire and Somerset. The feeling is this killer is most likely based locally but is trying to make it look like he's not. Our team had no breaks in the case, few leads and no suspects.'

I took over again. 'While that team continue their work we've been tasked with exploring the case ourselves. We'll come at it with a fresh perspective. We'll be supplied copies of their case files, forensic reports, anything we need. We'll have very little contact with the Scotland Yard team directly. We are not in competition, it's a joint approach; there will be a flow of information back and forth. We'll share our findings and they'll do the same.

'What we shouldn't do is slow their progress by

bombarding them with questions while we catch up. Our team, the three of us in this room plus forensic pathologist Heidi Hamilton, will investigate independently. We're tasked with examining new angles and alternative possibilities. I consider it vital, imperative in fact, we are not influenced by Scotland Yard's findings. We wipe the slate clean and come at this case our own way. We analyse the data we're provided and run our own investigation from the ground up. We draw our own conclusions. As a small team we're going to need to work hard and fast. We're not going to have all the resources afforded to Scotland Yard but the benefit is that as a small team we can be nimble, responsive and we don't have anyone second-guessing our decisions or theories or breathing down our neck. For the most part we're going to be left alone to do what needs to be done. Does anyone have any questions?'

'On a purely practical note, am I working for Dorset Police or the Metropolitan Police?' asked Cotton.

'Scotland Yard are funding this so for the time being you're on loan to the Met. A bit like a star player on loan to another team.'

Rayner winked at her. 'Hear that? You're a star player. Shall I call you Messi, Ronaldo or Neymar?'

Cotton blushed. 'I'm not sure who they are. I'm guessing they're footballers?'

Rayner shook his head in dismay. 'You're having me on, aren't you? Yes, they're footballers. Am I the only one in this room who knows anything about the beautiful game?'

'Is this a one-time gig?' asked Cotton.

'I don't know for sure. This is a trial run. If we're successful and add value I'm led to believe there will be other cases,' I said, honestly.

After a moment of silence I added, 'If either of you want out now is the time. I think we have an opportunity to do some very special work here but I understand this might not be the career move you had in mind. This team can only exist if we deliver results.'

I handed Rayner the pen and took his seat. 'If there are no objections, let's get started,' I said. Then added in a sombre tone, 'Hamilton called me last night. The serration marks on the Poulson boys are a close match to those on all the other twins. It's safe to say it was the same hacksaw. She's also as sure as she can be it was the same hammer.'

As he spoke Rayner pointed to each family in turn.

'This is the Anderson family. Parents Tom and Kelly Anderson, twin boys ten years old. No other siblings. All bludgeoned to death at their home in Croydon. This was the first attack, and from what we believe took place, the most unsophisticated. We gather the killer started with the boys. Their skulls were cracked open with a hammer. The father was found in the hallway and it is believed he woke during the attack on the boys and possibly went to investigate a noise or disturbance. It's probable there was a struggle where the killer and father fought before Mr Anderson was overcome and beaten to death in the hallway with a hammer. Mrs Anderson was found in the downstairs kitchen. It is believed she was trying to escape the assailant. Again, hammer blows to the head and body. Having killed the parents the killer returned to boys where he removed the head and limbs from the torsos.'

'Do we have any theories on why separating the body into pieces is important to the killer?' asked Cotton.

'I'm working on it,' I said. In truth I'd been wrestling with several theories but wasn't yet convinced by any one of them.

Cotton rubbed her brow as she spoke. 'This first attack is chaotic and poorly executed. Are we thinking he lacked control and simply couldn't wait to get to the boys or that he lacked a plan?'

Rayner pointed to a picture of the bloody mess of the father's body in the hallway. 'There is no way of knowing for sure but I would suggest he'd fantasised for a long time about these killings before finally giving in to his need. Yet, when the time came he was ill prepared and made a hash of it. After this attack he never deviated from killing the parents first. He learned from that mistake. It could have all ended that night if Mr Anderson had managed to overcome the assailant and the killer realises that.'

'Do we think the ten month time gap between this attack and the next is down to fear of how it nearly all went so wrong?' asked Cotton.

'My guess, it's more likely he simply fulfilled the need he had at that time and it satisfied him,' said Rayner. 'It's well documented that serial killers believe that by doing it once it'll stop the urge, but of course it doesn't, it has the opposite effect, it fuels it. The need soon outweighs the fear of being caught. These guys then convince themselves they're smarter than the rest of us and won't get caught.'

Rayner pointed to the next family on the board. 'The Westbury family. One of the detectives investigating this family murder here in Dorset had read about the Anderson case and recognised similarities, he called Scotland Yard, and we took over the investigation.'

He ran us through each of the attacks one by one. I watched Cotton absorbing all the information and knew I had the beginnings of a great team. It wasn't long before questions were flying between us that I hoped could make a difference.

CHAPTER SEVEN

Rayner had clearly lived and breathed this case for a long time and his near encyclopaedic knowledge of it was impressive. 'The Westbury family lived in Shaftesbury, right here in Dorset, just like the Poulson family. The Westburys had twin boys of eleven years of age and a daughter of fourteen. The attack took place three days after the boys' birthday. The house still had party balloons and banners up.' Rayner moved between the whiteboard and a map on the wall where he pointed to the location. 'Here. Seven months later the Raymond family in the county of Hampshire, close to the Dorset border, were all murdered in a similar way. Twin boys aged nine years. This time no siblings.'

Rayner made notes of questions raised on a separate whiteboard. 'This attack took place in Wiltshire, once again close to the Dorset county line. The Chiles family. The boys were ten years old. This attack occurred six months after the Raymond family murders.'

'And the dice in the hands of each of the boys, what do we know?' said Cotton. 'All the children had a single dice placed in their hand. Either a left or right hand. The choice of hand appears to have no significance. All the sides of the dice scratched out except the number six.'

'Six? Why six?' I asked rhetorically.

Rayner wrote it up on the board. *Why dice? Number six?*

Rayner returned to the families. 'And now the Poulson family four months after the Chiles family. The killer starts with parents. It also appears that on this occasion he had the balls to walk the boys out of the house and onto the back lawn. Where he once again went through his ritual. Club them with a hammer, then butcher them. This time under the night sky.'

'It shows a whole new level of authority and desire,' I said. 'He's mastered the process, feels in control of his environment and is willing to take chances.'

'He appears to have more self-control, that's for sure,' said Cotton.

I added, 'Possibly, it also shows his fantasy has developed. When he started with the Westburys, going into the home must have felt daunting, no matter how many times he'd played it out in his head beforehand. There were too many things that could go wrong. And they did. He was learning his craft back then. Making mistakes is part of the learning process. It would have been hard work, difficult to think clearly, and that would have diminished his pleasure.'

'You think this is sexually motivated?' asked Cotton.

'I don't know,' I admitted. 'Nothing from the crime scenes or the victims themselves suggests that. That's not to say he isn't achieving some form of gratification after the act itself. He could be taking pictures or video.'

'Something that occurred to me,' said Cotton. 'In the case of the Poulson family, if there hadn't been a full moon he wouldn't have been able to see what he was doing.

Meaning, it shows he'd planned ahead. Or he simply deviated from his plan upon seeing the moon had lit the garden.'

'There were no security lights?' said Rayner.

'The ones at the back of the house didn't work. The wire was cut. It's likely the intruder cut the wires before entering the premises,' said Cotton.

'Good work,' I said.

We checked the lunar calendar and compared the dates of the other attacks. The Poulson attack was the only night that had a full moon.

'Maybe it was coincidence. He saw the opportunity to move outside and took it,' said Cotton.

'Ballsy move, if so,' said Rayner.

'Very unlikely. This guy has become a planner,' I said. 'The bigger question is now he's experienced it under a full moon, will he go back to killing indoors? Or will he wait for a full moon?' We all knew the answer.

'The next full moon is October thirteenth. It's the Hunter's Moon. It's in twenty-eight days.'

'Hunter's Moon,' said Rayner. 'Christ almighty, how could he resist that?'

The pressure in the room rocketed. I needed to keep us all on track. 'The first crime scenes were a mess. He learned he had to kill the parents before he could do what he was really there for. The early family murders were rehearsals. He started sloppy and has become more confident; he's now willing to take the risk of killing outside the home. We still have no idea why the dice are symbolic? Maybe the six on the dice is what's important, not the dice itself. It's the only side not scratched out. The bodies are cut into six pieces. Is there a link there?'

'Maybe it means he's going to stop once he's murdered six families?'

'If he does he might never be caught,' said Cotton.

'Better that than more families murdered.'

'Tell that to family number six.'

I stood up and poured myself a coffee. I needed caffeine. 'He's just getting started. He's enjoying himself. He's mastered his craft. It's getting easier for him. Why would he stop now? There's no reason to. Whatever fantasy he's fulfilling, it must be consuming every waking hour. He might be able to hide it but it's there, all day, every day. It's impossible to walk away from.'

'Then we stop him,' said Cotton. 'Whatever it takes. We stop this bastard.'

CHAPTER EIGHT

By late afternoon, Hamilton had arrived. Having worked late the previous night, she set off from London around lunchtime. As soon as she walked through the door, I brought her up to speed, all the while hoping her pathology report had yielded something of value.

Hamilton studied the room. We were already feeling the squeeze and it was plain to see we needed more space. I'd already made the decision that as soon as I could I'd call Dorset Police to see whether they had any office space available.

'It's a bit snug,' said Hamilton.

'You can say that again,' chuckled Rayner.

'I was hoping there would be a desk for you but it looks like it's been commandeered.' Rayner and Cotton had covered her desk with photos and Post-it notes.

'That's fine, I can't stop. Date night tonight.'

'That sounds exciting. Anything serious?' I said.

'Quite the opposite.'

'Really? How so?'

'I have a new man I need to put through his paces.'

'I see.' I didn't see but was a little lost for words.

'Since the love of my life fell in love with another woman,' I knew she was teasing me, 'I've discovered the sinful joys of men half my age.' She whispered as though I were a trusted confidant, 'They're so eager to please, they're not looking for commitment – which suits me at this moment in time – and wow, they're so knowledgeable, and adventurous.' Hamilton chuckled. 'I've always known how to make you blush, James. It's one of the things I adore about you.'

'I'm not blushing, Heidi.' I raised an eyebrow. 'Well, maybe a little.'

I changed the subject by introducing Emma Cotton, then after seeking Rayner's full attention Hamilton addressed us all.

She went over the pathology report. It threw very little additional light on what we already knew. 'As well as nothing from the autopsies, disappointingly, no useful forensic evidence has surfaced yet, either. Though I narrowed time of death to between two a.m. and four a.m.'

'But? What is it?' I said. I knew her well enough to know something was bothering her.

'It's nothing,' said Hamilton.

'It's never nothing. If you have something, share it. No matter how small or how stupid you think it might sound.'

'It's just something I've been mulling over. I know I'm stepping out of my field of expertise here but something occurred to me, and it was only because the killer is choosing families with twins.'

'Go on.'

'He would need to find a way to select them. I mean, I wouldn't really have a clue where to start if I were looking for families with twin boys of a certain age. I guess I'd consider schools but you couldn't just start phoning schools and asking, could you?'

'You're right,' I said, smiling encouragingly.

Cotton rummaged over one of the desks and grabbed a print-out which she held up. 'We're looking at all possible connections with the twin boys from each family, such as schools, hobbies, sports clubs, holiday clubs, online gaming et cetera,' said Cotton.

Hamilton perched on the edge of my desk as she spoke. 'I've worked on enough serial killer cases to have learned a little of how they behave and it crossed my mind that unlike other serial killers, who might stalk or cruise around, find a victim, and wait for an opportunity to abduct or attack, this killer will have had to do some digging to find male twins within the age range he chooses. The boys are all between nine and eleven years old. Right?'

'Correct. There must be a national register of twins?' said Rayner. 'We're only just bringing ourselves up to speed. We're planning on looking into that.'

Cotton shrugged. 'I'll check it out.'

'Working along those lines, something else crossed my mind,' said Hamilton. 'I checked before I left and there are registries which adult twins can join voluntarily, those registries are typically used for research purposes.'

'Research?'

'Genetic, biological and psychological research.'

'Okay,' said Rayner. 'This helps us how?' The frown on his face suggested he was wondering where all this was going. 'Maybe the killer is finding the adult twin parent then checking to see if the kids are twins. Everyone knows twins run in families.'

Hamilton pulled a face.

'Are you saying that's a myth,' said Rayner.

'No. Twins running in families is only half true,' said Hamilton.

'The less sciency the better, please,' insisted Rayner.

'I'll try. Non-identical twins, like our dead boys, only occur when two eggs are fertilised by two sperm at the same time. A woman is more likely to release two or more eggs during ovulation if she has a certain gene, and it's that gene that runs in families.'

'I just thought of the boys as twins,' admitted Cotton. 'I never thought it might be relevant they weren't identical.'

'I still don't see how this helps us,' complained Rayner.

'Well, this is the exciting bit. All our twin boys were non-identical,' said Hamilton. 'None of the dead children were identical twins. None. What's important about that, is that non-identical twins can run in families. A couple is more likely to have twins if there are twins on the woman's side of the family. And I repeat. Those twins will most likely be non-identical.'

Rayner scratched his head. 'I don't get it, sorry.'

A smile spread across my face as the penny dropped. 'That's brilliant. You think we're possibly looking in the wrong place. We don't look for how he's selecting the boys at all. We start with the mother.'

'Exactly. What if he knows the mother? What if it's her who unintentionally informs the killer that she has twin boys. The other thing about non-identical twins is that they could be a boy and a girl. The killer has somehow found a reliable way of identifying non-identical male twins, between the ages of nine and eleven. I just think it's a possibility.'

'I'm with you now,' said Rayner. 'We dig into the mother's background. Figure out what links them. Relationships, clubs, sports, education, work, social media, associations.'

'Then cross reference all the mothers,' added Cotton. 'We find the commonality.'

'What do we think?' I asked.

'It's a plausible theory, and we've got to start somewhere,' said Rayner.

'So the killer has access to the information on the birth of twins, most likely via the mother,' said Cotton thinking out loud. 'Combing through who has access and then whittling down suspects will be a mammoth task.'

'Colossal,' agreed Hamilton. 'The thing is, what is interesting to me is that none of the twins were identical, that can't be coincidence. Identical twins occur when a fertilised embryo splits in two. Each child has the same genes and means they are the same sex and it's why they have similarities in appearance. More importantly to my theory and why we're able to hone in on the mothers is that there is no evidence that identical twins run in families.'

'It's a new approach to the investigation. It's better than going over the work done by Scotland Yard and simply looking for what they might have overlooked,' said Rayner.

'It's as good a place as any to start,' agreed Cotton.

Hamilton's smile said it all. 'The power of science,' she said. She checked her watch. 'I'd better get going; it's a long drive back.'

I walked Hamilton back to her car.

'They're going to be more motivated than ever. A fresh approach in a case like this is as exciting as new evidence,' I said.

'Tomorrow, I'll visit the forensics team again. I'll see if anything new has turned up. I'll keep you posted,' said Hamilton. 'Being in London means I can make sure you're kept in the loop when new leads turn up. We're going to catch this guy.'

I tried to smile. 'I hope so. I just hope we do it quickly.'

'You know I believe in you, and so do those two.' She glanced back towards the office where Cotton and Rayner were working inside. 'I've told you many times that the thing I like about science is that there's certainty. I don't know how you do what you do and I don't want to know but if anyone can stop this guy, you can. You and your team. Stay strong.' She kissed me on the cheek, got into her car and wound the window down.

I leaned close. 'What we both do is similar in some ways. Just like science, when looking for the answer there has to be a process of elimination.'

I watched Hamilton drive away. My mind turned to the next full moon, the Hunter's Moon, in just twenty-eight days.

I was gambling the direction this case now took on Hamilton's theory that our time was best spent finding a link between the mothers and the killer. If I was wrong, and we couldn't find a link soon, another family would die.

CHAPTER NINE

I arrived back at the now empty Poulson home to take another look. It was early evening and I planned on spending the time leading up to the hour the attack took place learning what the killer experienced, wanting to sense how the Poulson family home looked on the night he attacked. It's well documented that serial killers often watch their victims, going over in their head how the event would play out. Planning and fantasising.

I parked on a grass verge in Ravenwood Lane, a private wooded lane that leads to the gated entrance of the Poulsons' long driveway up to the house.

As the crow flies, the nearest neighbour was a little under half a mile away. Not close enough to witness whether there had been any unusual activity on the night in question.

I swapped my shoes for Wellington boots and began walking towards the house. It had been raining again, the ground was soft and the air smelled damp. Up ahead the iridescent feathers of a cock pheasant caught my eye as it ran across the lane ahead of me and into the large field neighbouring the property.

I reached the driveway and stood for a while picturing where I might position myself to observe the house if I were the killer. I'd want cover from any potential rainfall, a place I wouldn't be seen from the house or from Ravenwood Lane should anyone unexpectedly approach the house on the evening in question. I'd want to feel comfortable and able to relax.

I walked on slowly, looking around as I moved. He'd want to see lights being switched off when the parents retired to bed. Their bedroom was at the front of the house, top left window, so the killer would have wanted to observe the front of the house. I walked backwards up the Poulsons' driveway looking from left to right, scanning the garden, lawns, hedgerows, fencing and trees. The paddock, now empty, offered no cover.

I crossed the lawn, instinctively drawn to a large Alder tree punctuating the hedgerow on my right. I squatted down and leaned against the tree's dark fissured trunk. I edged around its base, attempting to hide myself away while staying in visual contact with the house. Pushing myself between the tree trunk and a tall hawthorn hedgerow I found myself on the other side in an adjoining field. The thick hedgerow now screened my view of the house almost completely. I looked back towards Ravenwood Lane behind me. If I stayed low, the hedgerow between Ravenwood Lane at the far end of the field shielded me from onlookers. I continued on in the direction of the house. Through the thick hedge it was almost impossible to see the house on the other side. I wondered if I was wasting my time.

Ahead of me the hedgerow was disrupted. Twigs and branches had been cut away and tossed aside. As I got closer I could see the hedge had been hollowed out on this side only. On the Poulsons' side the greenery remained, which was why I hadn't noticed before. Carefully, I peered inside.

From here I was looking directly at the Poulson house. Had I been wearing dark or camouflaged clothing, I was sure it would be nigh on impossible to see me from the Poulsons' garden.

You watched them from here, didn't you? I said to myself. *You could have stayed here for hours had you wanted to.* I got on the phone to Rayner. We needed to get a forensics team back out here.

I began walking towards the house once more. As I pushed my way past the Alder tree and onto the Poulsons' front lawn a white Range Rover moved along Ravenwood Lane. I heard the engine stop. I stood and watched for a moment then went to see who had arrived. As I approached the gateway a male figure appeared. He looked to be in his seventies, trim and well dressed, his skin tanned, his silver hair fashionably cut. His bright blue eyes fixed on mine. 'Chief Inspector Hardy?' His voice was gravelly. He held out a smooth manicured hand, which I shook. 'I was told you'd be at my daughter's home. My name is Patrick Simpson, I wondered if I might have a word? I have a proposition for you.'

CHAPTER TEN

As Patrick Simpson and I walked along Ravenwood Lane, I could feel his eyes appraising me. 'I'm sorry for your loss,' I said. 'Truly, I am. We're doing all we can to find the person responsible.'

Simpson's eyes fixed on mine. 'I don't expect you to understand the depth of despair I'm feeling. I come from a small mining village in Wales. Mine was a family of miners; my father was a miner, as was his father before him. I left school at fifteen with nothing, no qualifications and was expected to follow in my father's footsteps. By seventeen, I knew I wanted more and against my parents' wishes, I joined the army. By twenty-two I had left the army and started the first of many businesses. By thirty-one I had made my first million. My purpose in life has been to find my own way and create my own opportunities. As soon as I married and started a family my focus shifted and I wanted to make sure they never went without. Fifty years later I'm a multi-millionaire.' He reached out and grabbed my arm. 'My money means nothing without my family to share it with. My wife, Yvonne, the love of my life, died of cancer six and half years ago. Money couldn't save her, she had every treatment available. And now this, my daughter and grandsons taken. I'm alone, Inspector. My Elizabeth, little Jake and Gregory, and my son-in-law Ryan were slaughtered by some deranged...' He choked back tears. 'After a lifetime of building wealth everything of any real value has been taken from me.'

'I understand you're hurting...'

'With all due respect. You have no idea,' barked Simpson. He squeezed my arm harder. I looked down at his hand and he let go. 'I'm sorry, Inspector. I want this bastard to pay. I want there to be no place for him to hide. I want him found and I want him to know pain and suffering before his miserable life ends, preferably at my hand.'

I pretended not to hear the that. 'New Scotland Yard have a team dedicated to the investigation. I'm part of a very small unit who are simply complementing their efforts. You ought to speak to the Yard; they'll keep you informed of developments better than I can. I can give you their number.'

'You think I came to find you without doing my homework? I know who you are. Scotland Yard are getting nowhere. That's why they called you. If they had done their job and caught this inhuman fuck my precious Elizabeth would still be alive. My grandsons would not have been butchered.'

'I'm not sure how I can help.'

'I want to know what you need.'

'I don't understand,' I said.

'I think you do.'

'Really. I don't.'

Simpson took a thick padded white envelope from inside his jacket. 'Inside is fifty thousand pounds. Also, my personal mobile phone number. Hire whoever you need to.

Buy whatever information you must. Knock down doors and twist arms, whatever it is you need to do. There's plenty more where this came from. Take it.'

I stepped back and put my hands in my pockets. 'I can't take your money. It doesn't work like that.'

'Why not? I know the police are underfunded. I'm simply making funds available. This is purely a business transaction.'

'For one thing it's illegal. If I take your money I could lose my job and I'd be off your daughter's case. Mr Simpson, this case will be solved through good police work.'

'What if I hire you privately?'

'I'm not for hire.'

'What if I put a bounty on this man's head? I'm thinking of going to the newspapers and putting a price on his head and offering a reward for information leading to his arrest.'

'Mr Simpson, if you do either of those things you are making the police's job more difficult. I know it seems like the logical thing to do and I understand you want to help but it won't. I promise you. What will happen is the team dedicated to finding the murderer will be swamped with leads. Most of which will be from crackpots and time wasters. The team's time will be diluted and their focus removed from the evidence they have. I urge you to do nothing.'

Simpson's posture changed; he looked like a broken man. He was used to being in control. Having lost everything he held dear he was struggling to make sense of his life. He wanted to keep his mind active, find purpose, be a part of something that would bring the man who did this to justice. I guessed he hoped it might bring him closure. Who was I to tell him he couldn't? All I knew was that, right now, his money wouldn't help find his family's killer.

'Was your daughter a twin?'

Simpson looked at me dumbfounded. It was like I'd given him a kick in the chest. 'Yes. But, how did you know? Charlotte died six days after being born. She was the sweetest little...' He choked up.

'I'm sorry. I didn't mean to upset you further.'

He took a deep breath and forced himself to continue. 'Have you at least spoken to Elizabeth's ex-business partner? He was at the house late the day before. On the phone Lizzie told me herself he was going to visit. He was always trying to get her involved in some new business venture. He might have seen something or someone.'

I took out my notebook. 'He was there?' I asked.

'He wasn't there long by all accounts. But he was definitely there.'

'Why hasn't he come forward?'

'You'd have to ask him that.'

'What's his name?'

'Janek Bonne. He's currently living on a yacht at a marina near Poole.' He showed me a picture. 'Elizabeth sent it to me; she knows I love yachts and was on the lookout for one myself.'

I copied down the details.

'I'd like you to keep me posted on developments,' he said. He gave me his mobile number.

'I'll do what I can do. I can't make any promises.'

Simpson shook my hand and went back to his Range Rover. He was a broken man who wanted nothing more than to help and feel useful. I felt bad I'd had to disappoint him.

As I leaned against the boot of my car and changed my Wellington boots for shoes, I felt both excited at the possibility of forensic evidence from the hedgerow and frustrated that it appeared no one had known about Janek Bonne being at the residence the evening before the murders. I needed to speak to him urgently; without knowing it, he could be the key to unlocking this investigation.

CHAPTER ELEVEN

Poole Marina can berth up to seventy-five boats and can accommodate vessels up to seventy metres. Finding Janek Bonne's yacht should have been simple enough but for a city boy like myself, who doesn't know his port side from his poop deck, it wasn't long before I found myself walking up and down scratching my head.

When Cotton joined me I hoped we'd have more luck in finding which yacht was his. 'What are we looking for?' she asked.

'She's called *Heart of Serenity*.'

A bald, red bearded man in blue overalls scowled at us over Ray-Ban sunglasses as we checked the name of each boat in turn. He had what looked like a pump in his hands as he stood on the deck of the white and gold yacht, *Barbarossa*. We smiled politely as we passed. He kept an eye on us.

We read names off a few more yachts which to my untrained eye all looked similar, other than the size. Cotton turned and walked back to the red-bearded man.

'We're looking for a boat called *Heart of Serenity*,' said Cotton.

'This here's *Barbarossa*,' he said, stroking his beard.

'Barbarossa means red beard in Italian,' said Cotton. 'I get it.'

He continued staring at the pump in his hands. He took a filthy rag from his pocket, spat on the pump, wiped it and began reading out loud a code stamped into it.

'We'd like to speak with Janek Bonne. I believe he owns *Heart of Serenity*.'

He sighed. He put down the pump, wiped his greasy hands on the rag before tucking it back in his pocket and came closer. 'Why might that be?'

Cotton held out her warrant card. 'Police.'

Redbeard adjusted his sunglasses and took a long look. He didn't appear impressed. He scratched an eyebrow with his little finger and sucked his teeth. '*Heart of Serenity* is that way. Forty-five footer she is. A motor yacht, and an absolute cracker. She must be about, um... twenty boats up. Maybe more, maybe less. You're lucky. Janek's motorbike is still in the car park, I saw it there less than thirty minutes ago, so I guess he must be home.' He stopped pointing in the vague direction of the boat and moved his finger to point towards the car park behind us. A silver touring BMW motorbike with large panniers was parked in the corner. 'Nice bloke, is Janek. Sharp as a shark's tooth. A free spirit of sorts. New to life on the water, he is. He's been all over Europe on that bike of his. So many fascinating stories. Travel like that gives a richness and depth to a person's character. I have stories of my own of course.' He chuckled to himself as though remembering a story that had tickled him. 'I hope he's not in trouble.'

'Why would you think he's in trouble?' I asked.

'No reason. He seemed a little off last time I spoke to him.'

'That's interesting. Off, in what way?'

'Had a lot on his mind, he told me. You know, I've really got to get this pump fixed.' Redbeard turned his back on us and resumed fiddling with the pump.

'Conversation's over,' said Cotton, looking at me.

'I think you're right,' I said.

We made our way past hundreds of thousands of pounds' worth of yachts. Some possibly costing more than I'd see in a lifetime.

A cat hopped off a boat ahead of us and with its tail in the air tried to garner our attention. Cotton stroked the cat as we walked past then pointed up ahead. 'That looks like *Heart of Serenity*.'

There was no sign of anyone home as I stepped aboard. Tinted windows meant I couldn't see inside. I knocked on the door to the galley. I knocked again. I tried the door and it opened. I looked at Cotton. Opening the door some more I leaned inside. 'Mr Janek Bonne, this is Detective Chief Inspector Hardy. Police. Are you home? I wondered if I might have a word?'

With no reply I made my way awkwardly down four steps into the main cabin and galley. The smell of something spicy filled my nostrils. On the hob sat a pot of cold curry. On the dining table was a congealing plateful and a naan bread. A fork rested beside it and next to that an almost untouched bottle of beer.

'This kitchen's better than mine at home,' said Cotton.

'It sure is something,' I agreed.

'White leather seats. I wish. Watson, my cat, would love sinking his claws into those cushions.'

Cotton went to a door to the left of the steps and found the guest cabin. I went through to the master bedroom.

Behind me I could hear Cotton opening and closing drawers and cupboards.

Biker's boots, leathers and underclothes sat in a messy

pile on the floor. Against the neat and exquisite interior of the rest of the yacht they looked out of place.

I heard pipes creak and water drips. A tinted glass door beside me was a little wet and water-stained. I guessed it must the shower.

I spoke through the shower door. 'Mr Bonne, this is the police, are you there?'

I knocked.

'Mr Bonne, are you in the shower?'

No response.

I looked at Cotton who was now standing beside me.

She nodded, indicating she agreed we needed to open the door.

I grasped the handle and slowly opened it.

'Shit!'

A naked man was slumped in the base of the shower. He had a leather trouser belt around his neck. I rushed in, and checked for signs of life.

Cotton came running. She stood well back to give me room in the cramped space.

I couldn't get to the belt around his neck so I pulled his legs out of the shower, then rolled him onto his back as best I could. I removed the belt and checked for a pulse, although I already knew what the outcome would be. 'He's dead,' I said, realising I was stating the obvious.

I stepped aside to allow Cotton room to see.

She inhaled sharply. 'Do you think it's Janek?' Cotton took out her phone and called it in while I looked around.

We both put on gloves to preserve what was now a crime scene. I carefully opened a wallet on the bedside dresser and took out the driving licence. I went back to the shower and pushed the brown shoulder length hair away from the face.

'It's Janek,' I called to Cotton. I held up the driving licence photo.

'That's one hell of a coincidence, don't you think?' said Cotton. 'The first potential break in this case and it's evaporated before our eyes.'

There was no sign of a struggle. I went through cupboards and drawers, I wasn't sure what I was looking for, hoping I'd know when I found it. I moved between each room. Cotton did the same.

'Hardy, check this out,' called Cotton. She was back in the shower room with the body. She showed me Bonne's mobile phone which I'd missed earlier but had been in the corner, partly beneath him. 'He'd been watching pornography. Looks like his death was an accident, possibly autoerotic asphyxiation.'

'Jesus,' I said. 'How did you know the password?'

'I didn't. The phone has facial recognition. I just held it in front of his...'

'Really? I'm not sure whether to be shocked you did that or impressed.'

'Impressed. Definitely,' said Cotton.

A motorcycle helmet sat on the kitchen worktop. From a plug socket on the wall a power cable ran over the surface and dangled over the edge. I recognised it as one used with a laptop. I looked around the room, lifted seat cushions and checked under the bed mattress but found nothing. *What am I missing?*

I sat down on the sofa as though I were Bonne. I looked around for where I might hide a laptop if I lived on the boat. Nothing jumped out at me. I stared at the motorcycle helmet and power cable. 'Have you seen a laptop?' I asked.

'Not yet,' said Cotton. 'Why?'

I got up and pointed to the cable. 'I wondered whether someone took it.'

'You think he was robbed? He wouldn't be the first dead man to be robbed by some low-life.'

I took a closer look at the motorcycle helmet. It had a camera on the side. 'What do you know about head cameras?' Cotton stopped going through a small bookcase and looked at the helmet.

'It's worth a look,' said Cotton. 'Maybe the camera caught something the night of the Poulson murders. I think I know someone who'll be able to access that for us.'

I reached up onto the kitchen shelf above and opened a coffee tin, then a sugar tin and finally the tea caddy. I pulled out a rolled up bundle of cash. I showed it to Cotton and pointed. 'If the laptop was stolen by a thief then the culprit was pretty useless. First place most thieves know to look, normally.'

'Maybe the incompetent thief was disturbed and fled?' quipped Cotton.

'Yep, maybe,' I said. 'I could accept that but Bonne hasn't touched his meal.'

'And? I don't follow.'

'What I don't accept is that he cooked his curry, dished it up, opened a bottle of beer and then thought he'd take a shower and do what we're supposed to think he was doing in the shower.'

'The alternative is that his death was staged.'

I knelt down and picked up a shard of broken crockery. If I had to guess I'd say it looked like a piece of a mug. I checked the bin inside a cupboard. It was empty, and there was no bin bag. I looked at all the cupboard doors, around the edge of the worktop, paying close attention to the corners. Standing back and observing the room as a whole, I noticed a black scuff mark across the bottom drawer of a set of three. 'Let's keep an open mind for the time being. It looks to me like some sort of struggle took place.'

CHAPTER TWELVE

Cotton, Rayner and I stood around a screen in my private office. Cotton's colleague, Becky Wang, had come over from the Bournemouth police cyber unit and was working through the footage from Janek Bonne's motorcycle helmet camera.

'I uploaded the video footage to Scotland Yard's secure server. It gives us as much secure space as we'll ever need. It means they can analyse it too, if they want,' said Wang. She adjusted the size of the footage on the screen, sipping from a mug of hot lemon tea. As she worked her head bobbed from side to side, her silky straight black hair bouncing around until finally she was ready. She relaxed back in the chair. 'I checked the time stamp on the footage and it's spot on,' she said. 'It's a top of the range head-cam so the footage quality is excellent.' She gave the keyboard one last tap.

'Boom! Ch-ch-check it out.' We watched as Bonne started his motorcycle. The picture was crisp and the sound good. From the evening light and the recording's time stamp we knew the recording was from seven-thirty on the evening before the murders.

A voice called out and Bonne turned to look.

'Bye, Janek, it was good to see you. Be careful on the roads,' said Elizabeth Poulson. She was smiling and waving. Ryan was standing behind his wife with his arm around her shoulders. In front of their parents the boys, Jake and Gregory, were crouching in the doorway. They appeared excited by the motorbike. Huddled together the boys pointed in the direction of the bike and talked together.

Bonne revved the engine a couple of times to make the boys laugh. Elizabeth chuckled and waved a hand at him to make him stop. The boys giggled some more. It was clear they were all good friends.

'Have a great time on your travels,' said Ryan. 'Say hello to Iceland for me, and all those gorgeous Icelandic women, you lucky so and so. Are you sure I can't come with you?'

Elizabeth gave her husband a playful dig in the ribs. 'Don't even think about it.'

Janek spoke. 'See you, I'll send a postcard from Reykjavik. I'll call you when I get back.' He gave a thumbs up to Jake and Gregory.

The motorbike began to move. It headed down the Poulsons' driveway, slowing at the open gate before turning left. Bonne made his way along Ravenwood Lane, the camera bouncing as the bike navigated the lane's uneven surface.

Bonne's bike approached the end of Ravenwood Lane. It came to a halt as he checked the traffic. His head turned left and then right. Several cars passed in both directions. He was about to pull out when a small white van to his right, its indicator blinking, slowed to turn into Ravenwood Lane. Bonne kept watching the van as it slowly approached and started turning, but instead of entering the lane it swerved and picked up speed as it continued on.

'Idiot,' Bonne cursed. The motorbike pulled out as the traffic cleared and we watched for around thirty minutes.

Eventually Janek arrived at the marina where he parked and switched off his head-cam.

'Nothing,' said Rayner. He stretched and yawned.

'Can we go back to where the white van is slowing down?' I said. I wasn't sure what I was looking for but it was the only thing that stuck in my mind.

'What did you see?' said Cotton.

'It's the only part of any interest,' said Rayner.

'Apart from Bonne's speeding and committing every traffic violation known to man,' said Wang.

'It was a bit like watching the Dakar Rally,' agreed Rayner.

'Here we go. Wait a second.' Wang stopped the footage as Bonne checked the traffic, his head turning left to right.

'The van was definitely intending to turn,' said Rayner. He pointed his thick forefinger at the screen.

'Freeze it,' I said 'There.' I pointed at the van. 'Can we get a better image, a close-up of the driver?'

'I don't think so. The driver is in darkness. I might be able to lighten it; there are a few things I can try, but I also know from experience with this sort of image it's very unlikely we'll get anything worthwhile.'

'What about the registration? Can you run that and see what comes up, please,' said Cotton.

'Already underway,' said Wang. 'I'll work on the footage some more later tonight. I've really got to go, my babysitter will go bananas if I'm late home again.'

'Good of you to do this at such short notice. Do what you can with the driver and let us know,' I said. 'You've got my number, if anything turns up, call me.'

'I'll be in touch. Like I said, a worthwhile image of the driver is unlikely, even with enhancing software, but I'll give it a go.' She grabbed her coat off the back of a chair and I got the door for her.

Rayner looked at his phone for the time. I checked my watch. I was meant to be finished an hour ago for a family meal; it was now past seven o'clock.

'Let's call it a day,' I said. 'Best thing we can do is stay well rested, it'll keep us sharp. I'll be in the office from about six-thirty tomorrow. But you all keep your own hours. Whatever works for you.'

'I prefer an early start, but I'm going to follow up a few things tonight at home that I don't want to leave until tomorrow. I'll be in late morning,' said Cotton.

Rayner came over to me and spoke privately. 'I'll be in as soon as I can. Jenny's nurse is visiting tomorrow. I want to be there. She's still in a lot of pain and unsteady on her feet. She puts on a brave face but I know she's in a lot of discomfort most of the time. I want to see if I can get someone to look in on her regularly. The nurse might know someone I can hire privately.'

'If there's anything you need,' I said.

'I know. Cheers, mate.'

I locked up the office and set the alarm, then to clear my mind I went for a short walk around the block. Though the office is part of Mum's house, a short walk at the end of the day before re-entering through the front door was my attempt at separating work-life from home-life.

CHAPTER THIRTEEN

The florist's van inched along the road as the driver looked for the house number. The vehicle was covered in images of butterflies and flowers. The company name *Heaven Scent* was emblazoned along the side in a huge green swirly font. It pulled up next to the kerb and the driver got out.

Declan was unloading his car when he heard the florist's voice calling him.

'Excuse me, my love. By any chance does an Emma Cotton live here?' She tilted her head back causing her chin to stick out as she read the address on the card in her hand through her reading glasses. She then looked up at Declan.

Her grey hair was cut in a short choppy style. Her clothing choice of baby pink t-shirt, tight blue jeans and pale blue trainers gave her a youthful appearance which despite a forty year age gap made Declan look twice. He definitely had a thing for older women.

She raised her eyebrows, smiled and repeated the question in a different way. 'I'm looking for an Emma Cotton, I've got a couple of gorgeous bouquets for her, does the lucky lady live here?'

'Sorry, I was miles away. She's my neighbour. Next door.' Declan pointed at the house. 'She should be home.'

'Perfect. Thank you.' She opened the back of the van and took out the first bouquet. It was called *Cherry Blossom* and was a mixture of pink lilies, hot pink carnations, lilac freesias and soft pink gypsophila.

Declan watched the delivery while taking boxes of snacks and drink from the car to the house.

After a pause and a ringing of the doorbell a second time, Emma opened the door.

'Good morning, a *Heaven Scent* bouquet delivery for Emma Cotton,' the florist smiled cheerfully.

'Um, okay,' mumbled Emma. She squinted against the daylight and straightened her pyjamas. Bleary-eyed, she took the bouquet and opened the envelope with the card inside. The card read 'I miss you. Let's try again. How about a drink? Alex xxx'.

The florist was humming to herself; she was part-way up the garden path on her way to fetch the second bouquet.

'Hold on a moment,' called Emma.

The florist turned, her cheery face changing with concerned confusion. 'Everything okay, my love?'

Declan kept his head down and pretended to be checking his party inventory. He pulled out a bottle of vodka and peered at the label.

'You know what, they're beautiful flowers, stunning, but can you take them away please. I don't want them.'

'I don't understand,' said the florist. 'Is something wrong?'

'No, no. It would be such a waste to keep them. I'm not going to be home much over the next few days, possibly weeks. They'd be more appreciated elsewhere. Can you take them to a nursing home or hospice?'

'If you're sure, my love. We can do that. It would be my

pleasure.' The florist had been in the job long enough to know not to ask questions when a woman refuses flowers. She took back the bouquet. 'Any place in particular you'd like them to go?'

'No. You choose,' said Emma. 'Sorry.' She closed the front door.

The florist saw Declan watching. She pulled a face and mouthed, 'That was awkward.'

Declan realised he hadn't seen Emma's male friend around in a while. He guessed they must have broken up. He was pleased. The bloke had come across as a bit up himself. In truth he thought he was a tosser. Not really Emma's type. Not that he knew what that was, he just hadn't felt they had been a natural fit.

CHAPTER FOURTEEN

Overnight, we had a name and address for the owner of the small white van seen on Bonne's head-cam footage. Two constables were sent to the two bedroom terrace house on Malmesbury Road in Charminster to locate the van. Unfortunately Paul Ackland, the registered owner, noticed the constables showing an interest and decided to run. A chase ensued but Paul Ackland was eventually apprehended after hiding within the grounds of the local primary school. That evening Cotton and I paid him a visit down at the station.

Ackland's right eye was swollen and bruised and his bottom lip cut. He ran his tongue over the cut. His oval head, cropped mousy-coloured hair, small mouth and large eyes set wide over his little nose gave him a sloth-like appearance. His demeanour however, was anything but; he looked ready to pounce. He scowled at us as we entered the room. We sat down and I placed a file of photographic evidence on the desk in front of me.

Cotton started the recording equipment and gave the date and time, her name and rank and mine. She stated we were interviewing Paul Ackland.

'I've done nothing. Why am I here? This is harassment. You know that right?' said Ackland.

'Harassment? How have you been harassed, exactly? You ran from officers who wanted to question you. That's the only reason they brought you in.'

'I ran because I've done nothing. What do you want from me?'

'We have a few questions.'

'All right. Nothing to hide. I'll go along with that. Always happy to help the law.'

'Why did you run?'

'I got spooked. Me and the law, we don't always see eye to eye.'

'I see from your record you're acquainted with the judicial system,' I said. I opened his police record.

'That's unfair. You can't judge me. I've served my time and I'm a changed man. I'm a product of shitty foster homes and social care. What you have there in that file is the old me. I've turned over a new leaf. I'm no longer going to allow how I was screwed over as a kid dictate my future. I've found steady employment and I'm staying on the right side of the law. That said, I see the police and I expect the worst. Sure you understand. I get jittery, that's all.'

'Jittery?'

'Yes, jittery.'

'Okay. As I understand it you waived your right to a solicitor. Would you like to change your mind? Would you like a solicitor present?' said Cotton.

'Don't need one. Done nothing wrong. And you haven't arrested me. I'm here because as a citizen I want to help.' He ran his hands over his oval head, smoothing his short downy hair.

I pointed to Ackland's right eye and said, 'Your eye. Looks painful. How did that happen?'

'Had an argument with the missus. She gets the hump sometimes. You know how women are?'

'I'm not sure I do. Enlighten me. Tell me about your relationship and how you wound up with a black eye and a split lip'

'Are you shitting me?' Ackland sighed and drummed the table with the tips of his fingers. 'Look, it wasn't her fault. I mean she did it, yeah, she walloped me, but I deserved it, I suppose. Tara found some lace undies in my jacket pocket.'

'Tara's your wife?'

'Yeah.'

'Undies that weren't your Tara's. And that upset her?'

'Look, Tara thought I shagged one of the girls at the club.'

'The club?'

'I work at a strip club. I oversee security.'

'Which club?'

'Venus Moon Gentlemen's Club.'

Cotton made a note.

'How does Tara feel about you working in a strip club?' I asked.

'I wouldn't say she's delighted about it. She's on my case all the time. She gets it into her head I'm screwing the girls.'

'And you're not?'

'No. That would be unprofessional. They're not whores; they're dancers. And anyway, look at me. I'm not exactly Brad Pitt am I? I'm more Gollum than Clooney. And the girls are all, you know... hot. They can have whoever they want. And it certainly isn't me. They see me more like a big brother. I look after them.'

'How did the underwear end up in your pocket?' asked Cotton.

'One of the girls put a pair of knickers in my jacket for a

laugh. It was a prank. They must have thought it would be funny.'

'Judging by your eye, I'd have to disagree.'

'Me too. I had a word with the girls.' He touched his eye, it began watering. 'Anyway, when the missus found the undies she raged like a storm over the North Sea. She hit me with a saucepan. Can you believe, a sodding saucepan?' He chuckled and winced from the cut on his lip. 'Eventually, she calmed down, got it out her system and we're fine now. We're back to being the world's greatest love story.' Ackland winked. 'On the up side, you want great sex with your missus, best thing you can do is make her think there's another woman. Adds real zest. You know what I mean?'

'I'll bear that in mind,' I said with an incredulous shake of my head. 'Judging by your files I'd say you like to resolve disagreements with your fists.'

'Never once hit a woman.' He looked at Cotton.

'I'm not suggesting you would,' I said.

'Good. As long as we're clear.' Ackland's big eyes bulged as he stared at me.

I nodded. 'I'm clear.' For some reason I believed him.

'I know how to handle myself. I know how to fight. As a kid I learned boxing. Growing up the way I did you either better be funny or know how to fight. Let's just say I'm no Ricky Gervais. I'm no Tyson Fury either but boxing kept me off the streets.'

'Do you own a white van?' I read out the registration and watched Ackland's reaction.

'You know I do. What about it?' said Ackland with exasperation. 'Before the job at the club I was going to start a business.'

'Doing what?'

'A bit of this 'n' that.'

'Could you be a bit more specific?'

'An electrician. I got qualified while in prison. I told you, I got my life in order.'

I flicked through a few pages in Ackland's file. 'It says here you were once charged with sexual assault. A boy, thirteen. The charges were dropped when the boy later withdrew the allegation.'

'Fuck you. You bring that up? You're an arsehole. That's bullshit. Utter fucking bullshit. He made it up. I never touched the little fucker. He was some crazy kid I knew from my time in care. That was years ago, man. Why are you dragging that up? That shouldn't be allowed.'

'So you're not into young boys,' said Cotton.

'Fuck off. That all happened years ago. I'm no paedo. And I'm not queer. All right?'

I took three photographs from under the file and placed them in front of Ackland. 'We searched your van. It's been impounded. The forensic team are examining it.'

'What the hell? You can't do that. I need that van to get to work.'

I pointed to the photos in turn. 'We found blood in the van. It's being tested.'

'I don't know why there's blood in the van. It could be mine.'

'Have you cut yourself recently?'

Ackland pointed to his lip. 'Duh!'

'There's more blood in the van than would come from a split lip.' I pointed to the next photograph. 'We found this cleaver and saw in the van. Why does an electrician need a cleaver?'

'They're not mine.'

'If we test them are we going to find traces of blood on them? Your fingerprints?'

'No.'

'We found clear plastic bags as well, Ackland. Can you explain that?'

'They're for work.'

'Where were you three nights ago?'

'Dunno. Probably at the club. I'd have to check. Don't have my diary on me.' Ackland mockingly patted his pockets.

I took out a photo of each of the murdered families. 'Do you know these families?'

Ackland looked at the photos and then at me.

'You recognise them?' I said.

'No. Who are they?'

'They're all dead. Each of these families is dead.'

'What's that got to do with me?' I could see panic in his eyes.

'Your van was seen close to the location of this family,' I pointed to the Poulsons, 'on the evening before their murder.'

'What? You think I had something to do with this?' He was getting very agitated and bouncing around in his seat.

'Did you?' I asked.

'Whoa! Hold on. Are you crazy?'

'Why were you there?'

'I wasn't.'

I took out a photograph. 'Do you know this man, Janek Bonne?'

'No.'

'Ever been to his boat?'

'No. If I don't know him, why would I have been to his boat? I've never set foot on a boat in my life. Maybe a rowing boat once, at the park.'

'Did you murder him after he saw your van near the Poulson home?' I placed a photo of the house in front of him.

'The Poulson home?'

I pointed to the family photo again.

'How do you know Janek Bonne?'

'I told you I don't know the fella.'

'Were you aware his head-cam had seen your van close to the scene of the murders?'

'I've done nothing. I don't know anything about any of this. You've got the wrong man.'

'I don't think so. You're hiding something.'

Ackland pinched the bridge of his small round nose. He ran the tip of his tongue over his split lip, which was now bleeding. 'I'll be straight. Just don't start twisting what I tell you, all right? I was near the house. I know because I told the missus as much when I saw on the news that family had been done in. But I didn't kill them. I drove near where they lived, all right? That's all. I swear.'

'I know you were there,' I said, as though I'd known all along. I'd known his van was there, now he confirmed he'd been driving it. 'You're not telling me anything new. Once we get the DNA from the van you'll have limited options. You're better off talking to me now. Tell me everything right now. Come clean.'

'I've changed my mind. I want a solicitor provided. You're looking to pin this on me, I can see it on your face. I ain't done nothin'. I don't know what your game is but you're off your head.'

Cotton stopped the interview. And we both got to our feet. I collected the photographs, all except the Poulson family photo which remained in front of Ackland. 'You get your solicitor. We'll be back. This isn't over.'

Ackland looked down at the photograph of a smiling Poulson family. He turned it over and pushed it away.

CHAPTER FIFTEEN

Paul Ackland looked less confident than the last time I saw him as he sat beside his solicitor. His tiny chin was tucked in and his large eyes followed me as I prepared to hear what he had to say.

Cotton pressed the button on the interview recorder.

His solicitor, Ian Lincoln, finished writing notes on his legal pad. He played with his expensive-looking pen and stroked the stubble on his chin while eyeing Cotton up and down. He adjusted the maroon silk handkerchief in the breast pocket of his blue suit. He turned, expecting me to take the lead.

Cotton spoke calmly and coolly. 'Mr Ackland, we've put you in the location close to the Poulson family home around the time the family were murdered. I'd now like to go over some other dates with you. Where were you on—'

Lincoln held up a manicured hand. I got a waft of his aftershave. My guess was Lincoln wanted to assert his authority or impress his client by immediately interrupting. 'Mr Ackland has indeed admitted his van was in the area at the time the Poulson murders took place. The truth is he was on his way to visit some acquaintances.'

'Friends?' said Cotton, directing her question at Ackland. 'Who are these friends? I'd like names please.'

'Let me stop you there, Sergeant,' said Lincoln, his smile dazzlingly white against his tanned skin. 'They're acquaintances more than friends.'

'Yeah, I don't really know them that well,' chipped in Ackland.

'Detective Inspector,' corrected Cotton before continuing. 'These acquaintances that you don't know that well, can they confirm you were with them at the time of the murders?'

'I'd have to check,' said Ackland. 'Not everyone is as trusting of the police or as cooperative as I am.'

'You mean you want to speak to them and persuade them to give you an alibi?' said Cotton.

Lincoln checked the time on his thick, expensive-looking watch. 'Mr Ackland's time is precious and it seems it's being wasted.'

'We're investigating the murders of five families and Mr Ackland was seen attempting to enter the private lane leading to the house of a family murdered a few hours later.'

'He already explained, he did not enter the lane. What you might or might not have seen was possibly my client almost taking a wrong turn. Last time I checked, that's not a crime, Detective Inspector.' Lincoln lifted his square jaw and raised a dismissive eyebrow.

'That's right, I might have taken a wrong turn,' said Ackland.

'We're still waiting for you to account for your whereabouts at the time of the murder of the Poulson family and of the other murdered families. If you can do that, this will be over. Shall I go over the dates and times again?' Cotton took a sheet from a file in front of her.

Lincoln held up a hand. 'That's not necessary.'

Ackland leaned in close to Lincoln, whispering behind his hand. The solicitor nodded. They conversed in hushed voices while Cotton and I looked on. Eventually I interrupted.

'What is this?' I said. 'Do you have something you'd like to share or shall we continue?'

Lincoln adjusted the large knot of his maroon necktie. 'Mr Ackland has not been charged with any offence. He has been extremely cooperative. However, he'd like this matter cleared up so that he can go about his daily business without fear of harassment from the police. He would like to come clean about his movements around the time of the unfortunate deaths of the Poulson family. There are some things he's not proud of, but nevertheless he'd like to make a statement that he hopes will put this matter to rest.'

Something didn't feel right. What was I missing? I must have looked confused.

'Not about killing that family,' spluttered Ackland. 'I had nothin' to do with that. I want to tell you about what I was doing when that biker bloke saw me. It's not what you think.'

'It's important you take into account that Mr Ackland's statement is voluntary. He may have been present, unintentionally of course, when a crime was being committed. This is why he's been a little hesitant to be as forthcoming as he might regarding his whereabouts at the time in question. What's important is that this fishing exercise of yours ceases.' He leaned towards the recorder and spoke into it. 'My client had nothing to do with any murder.'

'Will you get to the point?' I said. Lincoln was beginning to really grate on my nerves.

'Of course,' said Lincoln. 'However, are we clear that no charges should be brought if it is found my client was in the presence of others who might or might not have been committing a rather minor crime?'

'Let's hear what he has to say,' said Cotton.

'He realises you're investigating a very serious crime and doesn't want you wasting any more of your time linking events to him.'

'Crimes,' corrected Cotton again. 'We're investigating crimes, the murder of children. If you can help, Mr Ackland, I suggest you do.'

I put my hand up and shut down Lincoln who was about to open his mouth again.

'Let's hear what he has to say, shall we?' I said.

Lincoln bristled uncomfortably. His slick hair gleamed under the harsh lighting. He twisted a cuff-link as Ackland spoke. Occasionally, he nodded encouragingly.

'I was there with two mates. We're doing the farmers a favour. We're keeping the numbers down and keeping them off the farmer's crops. It's conservation, that's what it is. No different to what happens in nature.'

It took me a moment to understand what Ackland was talking about. 'Poaching? Is that what you're saying?'

Ackland looked at Lincoln. He turned to me and nodded. 'Yeah. Deer. Venison is good eating.'

'The blood in the van?' I said.

'Uh huh. We portion out the meat with the cleaver and saw. Bag it up and sell it out the back of the van. I ain't proud. I've just had a few unexpected bills lately. I'm doing what I have to do to make ends meet.'

'You have the wrong man,' said Lincoln proudly. He looked smug. 'Mr Ackland is innocent. A lesser man might say he's been harassed.'

Cotton slammed the file closed. Lincoln jumped. 'Why the hell didn't you tell us this sooner? Do you have any idea how much time you wasted?'

'Sorry. Everything escalated. I didn't think it would go this far.'

Lincoln got to his feet and placed a hand on Ackland's shoulder. 'I suppose Mr Ackland is free to go? He's not been charged. You have no reason to hold him here a moment longer. He's been extremely cooperative. He's clearly innocent.'

'Innocent? You call poaching being innocent?'

Lincoln's smile evaporated. His face flushed red.

'I want names. I want the exact location,' I said.

'Yeah, yeah. You got it,' said Ackland. He looked relieved.

'I want a written statement. If it turns out you're telling the truth and that is your alibi then you'll be charged with poaching.'

Ackland turned to Lincoln.

'A slap on the wrist and a fine, nothing more,' said Lincoln reassuringly. 'Rare occasion there is a short custodial sentence, but very rarely. You'll be fine. Let's go.'

Cotton ended the interview, got up and showed them out.

I felt sick to my stomach. Not only did we waste hours on this idiot but now he was celebrating that his illegal pastime had given him an alibi.

CHAPTER SIXTEEN

Nurse Petra Budden helped Jenny with her shoes. Rayner watched through the door as the pair of them chatted. It was heartbreaking to see how Jen had struggled through her physiotherapy. He needed a moment before joining them. He took a deep breath and opened the door.

'It looked like it went really well. How was it?' he said, doing his best to sound upbeat.

'Hard,' said Jenny flatly.

'It was hard work,' agreed Petra. 'But you did amazingly. I know you've heard it numerous times but I'm going to say it again, it's really important to do the exercises and stretching. The skin will stretch given time and it's important to keep the joints mobile and to retain and build muscle. It's also important to pay attention to your body and rest when necessary.'

'All that's a damn sight easier when you're not six months pregnant,' grumbled Jenny. She put out her hand and Rayner helped her to her feet. 'Thank you, Petra.'

'We appreciate all you're doing, see you next week,' added Rayner.

'You will. Same time. Stay positive and the more you

move the quicker the recovery. Just be careful. This is a marathon not a sprint.'

Jenny patted her baby bump. 'I don't sprint anywhere these days.'

They took their time and once at the front of the hospital Jenny waited while Rayner went to get the car. He pulled up out front and helped her into the seat. Once on the road she was quiet, staring out of the window.

'Would you like some music on?' said Rayner.

'I'm okay. You can if you want.'

'No. I'm okay.' Rayner watched the road and glanced a few times at Jenny. She was in a sombre mood again. 'What's up? And don't say "nothing".'

She shrugged.

'Is it your legs, are they hurting?'

'No. They're not too bad. A bit tender.' Her face looked stormy. 'The case you're working.'

'What about it,' he tried to sound breezy. She never usually asked about his investigations and when she did it was because she had concerns.

'I read in the paper about what he did to those families. What sort of person does that to children?'

'Jen, I asked you not to. Not now, not while you've got so much going on. Focus on you. You know what these investigations can be like.'

'I didn't mean to read about it. I opened the paper and there it was. Normally—'

'I know. Normally, you can keep yourself occupied and leave me to it. Please don't worry, this guy is a coward. He'd take one look at me and run for the hills, I swear.'

She looked slightly reassured. 'You're sure?'

'I promise. You have nothing to worry about. He's probably some pathetic shit who gets off on hurting kids. When we find him he'll piss his pants and start crying like a fucking baby.'

'Don't talk like that. You're better than that.'

'Sorry. Just making my point.' He was hardly sleeping nights and on edge all the time. There were long periods, especially in the mornings, when he felt on the verge of tears. He looked down at their bump. He'd noticed how these days she was more sensitive about the way he spoke in front of the baby. Yet, he knew he was swearing and being less respectful to others pretty much all the time. Due to constant anger, he felt he was having trouble keeping it together.

'Be careful. The baby and I need you.'

Rayner reached out and squeezed her hand. 'You know me.'

'I do know you, which is why I'm saying it. When you and James are together you do stupid things. I love James, you know that, but I wonder if he always remembers his responsibilities at home. He can be like a dog with a bone and I don't want him putting you at risk for some misguided loyalty to the police service.'

'What? Misguided? Where the hell is this coming from? I know where this is coming from. You're blaming James for what happened. The house fire wasn't his fault.'

Jenny was taken aback by his sudden outburst. 'I'm not blaming him. Of course I'm not. It's just—' she turned in her seat to look at him.

'Just what?'

'Your loyalty to him. It's like the pair of you are still in the school playground taking on a bully.'

'What you're saying is that he leads and I follow. I'm not some faithful puppy that follows him around.' He had to slam on the brakes when he suddenly realised the traffic lights ahead had turned red.

'Careful,' said Jenny. 'This came out wrong. I know you're not. It's just you're like brothers. I don't know what I'm trying say. Just be careful. Don't do anything stupid.'

'Think for yourself. That's what you're saying,' grunted Rayner.

'Yes. I suppose it is.'

Jenny watched as he stewed over their conversation. She adored his unquestioning loyalty for those he loved. Yet since her pregnancy and the fire at James's house, when both she and Gabriel nearly lost their lives – started by someone he and James had sent to prison – the way he followed James was something that bothered her a great deal too. She knew their bravado was as much him as it was James but she felt she had to put it out there. It might make him think twice before doing something dumb.

'You know I'd never do anything to put you or the baby at risk, don't you?' said Rayner.

'I do. Equally, I want our baby to grow up with a father.'

Rayner kept his eyes on the road. He nodded and quietly grumbled to himself.

Jenny could see she'd got her message across. She kissed her fingers, reached over and planted it on his cheek. 'Love you.'

'Love you too.' He glanced at her and smiled. 'I'm not Robin to his Batman you know.'

'I know.' She chuckled. 'You're more like... Sheriff Woody and Buzz Lightyear.'

'Oi!'

CHAPTER SEVENTEEN

Alex rang the doorbell a fourth time. Stepping away from the front door he took a good look at each of the windows. He went back to the door, knocked and rang again. Opening the letterbox, he put his mouth to it. 'Emma? It's Alex. I've been thinking we should talk.'

'Emma's not in.'

Alex turned. 'Her car's here.' He looked to the street where Emma's red Ford Focus was parked.

'That's right. She got picked up. Her boss swung by early this morning. I saw them when I was going out for my run.'

Alex looked up at the windows one more time as though the information was unlikely to be reliable. 'That's kind of a relief. I've been trying to get hold of her. I remember now. She's on a big case. It slipped my mind. I've been up to my eyeballs opening a new dental practice. Head and shoulders above anything else on the south coast.' He walked over to the fence dividing the two front gardens and put out a hand. 'Duncan, isn't it?'

Declan didn't show his annoyance. He shook Alex's

hand before correcting him. 'It's Declan. And you're Alex. We've met.'

'Have we? That's right. Cake boy. You bake cakes. You're the one trying to make my girlfriend fat.'

'My mum bakes,' said Declan. He wasn't going to rise to this arrogant prick's bait. 'It raises a lot of money for charity.'

'Well, Emma's not a charity case. Maybe you could ask Mummy to cut back on the baked goods. In the politest possible way, of course.'

'Really? Surely that's Emma's choice?'

'A word to the wise, between you and me, I think she's too polite to say anything. I'm pretty sure most of the time the cakes end up in the bin.'

'I'll have a word with Mum. Sensitively.' Declan released his jaw which he realised he was clenching.

'You work out?' said Alex.

'A bit.'

'I'd say more than a bit. I do a bit of cardio myself. Triathlons when I get the time. And you?'

'Some boxing. Mixed martial arts.'

Alex did a karate chop in the air before patting Declan on his muscular shoulder. 'Just kidding. I don't want to wake the sleeping beast.'

Declan smiled. He was about to walk away but couldn't resist. 'I haven't seen you around so much lately. I thought perhaps you and Emma had broken up.'

Alex's smugness evaporated. His eyes hardened before slowly softening. 'We've both had work commitments and we're taking it slow. The way you do when you know it's the real thing.'

'Okay. That's one way I suppose.' Declan nodded knowingly.

Alex became playful. 'Between you and me, and I'll

throttle you if you let the cat out of the bag, I've planned a little surprise for Emma. A long weekend in Paris. I think it's most beautiful during the autumn months. What woman could resist?'

Declan felt deflated. He was ready for this conversation to be over. 'Sounds amazing. Look, I've got to run. Good to see you again. I'll let Emma know you dropped by.'

'Don't bother yourself. I'll probably catch her at work. Anyway, I'm sure you have more cakes to deliver.' He clucked his tongue and winked. 'See you around.'

Not if I see you first, you complete... thought Declan. What on earth does she see in him? Who says money can't buy you love?

He watched as Alex climbed into his white Jaguar XF, turned the car around, and accelerated away without so much as a glance in his direction.

His mother opened the front door and placed a tentative foot on the doorstep. She leaned heavily on a walking stick. With her other hand she held a rubbish bag from the kitchen pedal bin.

'What are you doing, Mum? I can do that.' He raced to her; ensured she was stable.

'I can do it. Stop fussing.' She brought the other foot out onto the step and placed a hand onto the wall to steady herself.

'It's a new hip. Where will you be if you fall because you're being impatient?'

'I suppose. I just wanted to do something useful. Sitting around gets me down. I'm supposed to do some light exercise.'

'Wait there. I'll put this in the bin and we'll go inside together.' He took the bag from her hand.

She smiled and roughed up his hair. 'You're a good boy.'

He couldn't help but chuckle. 'For Christ's sake leave my hair alone.'

She looked over at Emma's house. 'Worried your hair won't be perfect for her next door?'

'Shush, Mum. Keep your voice down.' Laughing, he ran around the side of the house to the bin, dropped the rubbish inside, and trotted back as quick as he could. He took her arm and helped her inside.

'It must run in the blood. Your father and I had a similar age gap.' She giggled at her mischief making. 'She's a lovely girl. When are you going to bite the bullet and ask her out?'

He shook his head and gave an exasperated laugh. 'Enough. She's in a relationship with a rich dentist. Not only that, she sees me as the young lad next door.' He helped her into her armchair and passed her the TV remote.

'So you're not denying it's crossed your mind?' Her eyes narrowed like a TV detective.

'That's it. Change the subject. I'm not talking about this any more. I'm making you a cup of tea, then getting on with some work.'

'Come on, Deccy, I'm only teasing.'

'Biscuits or cake with your tea?'

'I hope you invited her to the party.'

'Biscuits or cake? Or just tea?'

'Cake, please.'

He disappeared into the kitchen.

She listened to him moving around. She knew he was thinking about Emma. She waited for her moment. Tap on and off as the kettle was filled. Cupboard door opened and closed. Cups on worktop. Tea bags in. Fridge opened. Milk in cups. Milk back in fridge. Fridge closed. Kettle hissed as water boiled. A broad grin crossed her face; she had to control her laughter so she could speak. She took a deep breath; called to him in the kitchen. 'You invited her to the party, didn't you? I can tell.' Her body hurt from holding in the laughter. She could hear him in the other room, he was laughing too.

'Might have done,' he spluttered.

CHAPTER EIGHTEEN

I stared at my morning tea, steam swirling and dancing before evaporating. Rayner and Cotton placed their drinks on the edge of my desk and each pulled up a chair opposite me.

'I thought we had something,' I said.

'I wanted it to be Ackland as much as you guys,' said Rayner.

'His alibi fits. The blood in the van was animal blood, most likely deer.'

'He really was poaching?'

'Yep. His two mates have been hauled in and questioned. O'Brien and Doyle both swear Ackland was with them. Ackland's not our guy,' said Cotton.

I sucked my teeth in frustration. 'So where are we at with Janek Bonne?'

'His mobile phone was recovered and I've been going through his list of contacts. I'm about a third of the way through. I'll continue that today,' said Rayner.

Cotton cleared her throat before speaking. 'I'm still looking at the mothers. They were all twins themselves, that's confirmed. I've spoken to their families and been able to establish at least two of them were participating in research,' she said. 'I have a phone call scheduled and I'm speaking with a researcher at the institute later today. But get this. I googled the institute's website and Janek Bonne is a founder.'

'Really? Great work. Was Elizabeth Poulson one of the mothers?'

'Yes. She was part of a research study. What I can tell you is that Janek Bonne and Elizabeth Poulson go way back. I'm still trying to establish their relationship. Could be nothing but I'll follow it up anyway.'

'Good. Keep going with that,' I said then turned to Rayner. 'What about forensics from the hedgerow. Did they get anything?'

'They pulled some fibres. Definitely clothing. Also, definitely hair. I'm still waiting to hear if they're of any help to us. I'll call again today to chase them up.'

'Good. I need to call the chief super and give him an update.' I pushed back in my chair. Our unit had to prove its worth. I was trying to keep my frustration in check. For the sake of my new team I'd really hoped Ackland was our man, but right now any report I gave Webster would look like we'd achieved little or nothing.

My mobile phone rang; it was Heidi Hamilton.

Cotton and Rayner got up to leave me to it. I raised my hand and they waited. When I ended the call I looked at the pair, disbelief on my face. 'That was Hamilton. DNA was found under Janek Bonne's fingernails and there was bruising on hands, arms and chest.'

'A fight?' said Rayner.

'Or someone else was with him on the boat for sex. Maybe he liked it rough. Perhaps things went wrong and the other party panicked and fled?' said Cotton.

'The table was set for one,' added Rayner. 'It didn't look like he was expecting company.'

'Maybe he wasn't expecting company. The other party turned up unannounced.'

'It would explain why the meal wasn't touched. He decided sex came first. Sex beats dinner every time,' laughed Rayner.

Cotton shook her head. 'Really? Did you just say that out loud?'

'What? It's true.'

'Perhaps his death was suicide; maybe he used his belt to hang himself?' mused Cotton.

'Certainly convenient, wouldn't you say?' said Rayner sarcastically.

'All we can do is keep an open mind. Suicide, misadventure, even murder. We keep going. We follow the evidence. Right now we have Bonne's unexplained death, him being the last person to see the Poulson family alive, his history with Elizabeth Poulson and the research institute that connects them both and the boys. At this stage we can't rule anything out. For all we know, he went back to the house later that night, for reasons unknown killed the family and then filled with remorse, committed suicide.'

'Why would Bonne kill Elizabeth Poulson and her family,' said Cotton. 'It doesn't feel right.'

'I'll look into whether Bonne had ties with the other families,' said Rayner.

I agreed with Cotton that there were still a lot of unanswered questions. A lot of speculation. Right now it was all we could do. From the look on Rayner's face I could see he felt the same. He knew all we could do was carry on opening doors until we found something solid behind one of them.

'So we're in agreement? We dig into Bonne's background?'

Cotton and Rayner agreed.

'What do we know about Bonne right this minute,' asked Rayner.

'From what I've found online,' said Cotton, 'I can tell you Bonne amassed a fortune from investments in businesses primarily in the field of science, but he had a varied portfolio. I can also tell you he was a very private person. Travelled widely. Liked adventure and challenging himself. Did a lot for charity. Was well respected. More recently, he'd become something of a philanthropist. Through the Bonne Foundation he's focused on research and well-being. The twin research was a tiny part of that.'

'It's conceivable he led a double life. Many psychopaths live two very distinct lives. A different public and private persona isn't unusual,' I said.

'We've come across that scenario on more than one occasion,' added Rayner.

'It means unless we redouble our efforts we'll only see the life Bonne wants us to see,' I said. 'We need to look at his private life, where he came from, childhood, family et cetera. Tell me about the institute researching twins that Bonne founded.'

'It's the Dorchester Science and Research Institute.' Cotton went over her notes. 'Robert Valentine leads the research. He's been at a conference in The Hague. Returned yesterday.' Cotton checked the time on her phone. 'In fact he's back in the office now.'

'Let's pay him a visit. Maybe he can throw some light on what twins might be of special interest to our killer. He can also tell us more about Bonne.'

Cotton nodded in agreement.

'Are you coming?' I said.

'Yes. Yes. I was just thinking. It's nothing.' She grabbed her coat off the back of her seat.

'Don't forget your call to the chief super. Webster'll want to know what we're up to,' said Rayner. 'You know how grouchy the old man gets.' He gave out one of his booming laughs.

'I'll call him from the car.' I grabbed my coat and downed my tea. 'I want to hear if forensics get anything more on those fibres from the hedgerow. Call me. Okay?'

Rayner went to his desk and made the call. 'I'm on it. I'll hound them. I'll also see what else I can dig up on Bonne.'

Cotton and I headed for my car. 'Are you okay? You don't seem yourself today.'

Her eyes shifted in a way that told me something wasn't right with her. 'Everything's fine. I'm good. A little tired perhaps. As you know, this is the biggest case I've worked; there's a lot to consider and it's a little hard to switch off at times. I suppose you know how that feels?'

'Unfortunately, yes. A case like this can too easily become all-consuming. The only advice I can offer is to try to be in the moment. When you're working focus on that, and if you're in your own time, doing whatever it is you do to unwind, then be focused on that. Don't be two places at once. It's easier said than done. My father tried to teach me that lesson; I guess it's only now I truly appreciate what he was telling me.'

'I understand. But honestly, I'm okay. Thank you.'

'You're sure?' I said, unconvinced. 'If anything is worrying you, you can always talk to me, you know that right? Unless it's relationship troubles,' I quipped. 'Then hopefully you know Monica is there for you. And if you really want to get away from it all remember, as far as Alice and Faith are concerned, you're like a big sister. They'd like nothing more than to see you again.'

'I know. Thank you,' she said. Her face looked anguished but she wasn't being forthcoming so I let it go.

She held out a hand for my car keys and said, 'I'll drive. It'll give you a chance to phone the chief super. From what Rayner says it's best you get that out of the way.'

CHAPTER NINETEEN

Robert Valentine welcomed us into his office with a firm handshake. He leaned in close and I noticed his floral aftershave. His dark good looks reminded me both in age and appearance of an actor I'd seen in a movie recently, one of Monica's favourites; the name Colin Farrell came to mind. His tailored shirt was open at the collar, the sleeves rolled up over his forearms. His tie lay across his desk, his suit jacket hung on the coat-stand in the corner of the room. He pointed to a couple of chairs on the other side of his desk. 'Please,' he said, 'take a seat, I won't keep you a moment.'

'Is everything okay, Mr Valentine?' I asked.

'I appear to have left my briefcase on the plane.' His dark eyes were warm and friendly as he moved around the room. He looked past us and chatted agreeably as he searched around the office as though the briefcase might magically appear. 'I'm sure I had it when I left the hotel. I suppose it could be in the taxi I took from the hotel to the airport. It's not the end of the world but you know how it is. It's more the inconvenience. The case had my latest research and even the dictaphone my children bought me for Father's Day, several years ago now, but precious memories. I'm annoyed with myself, I'm not usually so forgetful. Since Janek's death I've found it hard to concentrate.' He scratched the back of his head. 'We've all taken it hard. He was loved here at the institute. He was an easy man to like.' He gazed off into the distance.

He shook his head and then turned back to us. 'I'm sorry. Inspectors Hardy and Cotton, how can I be of assistance to you?'

'We're here to learn what we can about Mr Bonne and your work here with twins,' said Cotton. 'In particular these families.' Cotton passed Valentine an A4 sheet with details of the murdered families.

'I'm a little confused,' said Valentine. He smiled politely.

She pointed to the top of the sheet. 'We know for sure the Poulson family and the Anderson family registered with yourselves. We thought perhaps you could check on the rest of the names.'

Valentine scrunched up his face as he thought about it. 'Obviously, there is the matter of confidentiality.'

'It's part of a murder investigation,' I said. 'We're examining links between the families.'

Valentine's dark eyes widened. 'Murder?' He slumped back in his chair. 'Oh no. Are these the families murdered by that killer targeting twins?' He stared at the list again. 'Of course they are,' he said to himself. 'And you think they were all registered with us?'

'It's a possibility,' said Cotton. 'We don't know. We're hoping you can confirm that for us.'

He stroked his brow. 'Well, we do have many hundreds of pairs of twins from all around the globe,' he said.

'So it's possible they are all registered here?' said Cotton.

He became more reticent. 'Yes. It is possible.'

'Did Janek Bonne have access to the personal information of the twins, either adults or children?'

'No.'

'You're sure.'

'He funded our research. He was not hands-on in any way.'

'Did he have access to the results of the trials?'

'I'm not sure, possibly, I'd have to check. Hold on one moment. I hope you're not suggesting Janek was in any way involved in the murder of these families. Preposterous. If you knew the man you'd never suggest such a thing. He was a kind, peaceful and generous man. Everyone who knew him, loved him.'

'And yet he's dead, possibly murdered,' blurted Cotton. Realising her mistake she blushed.

'What! Janek murdered?'

'We don't know that,' I corrected. 'His death is unexplained at this moment in time.'

'We were led to believe it was suicide.' Valentine's thick eyebrows furrowed. 'It's all a lot to take in. The murdered families, and now Janek. And you think they're connected?'

'It's a possibility. We don't know at this stage of the investigation. It's why we need your help.'

'All we need is for someone to check the names against your database,' said Cotton. 'Perhaps someone could do it for us while we wait?'

Valentine's mind was elsewhere as he mumbled what sounded like something rehearsed from the company brochure. 'We take data security seriously. Adhere to the strictest data protection laws. Every twin's personal information is filed away on a state-of-the-art secure server. A leak is impossible. Personal information is safe.'

'That may be so but somehow a killer has obtained names and addresses around the south of England with boy twins of a similar age,' I said. 'And for all we know this could be the tip of the iceberg.'

'What about your clients?' asked Cotton. 'I mean, presumably someone buys the results of your research?' She already had a fair idea of the answer but we needed to keep Valentine talking. He appeared to be having trouble processing all this new information and might simply clam up.

I helped him out. 'From what we understand clients receive results of trials focusing on well-being, behavioural and lifestyle influences?'

'You're barking up the wrong tree,' insisted Valentine. 'Other research institutes look at clinical and genetic data. Maybe, one of them unwittingly shared their subject's private information. It isn't us.'

'We're exploring every avenue,' assured Cotton.

I decided to push my luck and make a claim I did not know for certain. 'The thing is we know one of the families, the Andersons, were only registered with this institute, and none of the others. It stands to reason that the addresses came from here. If we need to we will seize every computer in this building, and the personal computer of every member of staff.'

'You can't do that.' Valentine jumped to his feet, then slowly returned to his seat.

'We can and we will. This is a murder investigation and I'll do what is necessary to find the person responsible.'

Valentine could see I wasn't bluffing. 'I'll need to consult with colleagues before any decision is made.'

There was a knock at the door and a head of brown wavy hair appeared.

'I'm sorry, Robert. I didn't realise you were in a meeting.'

'Come in,' said Valentine. He waved a hand of encouragement.

A man who looked to be in his late thirties or early forties entered the room. The back of his shirt needed tucking in. Rather self-consciously he shoved his hands into his pockets. 'I didn't mean to interrupt. I heard you were back and wanted to bring you up to speed. We can speak later.'

'No, no. Stay. This is Inspector Cotton and Inspector...'

'Hardy,' I said, helping him out. 'Pleased to meet you. You are...?'

'Sorry, yes. Andrew Yates. I crunch numbers. Turn the twins' answers into percentages.' He laughed awkwardly.

'Andrew's being modest,' said Valentine, turning to us. 'Our Andrew here is a genius. He discovers valuable correlations of data that we can monetise for businesses around the world. He is the backbone of this institute. Every piece of data passes through his hands at some point.'

Yates's face turned pink. He patted his unruly hair then shoved his hand back into his pocket again. 'I don't know about all that,' said Yates. 'Are you here regarding Mr Bonne's death? He was a really great man. I heard it was suicide?'

'Possibly,' said Cotton.

'I suppose we never know what's going on inside someone's head.' He raised his eyebrows and looked at us.

'Did you know him well?' asked Cotton.

'No. I probably only ever met him a dozen times.' He opened and closed his mouth then looked around as though he'd run out of words, or used up his quota for the day. 'Actually, you know, I'd better get back to it. Nice to meet you. I'll catch you later, Robert.'

Yates closed the door behind him.

'Doesn't appreciate his brilliance. He's scruffy on the

outside but his mind is sharp and ordered,' said Valentine. 'Is there anything else? No? Okay. I'll talk to our legal team and see what we can do to assist. How about I call you in the morning?'

'Thank you.' I passed Valentine a card with my contact details. 'Sooner the better,' I added.

'Understood. I'll make a call immediately. Then I'd better get back to working out where I left that briefcase of mine. It only held my notes for the presentation. No lost data.' He laughed nervously.

As Valentine showed us out he chatted about his conference in the The Hague and how beautiful the city is. Once we reached the ground floor reception we shook hands and he left us. Andrew Yates was talking to a female colleague at the reception desk. On seeing us he ended his conversation and scuttled off along a corridor. I watched as he reached a door, punched in a code on a wall pad and disappeared inside. The female colleague went back to her duties. Turning away from us she picked up the phone and made a call.

'Looks like we're the talk of the town,' said Cotton.

'Yup. And so starts the rumour mill.'

CHAPTER TWENTY

'That's the one, Monica. Definitely,' said Faith. In her small hand she held a navy tweed waistcoat. She examined it like a fashion designer ahead of a big show.

'That'll go with all Daddy's jackets,' agreed Alice. 'Good spotting, sis'.'

Faith looked proud of her discovery. She lifted it up for them both to see. 'Can we get it?'

'I do like that,' said Monica. She gritted her teeth and smiled through the headache she couldn't shift. 'It's a lovely shade of blue and the material feels really nice. What do you think?'

The two girls nodded eagerly. They stood back while Monica went through the sizes on the rack. 'Got ya,' said Monica. 'Now we've just got to hope he doesn't tear it like he did the last one.'

'Perhaps he's getting a little wider around the middle,' said Alice.

Monica laughed. 'I'll let you put that to him. I'm in no position to say anything.'

'Yes, but you're pregnant. Daddy's not,' said Faith.

They all laughed and made their way to the checkout.

While the sales assistant scanned and folded the waistcoat Faith crossed her arms the way an adult might and said to Monica, 'I know it's not his birthday but I'm making him a card to go with the waistcoat.'

Monica was about to reply when her headache suddenly felt much worse. She reached out and grabbed hold of the checkout desk as her vision blurred. The girls did their best to hold her as she became unsteady on her feet. Looking panicked, the sales assistant called for help.

Monica eased herself down to a sitting position on the floor. 'It's nothing, it's okay. It'll pass. I'm all right.'

Faith sat beside Monica and held on to her, she put her head on her shoulder.

Alice waved to a second shopping assistant who was rushing over.

'My name's Pamela, I'm a first-aider. Are you okay? What seems to be the matter?'

'I'm fine, I'm so sorry, I felt lightheaded for a moment and had a bit of double-vision. A headache...' She pressed her hand against the back of her head. 'But I'm okay now. It's fine. If you can just help me up.'

Pamela looked concerned, unsure what to do. 'Why don't you sit there for a little while. To make sure you're okay.'

Monica looked around and saw other shoppers staring. 'I would rather finish up here and get going. But thank you.'

Pamela took Monica's arms and with Alice and Faith giving a supportive hand she got to her feet.

'I can get a chair if you want to sit for a while, take a breather? Would you like a glass of water?'

'No, thank you. I feel right as rain again now.' Monica presented her debit card and the assistant processed the payment and handed over the waistcoat.

'I'll tell you what,' said Pamela, 'why don't we go over to

the coffee shop where you can rest your feet.' Looking at Alice and Faith she said, 'I'm pretty sure if I have a word with my colleague we'll be able to rustle up some complimentary refreshments.' She winked at the two girls who she could see were pale and concerned.

As they walked Pamela spoke quietly to Monica. 'I'd like to call an ambulance. Get you checked over.' When Monica looked resistant she added, 'For the sake of you and the baby.'

'It's not necessary. We'll take a short break and then head home. I've been on my feet too long, that's all.'

'It's no trouble and it would put my mind at rest.'

'No, it's really kind of you but I'll be fine. I have my mobile. If it's necessary I'll call my other half.'

'If you're absolutely sure?' Pamela found them a table just inside the door of the store cafeteria. 'I'll explain the situation to my colleague and she'll look after you.'

'You've been very kind. Thank you.'

'Thank you,' echoed Alice and Faith and began scrutinising the menu. Pamela left them to it.

'Well that was a bit of unexpected excitement. Your little brother or sister is causing trouble again.'

'Are you really okay?' asked Alice.

'Yes, sweetheart, I'm fine.'

'I think baby would like some chocolate fudge cake,' said Faith grinning from ear to ear.

Amused, Alice and Monica looked at each other and then back at Faith. 'Well, you know what,' smiled Monica, 'I think we'd all like some chocolate fudge cake.'

CHAPTER TWENTY-ONE

'Baby is perfectly normal,' the sonographer said, followed by a little giggle. She spun around in her seat and peered at us through small wire framed glasses perched on the end of her thin nose. Her name badge read Tris which I assumed was short for something. It seemed to be her habit to end each sentence with a giggle no matter what she said. Tris wiped the gel on Monica's tummy and passed her some tissues to finish off the clean-up.

I shifted uneasily in my seat and repeated what I'd said on arrival. 'Monica collapsed. That can't be normal. Are you sure everything's okay?' I realised I might be being a little over-dramatic claiming she collapsed but I wanted to be sure she was all right.

'Yes, baby is fine,' repeated Tris. 'My suggestion is you speak to your midwife.' She put her hand on Monica's notes which I had to assume she'd read.

'I don't want to come across as a worrier,' I said, realising I was doing exactly that.

She scratched an eyebrow. 'Not at all. Carry on.' Giggle. She tilted her head, smiled and showed her teeth. Any minute now I expected a patronising pat on the head.

'Monica nearly passed out in the middle of a department store. I'm concerned the check-ups and tests have missed something?'

She narrowed her eyes and stroked her chin like an amateur actor going overboard to ensure the audience understood they were listening intently and weighing up some weighty question. She pondered a few seconds to be certain I'd quite finished before turning to Monica. 'It's best you to speak your GP or midwife. There are a few reasons you could have felt lightheaded. Your blood pressure might be on the high side. Or your sugar levels were a bit low. Make sure you eat regularly.' She opened the notes and gave them a perfunctory look, then turned to us both and offered reassurance. 'Your notes do mention slightly elevated blood pressure, so speak to the midwife as I said. My job is to check the baby, so I can't offer any medical advice on that score. I can only repeat that your baby looks perfectly normal for thirty weeks. And judging by today, it's also very active.' Another giggle.

'That's a relief, isn't it, James?' said Monica.

'Uh huh. Definitely.'

'An active baby must be a sign of a fit and healthy baby? I can live with that,' added Monica.

'That's right. It's just what you want. When you call your midwife or GP tell them exactly what happened and mention the headaches and blurred vision. It can possibly be a sign of pre-eclampsia, but they'll better advise you.'

'Pre-eclampsia?' said Monica.

'Don't be overly concerned. Make the call as a precaution. You can get ready now. I'll be outside, come through when you're done.' She gave another giggle as she got up and left us alone.

Sitting beside Monica, it was hard to take my eyes off

her. She looked radiant and happy. I was filled with so much love I thought I might burst. I felt in my pocket for the small box. I needed to wait. This wasn't the right time, but it seemed never to be the right time. As she pulled on her cardigan and adjusted her clothes, I took the box from my pocket. I put it behind my back and slid off the chair where I got down on one knee. My heart was pounding like a locomotive hurtling wildly along the tracks. My hands trembled and my mouth was dry. Monica was staring at the frozen image of our baby on the screen. I looked up at her and was about to speak when Tris knocked and came back into the room. I hid the box in the palm of my hand and pretended to be doing up my shoe lace. I thought about the embarrassment of being interrupted had I started my speech and a shudder ran down my spine.

Tris lifted her glasses off her nose and rested them on top of her head. 'I'm going to write up my notes,' she said. 'Do you have any more questions?'

I could see she was hoping I didn't.

'We're absolutely fine, thank you, Tris.' Monica looked down at me with a puzzled look on her face.

'We're wonderful. I mean, everything's okay. Thank you.' I jumped to my feet, thrust the small box into my pocket and helped Monica off the examination table.

'Are you okay?' asked Monica as we made our way out of the hospital. 'You seem on edge. I can come to these examinations on my own. I know you're busy. You don't need to come to every one if you don't have time.'

'On edge? I'm okay. Uh, I might be a little distracted but I love coming with you.'

'Perhaps next time I'll come with Sylvia, I think your mum would enjoy it.'

'That would be nice. She'd like that.' *So would Tris*, I

thought. We reached the car and I took the keys from my pocket. I opened the door and Monica got in. I felt the small box in my pocket. *Would the time ever be right?*

CHAPTER TWENTY-TWO

With his laptop bag slung over his shoulder Andrew Yates looked around nervously as he walked to his car through the institute's underground car park.

Opening the door, he placed one knee on the driver's seat and with the car's steering wheel digging into his ribs, reached over and slid the laptop bag as far under the passenger seat as possible. Satisfied, he sat back in the driver's seat and pulled on his seatbelt. As he reached out and put the keys in the ignition there was a knock on the side window.

Robert Valentine turned his hand in a winding motion. Yates lowered the window.

'Whoops. Sorry, Andy. Didn't mean to startle you,' said Valentine.

'That's fine. Bit jumpy. Too much caffeine today, perhaps.' He tried to laugh.

'Have you got a moment, I was wondering if we might have a word?'

'Of course,' said Yates. 'Everything okay?' He shifted his body to block the view of the passenger seat, even though he was sure the laptop bag wasn't visible.

'It's just you came to my office earlier, when the police were there, and I assumed you wanted to talk? Only, I didn't see you this afternoon. I'm checking there isn't anything important you needed to discuss.'

'Oh, that, um. It was nothing. There was a glitch in the software while you were away at the conference in Holland. I called the hotel and the conference venue and left a message. I was checking you got it.'

'Yes. I got your message. Not that I can remember what it said. It's been a crazy few days, especially with the news of Janek's death.'

Yates nodded in agreement. 'Anyway, today I was just going to let you know it's been sorted. I left some diagnostic tests running and managed to fix the bugs. I knew they'd take a while so I took a day off. I'm a little behind with the new data but it'll be ready by the end of the month. I'll give you an update on the latest set of results by the middle of next week. Is that okay?'

'Perfect. I'm glad everything worked out. Did you enjoy your day off?'

'My day off? Yes, yes. I didn't do much. I went walking. Packed a rucksack, grabbed my map and headed out across the hills.'

'With your walking group?'

'No. It was a last minute thing so I went alone. I like the group walks but sometimes it's nice to be in one's own company. It's easier to appreciate the surroundings as you walk. Gives you time to think. Difficult to do that in a group. Constant chatter.'

'I know what you mean. Well, I'll leave you to it. Have a good evening.' Valentine turned to walk away.

'The police. A few routine questions, I guess? Not interested in anything in particular?' asked Yates.

'They want access to the data.'

'What? Why? It was suicide.'

'They're looking into a murder.'

'They think Janek was murdered?'

'No. I don't think so. I don't know. They're looking into several murders.'

'I don't understand.'

'The victims are families with twins. There's been another family killed. They believe the families are all in our database.'

'Hang on. So they think Janek was involved?'

'I don't think they know what to think. They want us to cross-reference names and addresses of the families murdered with our database.'

'Are you going to let them? I hope you told them no. We can't have police crawling all over my database. Families might stop coming forward if we can't offer an ironclad guarantee that their information is private and secure.' He could feel his face flushing. The thought of unwanted guests poring over his research made his skin prickle.

'You're right, Andrew. I'll do all I can. The legal team are looking at it. It's a moral question as well as a legal one. If we can help in some way, perhaps we should. And if Janek was involved, which I don't believe for one second he was, and we hindered the investigation... how would that look?'

'It's not my place to say but if you do help I would suggest access to the records be restricted. I mean, you wouldn't give them carte blanche access. Who knows what they might start digging into. They say they want one thing and then before you know it they're prying into other areas. You have to be really careful. It could open a whole new can of worms.'

'I see your point. No, no, it won't come to that. If it came to it, we'd check the details ourselves and pass on the information. I'm sure they won't need to actually go through the data themselves.'

'I wouldn't put it past them.'

Valentine's brow furrowed. 'My biggest concern right now is that Janek's name doesn't get dragged through the mud. His reputation and that of the institute must be protected.'

'We'll make sure of it. If they ever force us to release the records then I'd be happy to oversee it. I know you'll fight it as best you can. And I'm sure the murder of the families and Janek's death is nothing but pure coincidence.'

Valentine sighed heavily. 'I'll see what the legal team suggest. Let's talk again in the morning.'

Valentine headed to his car.

Yates watched him drive away. He took out his mobile phone and made a call. His hands were shaking. He took long breaths to control his anxiety. 'I might have a problem. If we're doing this, you need to make a decision, and we'll need to do it quickly.'

CHAPTER TWENTY-THREE

Before closing the study door Andrew Yates scooted across the carpet on his office chair and called downstairs to his fiancée, Brianna. 'I'll be down in five minutes. Just backing up some holiday pictures.'

'Okay. Don't be long. Dinner will be ready in fifteen minutes. I'm putting the pizza in the oven now.' The oven door opened and closed. 'Wine or beer?'

'Beer, please.'

Yates's lean fingers glided over the laptop keyboard. Instantly, a Google search returned news articles on the dead families.

Ping! An email arrived.

Yates read it and formed his reply. He took the memory stick from his pocket, slid it into the side of the laptop and within seconds he'd attached a file to the email reply. His finger hovered for a second before he tapped Send. *That's why you're paying me the big bucks*, he thought.

He did another search and looked up the two police inspectors he'd met in Valentine's office. Not a lot on Cotton. He skim-read an article on a recent case involving an escaped convict. He moved on to Hardy, working his way through the articles. Lots of articles. Many serious cases. He enlarged a picture of the inspector shaking hands with the prime minister; he was receiving an award.

Having checked his email with the large attachment had gone, he removed the memory stick. He plugged in his camera and left it backing up the photographs.

Brianna called up the stairs. 'Dinner!'

Yates cleared his browsing history and left the camera transferring pictures.

'Coming!'

He closed the study door and moved across the landing to the boys' room. 'Did you hear your mother?' he said as he pushed open the door.

The boys, Oliver and Dylan, didn't acknowledge him, instead they carried on playing. Yates watched as the boys' online alter egos fired a shotgun and waved a machete at zombies while scaling the Eiffel Tower. 'You want your dinner up here?' he asked.

'Not hungry.'

'Had dinner. We've had crisps.'

'Your mum's done a proper meal,' said Yates wearily.

The boys didn't answer. They remained slouched on their matching navy blue bean bags staring up at the big screen.

He looked around the room and at the bunk beds with matching duvet covers. The bottom bunk was covered in school clothes, homework and empty plates. A few crumbs and smears on the plates suggested they'd had peanut butter and crackers. Plastic tumblers and a bottle of fizzy orange sat beside the boys.

'Andrew, tell Mum we don't want anything,' said Oliver without looking up.

'Thank you, Andrew. Close the door on the way out,' said Dylan.

Yates's nose wrinkled but he bit his tongue. He closed the door and went down stairs.

Brianna was dishing up. She passed him a plate of pizza, chips and beans. 'Knives and forks are on the table,' said Brianna. 'Where are the twins?'

'They're not hungry. I tried, but you know how they ignore me.'

Brianna gave him a peck on the cheek. 'It's not you. They ignore me too. It's their age.'

'More likely the bloody gaming,' muttered Yates.

'Let's eat ours. I'll take them some up later. Do you know if they've done their homework?'

Yates shook his head. 'No idea. Probably not. Not unless their homework involved zombie eradication in the heart of Paris.'

'Well, at least with their new zombie game they get to learn some geography. They were dropping hand grenades from a gondola into the Venice waterways last time I checked.'

Yates sipped his beer.

Brianna tore some garlic bread in half and passed it to him. She pulled off a chunk and talked as she chewed. 'The boys like you. They're no different with their dad. Come sit next to me. Let's make the most of being alone.'

Yates sat down beside her and put his beer bottle on the coffee table. Exchanging it for the TV remote control, he asked, 'What shall we watch?'

'Are you okay? You seem a bit low,' said Brianna. She rolled up a slice of pizza and took a bite.

He put down the TV remote and his dinner. Turning to Brianna he said, 'The police were at the institute.'

'Really. What, about Janek's suicide?'

'They came to see Robert. They want access to all my data.'

'Why?'

'As well as his death they're investigating a series of murders. They think the victims might be in the database. I suppose they think it's all somehow linked. I don't know.'

She shrugged. 'So what's the problem?'

'I don't think he should let them loose on all that information.'

'It's the company's data. I know you like to think it's yours.'

'You say that, but I did all the work. Without me the institute would have no research results. They're making a fortune off my analysis. And what do I get for it?'

'A good salary. Healthcare. Pension.'

He humphed. 'It's not enough. I've seen the payroll. Valentine's raking it in. He also has stock in the company. I should have that.'

Brianna frowned. 'I didn't know you were so upset about it. Speak to Valentine, tell him how you feel.'

'I did. Don't you remember? He said we'd discuss it at the next review. Can you see what I mean? The arrogance of the man. Anyway, I shouldn't have to. I started at the same time as him, more or less. It's because he's a salesman that he's getting more.'

'That seems reasonable to me. Normal in most companies.'

'You don't understand. I'm not respected by anyone there. They need me more than I need them.'

'So demonstrate that. Do something that'll wow them.'

'I have done. I've done something they'll never forget.'

'Good on you. What have you done?'

'It's best I don't say. Not yet anyway. Let's see how it pans out.'

The twins came charging down the stairs. 'Where's ours? We want pizza.'

'It's in the kitchen.'

'Can you get it, Mum?' The boys began shoving each other and trying to kick one another's butt for fun.

Brianna sighed and passed her plate to Yates, who stared at it.

'Can I have fish finger sandwiches, Mum?' said Oliver.

'No. We've got pizza. You have that or nothing.'

The boy pouted and pinched his brother for laughing at him.

Yates put Brianna's plate of food on the coffee table beside his own. He got up from the sofa and went back upstairs to his computer.

CHAPTER TWENTY-FOUR

Having received no response from the institute regarding my request to establish whether all five murdered families had been a part of their research I now found myself at the home of Robert Valentine.

'Inspector, come in, come in.' Valentine opened his front door wide and ushered me in. 'You found us okay?'

'Yes, your directions were spot on.'

'I'm having a day off. It's a little chaotic, it's my youngest's birthday, Milly's eight today. Come through. Meet the family.'

'Thank you. You have a beautiful home.'

'All my wife's work. Interior design, not my thing at all.'

'I'm sorry to intrude,' I said. That was a half-truth. I felt bad turning up at the man's home on his daughter's birthday but I had a job to do.

'You're not. The party is almost over. Between us, your being here is a great excuse for me to get out of operation clean-up.' Valentine made sure his wife, who was filling a black bag with party plates, was in earshot.

'I heard that, mister,' said Angie Valentine. She stopped what she was doing and joined us. It wasn't until she came close to greet me that I could see she was a petite woman in her forties and not a teenager. She was immaculately dressed in a knee length pastel green skirt and roll-neck sweater with suede loafers. A silver crucifix hung around her neck. 'Robert mentioned you were on your way. Can I get you a drink, Inspector? We have gallons of orange squash and lemonade. I think we have some carrot and cucumber sticks too if you're peckish? It seems once again I overdid it with the healthy snacks.' She gave an impish laugh.

I smiled politely. 'That's very kind, thank you. I don't want to intrude any longer than is necessary.'

'I understand,' said Angie. 'Why don't the pair of you go through to the reception room, it should be tidy and private. All joking aside, are you sure you wouldn't like a tea or coffee?' She tilted her head and touched my arm warmly.

'Thank you, no. I'm okay.'

'Right. Off you two scoot.' With a chuckle she held up the black bag containing party cups, plates, straws and left-over party food. She took hold of the handle of the door leading into the conservatory where the children were running around with balloons. She pulled a face and pretended she was going into a war zone. 'Wish me luck. I'm going back in.'

Valentine showed me into the front room and closed the door. He gestured to an armchair beside a bookcase. 'Please take a seat.' Valentine collapsed into a chair opposite me. 'I never knew seven eight-year-olds could make so much noise. My ears are ringing. Do you have children, Inspector?'

'I do. Two daughters, they're growing up fast. My eldest is a teenager. And believe it or not, I have another on the way.'

'Fabulous. Congratulations. You have a look about you,

I can tell you're a family man at heart. Family is the most important thing in my life. It's one of the reasons I agreed to leave my job in the city and help promote research at the institute. I took a large pay cut but I've always been fascinated by human behaviour, and Janek was a very persuasive man.' Valentine spoke fondly.

'Do you come from a big family?'

Valentine held on to his smile but his eyes saddened. 'I was orphaned at a young age.'

'I'm sorry.'

Valentine's smile returned as he appeared to recall his childhood. 'I was raised by my aunt, Evelyn. I don't remember my parents. I was very young when they died. I was very lucky to have my aunt. She was a wonderful woman and I had a magical childhood. I loved her as I would have my mother. She never married or had children of her own. She poured all her love into me. She passed away at the end of last year. Gone far too soon. I was there at the end. I held her hand. She went peacefully. A truly amazing woman.'

Valentine got up from his chair and took down a photograph in a frame. 'This is her.' It was a black and white photograph of a woman and a child beside a piano in what appeared to be a theatre. 'That is my Aunt Evelyn and myself at a pantomime rehearsal. I was about the same age as my own daughter there. Jack and the Beanstalk. That was the panto.' He laughed and taking the photo back, said, 'Anyway, enough of this. You're here about the files, is my guess.'

I nodded and said, 'Indeed I am.'

Valentine sat back down opposite me. He appeared eager to help. 'From a legal perspective, due to data protection we cannot simply hand over the files naming everyone in our research. In fairness, I think both you and I knew that would be the outcome. I'm extremely sorry. I understand the implications of that, I really do. It's a moral quandary. I want to help catch your killer but I need to ensure the institute remains trusted by participants and clientele alike.'

I was bitterly disappointed. I knew it was long shot but knowing whether the killer was selecting his victims from the institute's data would have finally meant we had a direction in which to take the investigation. 'I don't have to see the entire list at this stage. I just need confirmation that those families took part in research.'

Valentine shook his head. 'Our legal team also stated that without proper reason it is unlikely you'd seize our computers. I'm really sorry. I wish...' He stopped as though something had just occurred to him. He got up from his chair. 'Most of our research involves adult twins. However, we encourage families with young twins to join us so we can study their development. When that happens we send a member of our team to meet the family and introduce the institute. For the children it's a friendly face. All this will soon be done over the internet.' Valentine became a little more hesitant as he spoke and lowered his voice. 'We did have to dismiss a female member of the child liaison staff.'

'Is that right?' I said.

'Inappropriate behaviour with one of the fathers. It appears they had known each other in their university days. The thing is,' he spoke in a whisper, 'his was one of the murdered families. Naturally, at the time, for the sake of all involved we kept her dismissal quiet. But under the circumstances—'

'And she visited many of the families with children?'

'Most. Yes. Colin Westbury was the father. Sheila Denning the staff member.' He went to his phone and copied her contact details onto a piece of paper and handed it to me.

'You think Sheila Denning might know if all five families were part of your research?'

Immediately, Valentine became a little less forthcoming. He looked troubled. He shrugged and shook his head. 'I can't say. Just talk to her. I feel giving you this information is wrong. I will deny you got this from me if I'm ever asked. She filed for unfair dismissal and a settlement was reached, contracts were signed.'

To reassure him I said, 'Her name simply came up during our investigation like everyone else working for the company.'

Valentine looked relieved. He tried to smile but there was little happiness in his eyes. 'Thank you,' he said.

'You've done the right thing.'

'I hope so. Good luck, Inspector.'

I got up to leave. 'One last thing. Did Sheila Denning know Janek?'

'No. Not as far as I know. To be honest, Janek was there at the institute's inception, right at the start when it was just Andrew Yates and myself, but he was a starter not a finisher. He quickly moved on to his next venture. I only saw him from time to time once we were up and running. There would have been no reason for him to have known her.'

CHAPTER TWENTY-FIVE

Sheila Denning leaned against the wall at the back of the pharmacy and stared at her shoes. The uniform was white with green piping around the collar and cuffs. Her red wavy hair was tied back. When she looked up at me, her blue eyes were defiant.

'I'm sure you know why I'm here?'

'Took you long enough.'

'Why didn't you go to the police? Ever think you might be able to help their investigation?'

'I don't know anything. Plus, I was told to keep my mouth shut. Lot of good that did me. I lost my job and my family. My husband, damn him, made sure my children knew what I'd done. Just to make them hate me too. I now work three part-time jobs so I can afford rent on a shitty flat. I have no friends left and I only see my kids once in a blue moon. Yeah. Worked out really well, thank you, very much.'

'I'm sorry,' I said with sincerity.

'Why? Who am I to you? You know what? I don't give a shit what you think. Ask me your questions so I can get back to work.' She crossed her arms over her chest and stared at me.

'When you worked for the Dorchester Science and Research Institute we know you started a relationship with Colin Westbury.'

'Correct. I knew him from our time at university. We were students at the same time. Different courses but same group of friends. When I visited him and his family for their IFOD, institute family orientation day, it was a surprise to see him again. A lovely surprise. Stupidly, we picked up where we left off. Don't know why we did it. I suppose we were trying to recapture the excitement of those carefree uni days. Sounds like clichéd bollocks when I say it out loud. But that's how it is.' Sheila examined her fingernails. 'I don't expect anyone to understand. Anyway, I'm paying for it now. And Colin's dead. Along with his wife and kids. Which in everyone's eyes, and I don't want to sound hard-hearted, makes me look like even more of a cold bitch.' She ground a small stone beneath her shoe.

'My team are investigating the murder of Colin and his family along with several other families with twins. I was wondering whether you ever had an orientation day with any of these families.' I handed Sheila a page with the names and photographs of each family. To her credit she appeared to study the paper.

'Yes. The Anderson, Raymond and Chiles families amongst many other families. Not this family.' She pointed to the Poulson name. 'Definitely not that family.'

'Are you sure?'

Sheila gave me a look that told me I was asking a stupid question. 'I'm sure. I was good at my job. I liked my job. I enjoyed the travelling. I liked meeting the families, most of them, and I especially liked meeting the children. It was a worthwhile career.' She pointed behind her with her thumb. 'Unlike now where I'm stacking shelves in a chemist where the highlight of my day is to embarrass teenage boys buying condoms.' She checked the time on her phone. 'Are we done? I'd better get back to it. Those shelves won't stock themselves.'

'A couple more things. Do you know who had access to the family data? I don't mean the research data. Specifically, the names and addresses of the families with twins that were children.'

Sheila stroked the side of her nose as she thought about it. 'Obviously, me, but not every family. I only got the details of families where the twins were children. And not all those. I never once saw addresses where the twins who joined us were adults. There was a guy who ran the numbers on the research. Always moaning about something. Pay, funding, bugs in the system, deadlines, interns, his kids, he had a list as long as your arm. What was his name?'

'Yates? Andrew Yates?'

'Yeah, that could be him. There was someone else before him, got the whole thing up and going, I can't remember his name. Something foreign sounding. Anyway, Andy and his team of about two or three people all managed the information. Also Valentine, obviously. Perhaps HR. I don't know about them. Of course, the institute sells the data to other research institutes around the world.'

'Did you ever hear the contact details being made public?'

'No. Never. They might have accidentally sent out the wrong data which included personal information. If it can happen to big global companies it could happen at that poxy institute. But I never heard about it. Plus, Andrew Yates was always worried about the risk of being hacked or the computer system getting a virus. He was always after more money for this, that or the other to shore-up security.

In short, any number of people could have seen the data but I'd say it was very unlikely to have been stolen or leaked.' She shrugged. 'But what do I know? They make out it's all secure but I'm sure if you worked there and you wanted to find an address you'd find a way. Look, I've got to get back to work. Are we done?'

'We are, for now. Thank you.'

Sheila punched the code into the panel on the wall and the heavy back door to the chemist unlocked. She pulled it open and turned to look at me. 'You know where to find me if you have more questions.' I saw her glance at my ring finger. 'Next time, come at the end of my shift, you can buy me a drink.'

I smiled politely. 'I'm in a relationship,' I said.

'Like that matters to a man.'

'It matters to this man,' I said.

'Good for you, Inspector. Stay true to her. She's a lucky woman.' She closed the door and went inside. I was about to walk away when the door opened again and Sheila looked out. 'Bonne,' she said. 'That was the name of the data guy. Before Andrew Yates it was Janek Bonne. He was the guy who founded the company but he also did some of the early data collation. When Bonne left to travel Yates took over. That's what I heard anyway. I think I only met Janek once. He was pleasant enough.' She winked at me and said, 'Gotta go.'

To passers-by I must have looked like a mad man as I stood muttering to myself while I tried to piece how all the families, Janek Bonne, Robert Valentine, Andrew Yates and the institute all fit together.

I felt my phone buzz in my jacket. It was a text from home wondering whether I'd be home for dinner. I texted back I'd be there. I needed some family time and to be close to those I loved.

CHAPTER TWENTY-SIX

'Why are you hesitating?' asked Mum. She closed the kitchen door.

It was just after ten at night and Monica was in bed reading on her Kindle. Alice and Faith were fast asleep upstairs, or were supposed to be. We'd had a fun evening of Mexican food and monopoly. I claimed to have let Team Alice and Faith win but in truth they were getting good and they knew it. So did Mum and Monica.

I was in the kitchen with Mum. I passed her a mug of hot chocolate. I sat down opposite her at the kitchen table and poured a large glass of brandy. I saw her glance at the glass and felt I had to explain. 'It's just a small one. I'm not developing a problem.' I set the bottle aside.

'Your father would disapprove of you drinking spirits alone on a school night.'

'I'm not alone. I'm with you.'

'Don't be a smart mouth, you know what I mean.'

I took a sip of the brandy and stared at the glass in a moment of awkward silence. I returned to her question. 'Hesitating?'

'You know what I'm talking about.'

'I don't.'

'You do know. I can see it on your face when you're with her. You're as happy as I've ever seen you. And yet you're holding back?'

I took another sip from the glass. Looked at my hand. My ring finger. The finger that had once held Helena's ring. I looked at Mum. 'The truth is I'm scared,' I said. 'Not of asking, although I've not had much luck finding the right time. What we have is so good. It worries me to change what we have now.'

'I'd hazard a guess that's the reason you're not finding the right time. You're being held back by that fear.'

'You're probably right.' I emptied my glass and poured another.

'You know your brother and you were always very different children. Bradley has always been someone who needs to be on the move. I assume that's why he joined the Royal Marines; he always has to be moving forward. He doesn't appear to be satisfied with what he has at any moment in time. It may be he never does. You know I'm lucky if I hear from him on my birthday or at Christmas and I understand that's just how it is. Your father's funeral was nothing more than a flying visit; Bradley came and went so fast it made my head spin. It's not that he doesn't love us all, I'm sure he does, but his pursuit of whatever it is that drives and energises him means he cannot slow down enough to settle.'

I knew what she meant. It was hard to remember I had a brother that I loved but hardly knew. His life was something of a mystery to me. 'He'll settle down one day I'm sure.'

'Maybe so,' said Mum. 'You, on the other hand are like your father. Your family is what motivates you. They are why you'll crawl out of bed at an ungodly hour having had less than enough sleep and visit a crime scene. Some might think it's catching the criminal that drives you. You and I both know the real reason you do it is to keep good people and families safe and secure. If tomorrow, by some miracle, there were no more criminals, you'd still find a way to make sure good people could sleep peacefully at night, and make sure your family is safe and has as much as you can provide.' She took the bottle of brandy and poured a little into her hot chocolate. 'A part of your problem is you spend your time looking back at what has happened. Take a leaf out of Bradley's book. Don't look back, look forward. You won't lose her, Jamie. You'll bring that sweet girl closer. I can promise you that.'

From upstairs came a call from Faith. 'Can someone tuck me in, my covers have fallen off the bed.'

Mum smiled at me and sat back with her hot chocolate brandy. 'Duty calls,' she said.

I knew she meant that in more than the context of tucking in Faith's bed covers. As I climbed the stairs I wondered, not for the first time, whether Mum was some sort of mind-reader who always knew what was troubling me.

CHAPTER TWENTY-SEVEN

Becky Wang was off duty and now in her own time sat in my office with her laptop. She had traced Bonne's travelling calendar to an online resource for travellers called Roaming Stones.

'His online diary was a mixture of video, photo and written. Every photo and video was time-stamped. This gave me a timeline for his travels on his motorcycle, it recorded when and where he was at any given time.'

Wang was doing an admirable job of keeping up with the questions I threw at her. I placed another Post-it note in front of her. 'This is the date the Anderson family were murdered. Are you able to confirm Bonne's movements at that time?'

'One second, I can get that,' said Wang.

Heidi Hamilton had made a flying visit from London and was looking on; she leaned back in my chair reading Paul Ackland's statement.

Cotton stood next to the whiteboard poised to write up whether each date corresponded with Bonne being in the UK. It was slow going until Wang found a part of the

Roaming Stones account that synced with Bonne's Google calendar.

'They all match,' said Wang.

'What matches?' said Rayner. He joined us in the office, throwing his jacket over the back of his seat and rolling up his sleeves.

We stared at the dates on the board as Cotton wrote them up.

'Janek Bonne travelled thousands of miles over the last three years. He's taken his motorcycle across much of Europe. Yet on each and every date a murder was committed he was right here in the UK. We even have him at the Poulsons' home on the evening before the murder.'

'We have a prime suspect,' said Cotton. 'We don't know for sure, mainly because his laptop is missing, but it's not too much of a stretch to assume Janek Bonne somehow had access to the contact details of all the families. We've also discovered that after his mandatory military service he went on to serve in the Royal Danish Army. He served in the Kosovo war and though decorated for bravery, he left the army under a cloud. We're looking into the details but it seems he slit the throat of an unarmed prisoner. He was court-martialed and imprisoned for a short while before being exonerated.'

'He left the Poulson house before they were murdered,' said Rayner.

'He must have gone back,' said Wang.

'Why?' asked Hamilton. 'Why did he kill them?'

'That's what we need to look at next,' I said.

'Made more difficult by the fact he accidentally pleasured himself to death in the shower,' said Rayner.

'Delicately put,' said Cotton.

'I'm stating a fact,' said Rayner.

'You're trying to be funny. Nobody's in the mood.'

'I'm just saying it's incon-bloody-venient.'

'Yeah. Well we know that,' said Cotton. 'No need to state the obvious. If you're not going to contribute, keep it shut.'

'Christ. Someone got out of the wrong side of the bed today.'

'Stop being a prick.'

Rayner raised his hands in submission. 'Sorry. Blimey.'

Wang watched in bewilderment as our moment of jubilation descended into cross words between two exhausted and frustrated detectives.

'Have you two finished?' I said. 'We're all tired but let's simmer down.'

Baffled by what had just occurred and keen to change the atmosphere in the room, Hamilton decided to ask a question. 'We don't know categorically his death was accidental.' She put down the statement and got to her feet. 'Let's imagine for a moment Bonne's death wasn't accidental? What if it was murder? I've examined the body and it certainly looks like auto-erotic asphyxiation but a death like that can be staged. Perhaps someone threw the belt around his neck and tightened it.'

'I don't know. To me Bonne looks good for this,' said Cotton. 'We just need to figure out his movements on the night of the Poulson murders. Could the footage from his helmet camera have been doctored by Bonne to give a different date and time?'

'I can look at that,' said Wang. 'It's possible he filmed it another night with the date and time adjusted to fit that of the night of the murders. It would make a great alibi. It would show him leaving the Poulson family alive and well.'

'Are we saying Bonne is a possible suspect but we want to keep an open mind?'

Everyone in the room nodded. 'Uh huh,' said Cotton.

I turned to Hamilton. 'Will you take another look at the body and see if there is any evidence one way or another? I'd like to know if we can discount foul play.'

'Of course,' said Hamilton. 'I've got to be going. I'll take a look tomorrow.'

Wang grabbed her stuff. 'I'll give you an update on the head-cam footage tomorrow.'

I waited for Wang and Hamilton to leave and as soon as the three of us were alone I turned to Cotton and Rayner. I didn't need to say anything; they both looked like naughty children.

'Sorry,' said Rayner. He looked at Cotton. 'Sorry. I make shit jokes when I'm stressed.'

Cotton was chewing on the inside of her mouth. 'No need. Sorry. I shouldn't have... You know.'

'We've got a job to do.' I handed the office keys to Cotton. 'Lock up when you're finished. I'm taking Hamilton to the train station. Don't stay late. Go home at a reasonable time, both of you. Do something fun this evening, something that takes your mind off the case.'

The atmosphere was frosty as I walked out the door. I knew them both well enough to know it wouldn't stay that way for long. They just needed a break and to take their mind off the case for a few hours. I left them to it.

CHAPTER TWENTY-EIGHT

Paul Ackland stood at the bar, his large round eyes barely blinking as he stared at what remained of his pint of ale.

'You all right, mate?' The barman, a young guy with his long dark hair up in a bun, a large beard and a black stud in each ear, partly filled a pint glass with Guinness, leaving it to settle before finishing the job. He took a bottle of gin off the shelf behind him and began preparing a gin and tonic. 'Haven't seen you in here in a while.'

'No. Been up country.'

'Oh, yeah?' He was unsure whether Ackland literally meant he'd been up country or whether he meant he'd been incarcerated. He decided his guest wasn't in a talking mood. He nodded at Ackland's glass. 'Get you another?'

Ackland lifted his drink and finished it off. 'Why not?' He handed his glass to the barman.

Ackland felt an arm land heavily around his shoulders. A deeply-lined, narrow-eyed, long-nosed face appeared and his heart sank; he wanted to be alone. 'Ackers, mate. How ya diddling?'

'Tinsnip, you all right?'

'Yeah, yeah, of course, of course.'

Tinsnip's real name was Stuart Daniels. He got the moniker because of his use of tin snips as a tool for intimidating those he deemed a threat to his liberty and business interests. He liked to 'prune' fingers and toes, sometimes ears and, on one memorable occasion, the end of a nose. Where he pruned depended on the severity of the offence and his mood on any given day. Tinsnip owned the Venus Moon Gentlemen's Club, the strip joint where Ackland worked. He had acquired the place when the previous owner had found the running costs too great and had handed Tinsnip the keys, or so the story goes. Others say the owner's son ran up a gambling debt he couldn't afford and Tinsnip accepted the Venus Moon in settlement, instead of relieving the boy of his extremities.

'Thought we might have a little tête-à-tête,' said Tinsnip. He smoothed down the sides of his fresh haircut, then straightened his suit jacket and trousers, paying special attention to the bunny girl cuff-links. 'We'll grab a table. I'll have a pint of lager. Jimbo will have a diet lemonade, he's watching his calorific intake, he's gotta watch the old diabeetles.'

Ackland looked at him quizzically. 'Diabeetles?'

'Diabetes, mate.'

'Of course.' Ackland twisted around and saw the huge shape of Jimbo. He was used to seeing him in the club at night; he looked even bigger in broad daylight.

'All right, Jimbo?' said Ackland.

Jimbo waved a fleshy hand. As he did his chest and stomach wobbled. He was panting heavily and sweating after the short walk from the car park to the pub. He lifted his white baseball cap and wiped his forehead with his sleeve. He was sporting a black tracksuit, the jacket unzipped to reveal a black t-shirt. Gold trainers dazzled at the end of outstretched legs. The irony of Jimbo wearing athletic clothing wasn't wasted on Ackland.

'Looking good, mate,' called Ackland. 'New shoes?'

Jimbo grinned, revealing his tiny teeth, one of which was gold. He lifted a foot to show off the trainer. 'Sweet as, bro.'

Jimbo, real name James Blair, had always struggled with his weight. At school the boys, nasty little bastards that they were, insisted he was as heavy as a jumbo jet and twice as wide, hence the name. As he matured, he stood up for himself, grew confident, and soon the name changed from Jumbo to Jimbo.

Jimbo was Tinsnip's right hand man. Before Stuart Daniels ever became Tinsnip, Jimbo was the one he sent to chase you down and collect on your debt, intimidating and breaking bones when necessary. Those days had long since passed, due in part to everyone knowing Jimbo had trouble walking far, let alone running anywhere. He could barely get up the stairs, so could no longer chase anyone down.

These days Tinsnip used a stealthier approach. He turned up unannounced when you least expected it. 'You can run but you can't hide,' he told people. And when he caught up with you... *snip, snip.*

Ackland put their drinks down on the table at the back of the near empty pub. Jimbo sat on a bench on one side of the table while Tinsnip sat on a wooden chair. Beside Tinsnip a stool waited for Ackland. He couldn't help feeling nervous. He had a good idea why they were paying him a surprise visit.

'Have a seat, Ackers,' said Tinsnip. 'Cheers for the drinks.'

'Yeah, cheers, Ackers,' said Jimbo.

Ackland perched on the bar stool. Jimbo sucked his lemonade through the paper straw, which almost immediately collapsed. Tinsnip waited until Jimbo had finished sucking.

'Do you know why we're here?' asked Tinsnip.

'You want to talk about the club?' Of course he knew but he preferred to hear what Tinsnip had to say before preparing his own gallows.

'You and I have a good relationship. I need people I can trust and I want to believe I can trust you. I consider us friends. As such, I want to hear what you have to say. That's why we're having a chat over a delicious looking pint, rather than the alternative which entails adding your digits to my bucket of fingers and toes. So, please don't piss me about.'

Ackland had heard about the bucket of digits Tinsnip kept in his chest freezer.

Tinsnip admired his pint and took a sip before continuing. 'You've spoken to the police. Why?'

'Why?' echoed Jimbo. He attempted to stir his diet lemonade with the collapsed and floppy straw.

'It was nothing to do with you or the club. Nothing at all. You have my word.'

'I knew it,' said Jimbo. 'Ackers is all right. I told you. You owe me a Big Mac.'

'Jimbo and I had a little wager,' explained Tinsnip. He turned to Jimbo. 'Shall we hear a little more before we decide who won the bet?'

Jimbo nodded. 'If you like. But you don't trust no one. You're paranoid. Ackers is all right. He's sound, bro.'

Ackland continued. 'There was a murder. Nothing to do with me. Nothing to do with the club. A family. In a big house. The mum and dad and kids, all dead.'

'Nasty,' said Jimbo.

'When was this?'

'It was my night off. I was doing a mate a favour. He needed a look out. I owed him.'

'What did the po-lice want to know?' asked Jimbo.

'Whether I saw the killer. Or anything suspicious.'

'And did you?'

This is where Ackland was going to have to be inventive with the truth. 'They had a witness who saw my van. They knew I was in the area. I told them the truth.'

'Which is?'

'I was poaching.'

'You what?' said Jimbo. 'Why would you do that?'

Tinsnip started laughing uncontrollably.

'I don't get it. Why is that funny?' said Jimbo. 'It's cruel. Poaching is bad, bro.'

Tinsnip pulled himself together. 'Ackers here hasn't denied he was there. That would be daft. Make the po-lice suspicious. They'd start sniffing around. No. He nipped their snooping in the bud. He put his hands up and said he done it. Good lad.'

Jimbo forced a laugh but looked confused.

Ackland laughed nervously.

Tinsnip's smile vanished. 'What about your probation? I can't have you going back inside.'

'I'm a free man. Probation ended a month ago.'

Tinsnip slapped Ackland on the back. 'Good man. You're doing a good job at the club. There's less trouble with the punters. Profits are up. The girls like you. I need people like you around me, reliable and honest.'

Jimbo said, 'Honest Ackers.'

'Yeah, he's a good man. I just had to check. You understand?'

Ackland swallowed and took a sip of his pint. 'Yeah, of course. I'll see you later?' He tried to show understanding rather than relief.

'You will, bro. We'll be swinging by the club later,' said Jimbo.

'And Ackers,' said Tinsnip. 'No more poaching. No more nothing. You understand? If you're working for me you stay clean as the proverbial whistle. Got it?'

'Yeah. I understand. The poaching was a one-time gig, I was settling up, I owed him. It won't happen again.' Working for Tinsnip in any capacity was undoubtedly moving in the wrong direction if his intention was to stay on the right side of the law, but at the moment he had little choice. And so far everything Tinsnip had him doing was legit. How long that would last he didn't know.

'Good man.' Tinsnip opened his wallet and counted bank notes. 'Here's seventy quid. Get a bloody haircut. A nice shirt and some decent shoes too. I need you to look sharp. This club is going to be a gold mine. Everyone loves dancing girls.'

Jimbo revealed his gold tooth again as he echoed Tinsnip's words. 'Everyone loves dancing girls!' His body shook with hearty laughter.

CHAPTER TWENTY-NINE

Robert Valentine knocked on the door and waited for a response. None came. He knocked again. 'It's me,' he whispered. 'Can I come in?'

'Okay.'

Valentine's eldest daughter lay on her bed with her back to him, hugging her pillow. She wore her school uniform and still had her shoes on.

'What happened, sweetheart?'

'Nothing.'

'Something happened, Kimmy. Your mother said you came out of school upset. She said the school called and left a message for her to call them back.'

'It doesn't matter.'

'You know me, Kimmy. I'm like Switzerland. I'm neutral. I won't take sides, just talk to me.'

'Do you have chocolate?'

'No. Do you want some chocolate?'

'If you don't have chocolate then you're not Switzerland.'

'Ha ha. Very good. I see you haven't lost your sense of humour.'

Kimberly rolled over and looked at her father. She'd been crying. Valentine perched on the bed and cuddled her. 'The day you were born was the happiest day of my life. You and your little sister have been blessings I never thought I'd experience. Now look at you, all grown up. A teenager. You're the most precious thing in my life and it hurts me to see you upset, so whatever it is, you can tell me. And if I can help I will.'

'It's boy trouble,' said Kimberly bluntly.

Valentine shifted uncomfortably, cleared his throat and said, 'There are some things you're better off talking to your mother about. It's not... you know... s-e-x.'

Kimberly groaned. 'Nothing like that.'

'Good. Then I can probably help.' Valentine stroked his daughter's hair and she put her arm over his tummy.

Kimberly looked up at her dad with big sad eyes. 'Noah cheated on me at the weekend. Everyone knows he and I were together. A group from the athletics team went to the cinema. Apparently, Noah and Sabrina kissed. The team saw it. Now the whole school knows.'

'How did everyone see it if they were at the cinema? Surely, it was dark.'

Kimberly huffed. 'You're not helping. They kissed afterwards. Outside.'

'Sorry. Just trying to understand. I thought Sabrina was your friend.'

'So did I. She's not a friend now. She's a fucking bitch.'

'Okay. Language filter. What about Noah? What did he have to say for himself?'

'He said it was an accident. He didn't mean to do it. She kissed him. He didn't kiss her. I told him to get lost. I swore at him. I might have then kneed him in the you know whats and punched him in the chest.' Kimberly showed him her fist and Valentine kissed it. 'It hurts. My wrist is really sore. A teacher saw me do it. I got detention for a week.'

'You punched him and kicked him in the privates?'

'I did. He deserved it.'

'He definitely deserved it,' said Valentine. The pair of them laughed together. 'Next time a slap around the face. It's better on the wrist and somehow more acceptable in the eyes of teachers.'

'There won't be a next time. I'm giving up with boys. Forever.'

'Good. That's what I want to hear. Stay away from boys.' He hugged his daughter tighter. 'It's up to me to tell your mother you've got detention?'

'Yes, please. Tell her it wasn't my fault.'

'I'll do my best.' Valentine kissed the top of her head and got up. 'Wish me luck.'

'Good luck. And Dad... Thank you.'

'You're welcome, sweetheart. You know if I ever see Noah again I shall be having words with him.'

'Good. One more thing.'

'What's that.'

'Ice cream. Can I have some chocolate fudge brownie?'

Valentine smiled and winked. 'I'll see what I can do.'

CHAPTER THIRTY

Paul Ackland knocked twice and opened the door to the dressing room. Eighteen women, at various stages of undress, looked up and smiled at him. Ackland could feel himself blushing. 'Ackers baby, sweetheart, come in. Don't be shy. Nice haircut. Love the shirt. Ooh, nice shoes.'

Ackland entered and closed the door behind him. 'Sorry to intrude.'

Trisha, whose dressing table was closest the door, had one foot on her chair as she fastened her stiletto. As she straightened up Ackland averted his eyes. Trisha's black silk kimono fell open revealing her breasts. She stroked his jawline and gave him a peck on the cheek. 'You're so cute. Looking hot, Ackers baby.'

Ackland cleared his throat. 'Time to be serious, ladies. Do you all understand the new rules?'

Two girls, Laura and Pammy, whispered between themselves, gave each other a high five then blew him a kiss. 'So strict,' one of them said. 'Are you going to put me over your knee if I misbehave?'

All the women began laughing and joking.

Ackland raised his voice in an attempt to get some order. 'My job is to keep you ladies safe while you're out there. I know there has been trouble in the past. The old management let things slide. I'm here now and I want every punter out there to have a good time, but not at the cost of your well-being. You feel unsafe or if a punter goes too far you let me know and I will deal with it. All right?'

'Thank you, Ackers baby,' called the girls in unison.

Ackland opened the door and slammed it shut to get their attention. The sound echoed through the room. The girls fell silent. They all turned and looked at him.

'I mean it. I'm serious. They keep their hands to themselves. You dance; that's it. And strictly no extras. No hand-jobs, no oral, that's all over. That's all in the past. Any of you try it, you'll be out. You heard the boss yesterday. No exceptions.

'One other thing. No drugs on the premises. You need something to get you through the night, I understand. But not in here. If you must, then do it before you walk through the door.'

The girls groaned.

Suzy Sins, who was the first act on, marched up to Ackland in her sparkling skimpy two-piece. She waved a finger with cocaine on the tip then rubbed it over her gums. She then kissed him while the girls all screamed with delight. 'How about if you and me are alone in the club later tonight? Can we do some then?'

The girls began chanting, 'Ackers! Ackers! Ackers!'

He waved them away. Try as he might he couldn't stop laughing. He opened the dressing room door and pointed upstairs towards the club. He shouted over the din. 'You need me out there you holler. Have fun. You all look beautiful.'

Closing the door behind him he heard the girls say, 'Aah. He's so sweet.' He laughed even harder and made his way upstairs. He checked the bar staff were ready by giving them a thumbs up. They returned the gesture. He passed the front desk who he knew was ready and headed for the front door.

Head bouncer, Gavin 'the Truck', was pumped and ready to go. He ran a tattooed hand over his shaved head and winked at Ackland.

'All right, Truck?'

'All good, mate.'

'Anyone even smells like trouble we don't let them in,' said Ackland.

'Suits me.'

'Pat them down. No weapons. No drugs. No bringing in booze.'

'Got it. No worries.'

'Remember what the boss wants. Tell each guest there will be no more touching. The girls dance and that's it. Be sure to tell them it's strictly dancing only.'

The two men bumped fists.

'The boss will be along later, let's show him what we can do. Start letting the guests in when you're ready.'

Music blasted and the room darkened as Ackland went back into the main room. As he passed he ran his fingers over the stage and found the booth in the corner where he had a lemonade waiting. He sat down and waited for the place to start filling up. *Let the lunacy commence*, he thought.

He took out his phone and watched a few seconds of a recording. He looked closely at the face. He knew what he had to do. The man in the recording would pay handsomely to remain anonymous. And once the sick bastard had paid up he would turn the recording over to the newspapers and make even more. They'd pay big money for an exclusive like his.

Half a dozen girls stood at the bar. They broke into smiles as they welcomed the first customers.

Ackland put away his phone and sipped his lemonade as Suzy Sins came out on stage and began dancing.

CHAPTER THIRTY-ONE

As she left the private booth Jess gave Ackland a look that told him she wasn't happy. He took her to one side and she whispered in his ear.

Ackland called Truck over to assist. They reached the private booth and Ackland pulled back the curtain. The guests, two men in their twenties wearing pastel coloured polo shirts and black jeans looked up in surprise. One was zipping up his jeans, the other snorting cocaine off the table alongside a wad of cash.

'You two. It's time to leave. You were told on arrival there is a no touching policy.'

'Come on, mate. No harm done.'

'You paid her for a dance, nothing more.'

'Nothing happened. Whatever she told you, it's a lie.'

Truck squared up to the man who was now standing while doing up the top button of his jeans.

'You had your dick out. There's cash and coke on the table. That tells me all I need to know,' said Ackland.

The two men stepped out of the booth and strutted past the bar towards the exit. Ackland and Truck followed.

When the two men caught sight of Jess, who was watching from the far side of the club, they started cursing and swearing at her.

Ackland gave Truck the green light. He grabbed the man who'd been snorting cocaine by the arm and back of the neck and began frog-marching him to the exit. Ackland did the same to the other guest. Once outside the building he left the two creeps to Truck and his fellow doormen.

Ackland returned to bar. Tinsnip and Jimbo had arrived and were being handed drinks.

'Trouble?' said Tinsnip.

'Nothing to worry about. A couple of chancers decided the new policy didn't apply to them.'

'It's busy. This is good,' said Tinsnip. 'You seem to have everything under control.'

Ackland nodded. 'It'll take a while for the new tighter rules to sink in but so far so good.'

Tinsnip put on his business face. 'If we run the club the way we discussed the girls will be happy. If the girls are happy they'll stick around longer and that means they'll have regulars who are willing to pay more for a private dance. And we get a percentage of everything each girl makes. A business like this starts and ends with the girls being happy.'

'Smart, innit, bro?' said Jimbo.

'You know your stuff,' agreed Ackland.

'I've been to a few clubs in my time,' said Tinsnip. 'It doesn't take a lot to understand how these places work. I just never thought I'd own one myself.'

Ackland's attention turned to a guest who kept getting up from his seat and reaching up for Lucy who had just arrived on the main stage. 'Excuse me, I'd better deal with that idiot.'

Tinsnip and Jimbo watched as Ackland marched over and had words with the customer.

'This place is going to make me rich,' said Tinsnip. He checked his fake Rolex watch. 'It's still early and look at the place, it's packed!'

'Damn right,' said Jimbo. 'It's a goldmine.'

CHAPTER THIRTY-TWO

The music grew louder as Alex tried to step around a couple who were seriously into each other on the doorstep outside Declan's party. 'Sorry. Excuse me. I just need to squeeze through,' said Alex. The two men stopped kissing, grabbed their beer bottles and shifted out of his way.

The hallway, stairs and each room he peered into was packed with revellers dancing, drinking and having a good time.

'I'm looking for Emma?' he said to two women waiting for the toilet.

'There's an Emma in the kitchen, might be her?' said one of the women.

'Thank you. I'll take a look.' Alex pushed on to the kitchen and looked around. She wasn't there. Through the kitchen window more groups were gathered on the patio. He negotiated his way past three men in hysterics who were making hot dogs and piling on chilli sauce for a dare.

It was dark and the garden was lit with wall lanterns and strings of fairy lights running along the fences. A small group sat around a patio heater and a larger group stood around a fire pit.

On a bench almost hidden behind the barbecue sat Emma and Declan. He'd finished telling a funny story and the pair were in fits of laughter. Emma's hand briefly rested on Declan's as she insisted his story couldn't be true.

Emma looked up and was confused and shocked to see Alex standing there. She took a large swig of her gin and tonic, got up and realised she was unsteady on her feet. 'What are you doing here, Alex?' She held his arm and took him aside.

'That's hardly polite,' said Alex as calmly as he could. He released himself from her grip. 'I just popped by to see if you wanted a friendly drink. When you weren't home I was concerned. Then I thought I'd see if you were here. I hadn't heard from you and I wanted to make sure you were okay.' He looked at Declan then back at Emma. 'Which you clearly are. And a little drunk to boot.'

'Why are you here?' she repeated. Then louder than she'd intended, 'We're over. You understand that, don't you? Well, do you?'

Alex looked around. People were watching, whispering behind hands and laughing. 'I think you're a little tipsy. I believe we're still friends. Isn't that how we left it? As a friend I wonder whether you've had enough to drink. Shall I take you home?' He went to put his arm around her.

'What the hell are you doing? Take your hands off me,' yelled Emma. She shrugged him off and stumbled backwards. 'I've had a couple of drinks. I am not drunk. It's called being happy. Having fun. Letting your hair down. Something you know nothing about.'

Declan stepped in. He put himself between Emma and Alex. 'Look, mate, it's a private party, I think you should leave.'

Alex stepped close to Declan and pressed a couple of fingers into his chest. 'Hoping you might get lucky, are you?

I've seen the way you look at her. Want to try some mature pussy do you?'

'That's out of order. I think you should leave. Now,' said Declan.

'I see your game. Ply her with a few drinks, hoping she'll be an easy lay?'

Declan squared up to Alex. In a split second his mind ran through mixed martial arts moves he'd gone over in training recently. He was ready to lay Alex out cold if necessary.

Alex could see Declan was itching for an excuse to prove his Alpha status. He stepped back. He put his hands up in mock surrender. 'Just kidding. Come on. Surely you can take a joke.'

'I can take a joke. You're not funny,' said Declan. 'I want you to leave.' He jerked his head towards the door.

'That's enough,' insisted Emma. 'Alex, please leave. I'll call you tomorrow.'

'Don't bother. You didn't answer my texts. I came round to make sure you were okay. Clearly you are.' He looked the pair of them up and down.

Emma sighed. 'Declan, would you get me a coffee?'

Declan was unsure what to do. He didn't want to leave her.

'Please,' said Emma.

Declan glared at Alex and pushed past him.

'Good boy,' said Alex. 'Off you trot.' Once Declan was out of earshot he moved close to Emma. 'You didn't reply to my note or my text messages. I was worried. Did you get the flowers?'

'I got all the messages. I got the flowers. I'm also in the middle of a serial killer investigation. Time is in short supply.'

'How long does it take to send a text? We're friends.'

'I should have messaged you. I'm sorry. It's been busy.'

'You said that. Yet you found time for this.' He looked around at the party behind them to emphasise his point. 'Little young, aren't they?'

'If you want to do this here and now, then okay. As I thought I had already made perfectly clear, you and I are over. I'm sorry but my life doesn't have time for mixed messages or bullshit so I will say this one more time. Our relationship, brief as it was, is no more. It would be better if we do not see each other again, even as friends. Is there any part of that you do not understand?'

Alex looked dumbfounded. He grabbed her arm. 'What did I ever do to you to make you so hateful of me?'

'Let go of my arm before I put you face down on this floor.'

He released her. Her eyes told him she wasn't kidding. 'I see what you are. You're still that same playground slut who let the boys put their hands in her panties behind the bike shed. You think you've somehow risen out of the gutter because you've fucked your way to the lofty heights of detective inspector? You're a joke.'

'If you don't leave now I will arrest you.'

'Screw you. I'm leaving. You're pathetic.'

'I never want to see you again. Understand?'

'Fuck your toy boy if you want to. He's welcome to you.' Alex turned and walked away.

Declan was coming the other way with a mug of black coffee in each hand.

When he reached him Alex stopped and hissed in Declan's ear, 'Your bitch has been around the block a few times, boy. She isn't great in bed but from my experience she definitely likes it hard and rough. I'd be surprised if you're man enough for her.'

Despite his urge to throw him out Declan ignored him

and kept walking. His concern was for Emma who was pacing and looking distraught.

CHAPTER THIRTY-THREE

For most of the morning Cotton had been quiet. On and off at her desk she'd had her head in her hands. She was on her fifth cup of coffee when suddenly she jumped up with excitement. 'I got something. The dice. They're not regular dice. I mean they work like regular dice but they're special. Turns out they're handmade. I sent some photos to an artisan dice maker and she believes they're made from a speciality wood. She's willing to take a look.'

'Where is she based?' asked Rayner. He was on the phone and had his hand over the mouthpiece while he spoke.

Cotton didn't answer at first; she paced up and down behind her desk. Presumably her mind putting the pieces together. 'Oxford. Two to three hours from here depending on traffic. It's got to be worth the drive. If the dice do come from a specialist dice maker and we can trace the buyer... we might be able to establish who put the dice in the hands of the dead boys.'

'I'll request a dice be couriered down to us immediately,' I said. I picked up the phone and dialled Chief Superintendent Webster. I got through but was put on hold. 'I'll make sure they get here today. I'll need to let the chief super know where you're going and the courier can meet you there.'

Cotton placed a slip of paper with the address on my desk. 'One step ahead of you,' she said, smiling for the first time that day.

I spoke briefly to Webster, hung up and gave Cotton a nod. Feeling jubilant, she tossed her car keys up and snatched them mid-air. 'I've got a good feeling about this. This could prove Bonne is the killer.'

Cotton and I turned our attention to Rayner who had circled Paul Ackland's name on the whiteboard.

'You have a problem with Ackland?' asked Cotton.

'Ackland's poaching friend, Terry O'Brien, who claimed he was with Ackland the night of the murders just confessed to not being with him,' said Rayner. 'He's withdrawn his statement.'

'What? Paul Ackland was lying?' I said. 'You've got to be kidding me?'

'Nope. Ackland no longer has an alibi for when the murders took place. He was in the area and he lied to us. Why?' said Rayner.

'How come we didn't see this coming?' I asked. I was frustrated and angry; Ackland had pulled the wool over our eyes.

Rayner shrugged. 'I guess he's a bloody good liar. It transpires O'Brien is on probation. A charge of poaching risked his going back to prison, so he changed his story.'

I stood with my back to the room, staring out of the office window as I asked myself how I could have missed this. Ackland had made a fool of me. 'Have both Ackland's witnesses admitted to lying?'

'Not as far as I know. Shane Doyle, the other fella

Ackland claims he was poaching with hasn't changed his story. Yet.'

'Does Ackland know this?'

'No.'

I turned to Rayner and Cotton. 'Let's keep it that way. We can press Ackland. We'll suggest they both withdrew their statements. Let's go and speak to him, find out why he lied to us. He's hiding something and we need to know what.'

'You still want me to go to Oxford?' asked Cotton.

'Definitely. Your breakthrough with the dice might be vital in linking the killer to the crime itself.'

CHAPTER THIRTY-FOUR

It was two-thirty in the afternoon and Paul Ackland was sipping from a mug of tea. He wore a Metallica t-shirt and jogging trousers; his feet were bare. 'Come in, if you must. Wipe your feet,' he said. He made his way to the sitting room. 'Close the door behind you.'

The small sitting room was surprisingly tastefully furnished. Two new-looking mid-brown sofas and an oaty coloured carpet. Ackland straightened the chocolate velvety curtains and opened a window to let in some fresh air.

'Welcome to my humble abode,' said Ackland. 'I'd offer you tea, but I'm sure you won't be stopping long.' He took a large sip of tea and put the mug down on a glass coffee table. His black eye and cut lip were healing. His t-shirt was riding up as he sat back on the sofa and I noticed bruising on his ribs and stomach. He tried not to wince as he got comfortable.

Rayner went to the window and looked out at the back garden. There were toys on the lawn and a plastic sandpit on the patio. 'Late night?' he said over his shoulder.

'That's the nature of working at a club. How can I help you gents? Actually, before we get into that I want you both to know that I realise poaching is plain wrong. I was misled into thinking we were doing conservation work and a favour to the farmer whose land we were on. I now realise we should respect and look after all the flowers, trees, birds, beasts and bees we share this beautiful planet with. I am therefore, becoming a vegetarian and I will also be coop-erate with the police and the RSPCA. I will be assisting them in their fight against poaching. I am literally poacher turned gamekeeper.'

Rayner slow clapped when he'd finished. 'Is that a rehearsal for the judge? Well it's very good. I'm sure he or she will be mightily impressed.'

'That might be so, and I hope he is, but more importantly it's the truth,' said Ackland.

I leaned forward in my seat and looked Ackland in the eye. 'It seems you haven't been completely honest with us. Your pals have changed their stories...' I didn't need to say any more, I could see from Ackland's face he knew what had happened.

'No. They can't have.'

'Do you want to tell us what really happened?' said Rayner. 'Your alibi no longer stands up. You've lied to us. We're investigating murder and we want the truth, because right now you're a criminal with a violent history, who was seen attempting to turn into the private lane leading to the house where a family were murdered on the evening before said murders. You can see how that looks to us?'

Rayner and I watched Ackland's face contort while his brain clunked and clanged as it tried to figure a way out of his predicament. Finally, he blurted, 'O'Brien wasn't there.'

'We know that. Don't tell us what we already know. We just told you that news flash,' said Rayner.

'You're in deep shit now,' I said. 'Why were you in the area the night the Poulson family was murdered. And also, there's the dead man who recorded your van on his motorcycle head-cam, Janek Bonne. I'm sure you can see how we might interpret all this?'

Ackland looked distraught. 'You need to slow down. I know nothing about any murders. All right? I was poaching.'

'Not with O'Brien you weren't.'

'No, it was just Doyle and me. That's the truth.'

'Bullshit,' said Rayner. He stepped close to Ackland and loomed over him. 'This is your very last chance to come clean or we're taking you to the station. Understand?'

'No. Wait. Look. I need assurances anything I say won't go any further than this room. Give me that and I'll tell you what I know.'

Rayner and I looked at each other and I nodded. 'Let's hear what you've got to say. Then we'll decide.'

Rayner backed off and went to stand by the window.

Ackland's manner became serious as he focused on his story.

'I was there, all right? I really was helping a mate out. Poaching. I didn't want to do it but I owed him. As I was about to turn into the lane I saw the motorbike coming out so I drove past. I drove around for a good five minutes then went back. I parked in the lane near the house. It's quiet there.'

'The lane leading to the Poulson house?'

'Yeah. Like I said, it's quiet. I got there early, before Doyle. I hid the van.'

'Hid the van?'

'Yeah. He was going to pick me up. The idea being that he shoots a deer or two, makes a couple of hundred quid. The best way to do it is to stash the carcasses until later the next day; you're more likely to be stopped at two in the morning by police, than two in the afternoon. But in the end we took a chance because I wasn't able to return later.'

'Carry on,' said Rayner. 'So far this sounds like the same bullshit you served up last time.'

'It's the truth, I swear. When I got there that night, he'd been out already. He had a pheasant and a brace of rabbits in the back of his van.'

'Where did you go from there?' said Rayner.

'I'm not sure. Doyle knew where he was going, we just chatted while he drove. We went to a field with a wood beside it and waited. He'd been there before, knew there were deer about. Eventually, we did the deed and I helped him carry the deer to his van. He then drove me back and we went our separate ways. That was it.'

'I don't understand,' I said. 'Why bring O'Brien into it if he wasn't there?'

'I don't know. I suppose I thought the story would sound more authentic. He said he'd help me out.'

'Seems he changed his mind,' said Rayner.

Ackland shrugged.

'How come you're so happy to tell us of anyone else's involvement at all? What happened to loyalty amongst thieves, and poachers?'

Ackland picked up his mug and drained his tea. 'The alternative is you think I murdered the family, right? Or the fella on the motorbike.'

Rayner grunted. 'Did you?'

Ackland snorted like the question was too absurd even to consider. 'Nah.'

'So what happened once Doyle dropped you back at your van?' I said.

'Call of nature. I went into the field close to the Poulson house. It must have been around two or three a.m. It was dark but the moon was out. It was really quiet. Like pin-drop quiet. As I headed back to my van I heard a weird noise. It sounded like crying. It was coming from the direction of the house. I was going to ignore it but I heard it again. So I went to take a look.'

'How close were you?' I said.

'Not that close. The noise must have carried. Anyway, I walked up the field beside the house to get a closer look. At first I couldn't see anything. There's a thick hedge between the field and the house. It was dark and I used the light on my phone so I could see where I was going. As I walked the sobbing got louder. It was really creepy. The noise was on the other side of the hedge but I followed the sound. I thought, if I got closer I'd see where it was coming from.'

'What did you see?' I leaned closer to Ackland as his story drew me in.

Ackland got up, wincing and momentarily holding his ribs with one hand, he reached inside a vase and took out a pack of cigarettes and a lighter. His hand was trembling. He lit a cigarette then put the pack and lighter back in the vase. He closed his large eyes as he filled his lungs. He sat down and looked at the cigarette. 'I quit for the kids,' he said. 'One won't hurt. All things in moderation they say.'

'So they say,' I said.

Ackland let the cigarette droop from the corner of his small straight mouth. He rubbed his wide flat chin. 'I turned off the phone torch and squeezed between a tree and the hedge. I stayed low and crept close. Ninja style.' Ackland's button nose crumpled as his mind wrestled with the memories. 'Two little kids. Followed by an adult. The kids were being walked away from the house. It was only shapes. But I know what I saw. The kids were walking slowly and he prodded them. To keep them moving.'

'It was a man?'

'Definitely.'

'How can you be sure?'

'The way he moved. His voice.'

'You heard his voice?'

'Yeah. It was creepy as hell. He said something like "Stop right there. Don't look around".'

'Did you see what he looked like?'

'No. It was dark. He was dressed in dark clothing. The boys were in their pyjamas, I know that much.'

'How could you see anything if it was dark?' asked Rayner.

'Dunno. The moon, I guess. That night there had been a really big bright moon. Like Doyle always says, a bright moon is good for poaching.'

'Carry on.'

'The boys held hands. Then he... smashed them in the head. Just once. Each of them.' Ackland lifted his arm and brought it down hard. Ash fell from the tip of the cigarette but he didn't notice. His eyes were now open wide and bulging as he stared into space. 'Dropped like...' He swallowed and cleared his throat.

'What happened next?'

'He was stood over them. Watching. For ages. He just stood there. Then, he opened his coat. Took something from his inside pocket. Got down on his knees. I guess he was cutting them up.'

'How could you see that?'

'I must have got closer. I don't remember.' Ackland was upset and angry.

'You didn't try to stop him?' said Rayner.

'How the fuck would I have known what he was going to do?'

I glared at Rayner. He wasn't himself right now. I understood why but I needed him to keep it together.

'He cut them up. I could see what he was doing. I heard

him panting. I think I heard the saw too, cutting through bone, but I might have imagined that. That's when I backed away. I got out of there. It was sick.'

'Did you see anything else? A vehicle nearby? Any distinguishing features about him. Hair colour, the way he walked. Height?'

'Average height. Average build. Not skinny, not fat, not tall, not thin. Average. He was white. But I could be wrong. It was dark. And no I didn't see a car with a notice in the window saying Psycho at Work.'

'Why didn't you call the police?'

'Really? "Excuse me officer, I'm calling in to inform you of a murder. I was just completing my poaching activities with a friend when I saw some bloke butchering two kids. Oh yeah, and I have a criminal record, but it wasn't me that done it." Something like that? That's why I lied. Call me stupid, but I don't want to risk going back inside.'

'If you're lying about any of this we will find out and we will come down on you like a ton of bricks. You understand?' said Rayner. 'This guy is very likely to kill again. If you're holding out on us then that'll be on you. I will personally make sure you go back inside. Got it?'

'It's the god's honest truth. It's exactly as I told it.'

I was processing the new information in my head. I looked up and said, 'As far as we know, you're the only person who's seen him. We're going to need you to do a composite sketch. And stay out of trouble; you're our only witness.'

'I'll do my best,' said Ackland. 'You know how it is. There are limited job opportunities around here for an ex-con.' He slumped back on the sofa, winced and grabbed his ribs. 'Any jobs going on the force? I'd make a good undercover detective, don't you think?'

'Very funny. If anything else comes to mind let us know.

We'll be in touch. One last thing,' I said. 'The bruises to your ribs?'

Ackland lifted his shirt to show us. 'Aw – it's nothing. After the club closed I got jumped by a couple of pricks who'd been thrown out.'

'You're not having much luck. Black eye, split lip and busted ribs.'

'It goes like that sometimes. I feel my luck's about to change.' He winked. 'Good things are just around the corner.'

CHAPTER THIRTY-FIVE

The dice-maker's workshop was a space at the back of a jeweller's. It was well lit with lamps and the work surface was extremely tidy. Callipers, indent punch, precision square and sandpaper all had their place. With a gloved hand Dina Fellowes placed the dice in a micrometre.

Cotton guessed her to be in her late twenties or early thirties. Her hair was tied back, dark purple on top, red in the middle and yellow at the ends like a magical waterfall cascading almost to her waist. Her gradient eyeshadow matched her hair. A stud in her lower lip shone under the light of the lamp.

Dina seemed fascinated by the dice and hummed to herself as she inspected it and made notes of the readings. Finally, she turned to Cotton with a look of pleasure on her face. Her eyes twinkled with excitement. As she spoke Cotton once again caught sight of Dina's tongue stud which was a miniature black and white dice.

'Exquisite. The dice is finely balanced. Certainly, any casino would be happy to use a pair of them. Though of course a casino couldn't use them. There are strict guidelines. My point is they are crafted beautifully. An exotic wood with inlays that add some heft.'

'What does that mean?'

Dina smiled warmly. 'I sound like a geek, sorry.' She held up the dice. 'Without analysing it, which you might want to do, I'd say the wood itself is rosewood. The inlays,' she pointed to each dot, 'are turquoise.'

'Can the dice be traced? Do they have a hallmark like silver or gold or a signature like a painting?' asked Cotton.

'There is no maker's mark. Tracing whoever made it would be nigh on impossible. It might be that whoever it belonged to made it themselves. You could try to trace the materials but they're commonly used.'

'That is a shame. I thought we might be on to something.'

'I'm sorry I can't be more help.' Dina was about to pass Cotton the dice. 'I could take some photographs and share them around if you like. I wouldn't mention they are part of a murder investigation.'

'That's very kind. I might take you up on the offer, but not right now. Thank you.' Though sharing the photos might reap the right result, the risk of having photographs of evidence shared was too high. They could reach the press or end up on social media.

'Do you know why the sides, apart from six, have been defaced?' asked Dina, taking a closer look at each side.

Cotton shook her head. 'Not yet. Still a mystery.'

Dina flicked the dice tongue stud back and forth as she thought about it. 'Of course, there's the obvious six-six-six. But the number six is also the first perfect number. In mathematics a perfect number is when all the divisors, not including the number itself are added together they equal the number itself. In the case of number six those numbers are one, two and three.

In some cultures the number six is also a symbol of luck. Virgo is the sixth astrological sign in the zodiac. In the Tarot number six is the card of the Lover. And there is the sixth sense. Six wives of Henry the Eighth. The six could refer to so many things.'

'And that's the problem,' said Cotton. She collected the dice and thanked Dina for her time.

'If anything comes to mind I'll drop you a line.' Dina looked at her desk, figured out where she had got to with her work and went back to it.

CHAPTER THIRTY-SIX

Driving back to the office from Ackland's flat Rayner received a phone call; it was an update from the forensics team. He turned to me with a face like thunder. 'No usable genetic material on anything taken from the Poulsons' hedgerow. The only thing they recovered of any use was dark fibres consistent with a fleece material,' he said.

We were both disappointed there was no DNA sample even though it had always been a longshot. 'The dark colour of the fleece is consistent with Ackland's description of the killer's clothing,' I said.

'Do you think Ackland's telling the truth?'

'If you're asking whether I think he's involved in the twin murders, I'd say at this stage it's highly unlikely but I couldn't rule it out. I'm going to hold judgement until we check out his whereabouts around the times of the other murders.'

'Putting Ackland to one side, do you see Janek Bonne as the killer?'

I picked at the steering wheel with my fingernail. 'I really don't know. I don't like coincidences and it's one hell of a coincidence that Bonne was at the house, knew the

Poulson family, very likely had access to the database at the institute and was back in the country around the time of all the killings. What I don't like is that he died within a few hours of the Poulson family. Maybe the death was an accident or maybe it wasn't; there are just too many things I'm not happy about.'

'From what we know there is no evidence Bonne was particularly stressed, had suicidal inclinations or had ever tried to commit suicide in the past. By all accounts he was laid back and chilled.'

'Which means his death was an accident.' I sighed heavily.

'You okay?' asked Rayner. 'I can drive if you want.'

'No. I'm good.' I smiled weakly. 'I feel with Bonne's death that we're being drawn away from the primary investigation but I don't want to let it go, I have a gut feeling there is a connection. Janek's death might have nothing to do with the killing of the twins but could just as easily be the key to solving it. I'm also frustrated we wasted time on Ackland.'

We drove in silence for a while. My frustration was reaching boiling point. We were at a point where information gathering was creating more questions than answers. We needed to refocus our efforts.

'I'll keep on Ackland. We need to rule him in or out. I'll make sure his alibi is rock solid for the dates of the other murders. I'll also look for any connection there might be between him and Bonne,' said Rayner.

'Good. Do that as quickly as you can. Hopefully, Cotton gets something with her lead on the dice.'

CHAPTER THIRTY-SEVEN

Emma got back from Oxford around eight-thirty and it was dark out. She hadn't stopped for dinner and was feeling hungry, but during the drive she had made the decision to go to see Declan and apologise for spoiling his party.

She took a deep breath and rang the doorbell. While she waited for the door to open she ran her fingers through her hair, adjusted her clothes, checked her breath in a cupped hand and wished she'd thought about mints and lipstick. She stood up straight as the door slowly opened.

'Hello, Emma. Are you okay, love?' It was Declan's mum.

'Hello, Sue. I'm okay. I'm sorry to bother you so late. I was wondering whether Declan was home. I think I owe him an apology.'

'Really? Oh, okay. Come in, sweetheart. Declan's here. In fact he was just telling me off for getting up to answer the door. He does fuss. I tell him I need to keep moving but he says I'm doing too much.' She stepped back and held the door open. 'He's a good lad, just don't tell him I said so. You go first. I'm a bit slow on my feet, what with the hip op. Just through there into the sitting room. Where's Deccy? He was here a second ago.' She yelled upstairs. 'What are you doing up there? Emma's here. Emma from next door. She wants to talk to you, I hope you haven't been breaking the law again. Have you washed your face, cleaned behind your ears and brushed your hair today? And put on a fresh t-shirt.' She joined Emma in the sitting room. 'I do love embarrassing him. Can I get you a cup of tea, love?'

'No. I'm fine. Thank you. I can't stop long, I just need to have a quick word.'

Declan appeared. He looked flustered and sounded breathless.

'I'll make myself scarce. Give you two some privacy.' As she passed Declan she gave him a wink. He gave her a 'pack it in' look.

Emma didn't notice.

Declan closed the door and sat down opposite Emma. She fiddled with her watch. In an instant he noticed how slim and feminine her wrist was. His eyes traced her neckline and moved to her small ears, where a pale blue earring twinkled. Her eyebrows were fine and her lips and skin looked soft.

'I came to apologise. About what happened at the party. I'm sorry. I shouldn't have brought my problems to your doorstep.'

He shook his head and looked confused. 'There's nothing for *you* to apologise for. He's your boyfriend and all that, and I probably shouldn't say, but he behaved like an arse.' Declan shrugged. 'He was disrespectful and you put him in his place. As far as I'm concerned you did the right thing.'

'The truth is, I'm embarrassed. It put a downer on your party. It ruined the evening, it must have.'

'You didn't ruin anything. Your being there *made* the party for me. Talking to you and us laughing together, that's all I remember from the evening. And it's all I've thought about since.' Declan's heart did a double back flip. He scanned her face to see whether she got his meaning. She did. Her cheeks flushed. She tried to hide it but the corners of her mouth turned up. She swallowed. Her lips twitched. She lowered her eyes for a moment then looked up at him. His heart did another double flip, this time followed by a double pike. *Where had this explosion of confidence come from?*

'That's very kind of you, I'm relieved,' she said matter-of-factly.

Now it was his turn to feel embarrassed. He'd gone out on a limb and she'd replied with pleasantries. The room suddenly felt too hot. He had two choices; wait for the ground to open up and swallow him whole, or keep going. He took a deep breath. 'I hope it wasn't a complete disaster for you?'

'No. I enjoyed it too. In fact, it's been a while since I laughed so much.'

Declan felt relieved and emboldened.

'We could do it again?' he said.

'Another party?'

'No. The two of us. A drink.'

'Crikey.' Emma tucked her hair behind her ear and folded her arms. 'It's not that I don't think I'd enjoy it, but now is not a good time. I'm trying to sort out whatever this is with Alex. And I'm flat out at work.'

'You think I'm too young.'

'No. It's not that. Then again, I am a lot older.'

'Nine years is nothing.'

'I think it's nearer ten.' Emma kicked herself. Answering so quickly meant it was clear she'd worked it out. She should make her excuses and leave. For some reason she didn't want to. She felt relaxed around him, comfortable. His polite persistence wasn't unwelcome either. She liked it.

'I don't want to speak out of turn and please don't take this the wrong way but it seems to me that for whatever reason the relationships you've had to date haven't worked out. I wonder if it could be down to the choice of men.'

Emma felt her heart being needled by a fragment of truth. 'I don't make ideal relationship material; I don't put in the time.'

'Maybe it's time to try something new. If you found the right man, perhaps you'd find the time.'

'Perhaps. If you know the right man could you point him in my direction.' She cringed at her poor attempt at a joke, it had sounded better in her head. What was happening? She'd reverted to the teenage awkward, tongue-tied version of herself she remembered.

Declan leaned closer, he was on the edge of his seat. It felt like make or break time. 'How about we go for a drink, as friends, have some fun, and see how it goes? Nothing heavy. If we do have a good time, we'll see if we want to do it again.'

'I don't know.'

'Say yes.'

She sighed. 'I'm really not sure it's a good idea.'

'Just say yes.'

'I—'

'A drink. No strings.'

'One drink. No strings.'

'You have my word.'

'As friends?'

'Friends.'

'Okay. One drink.'

They both sat and smiled at each other. Not sure what to say next. For now, smiling and looking was okay.

The door opened and in came Sue with two cold drinks and a plate of biscuits on a tray. 'Knock, knock. Sorry to interrupt. You two seemed to have a lot to talk about, I thought you might like some refreshments.'

Declan got up and took the tray from his mother. He frowned at her.

Emma got to her feet. 'That's very kind, but I really should be going.'

'Please don't leave on my account, love,' said Sue hastily.

'We're all done,' said Declan. 'I'll show you out, Em.'

'Thank you, Sue,' said Emma. 'Another time, I promise. I'll pop round and we'll have a proper chat.'

Declan led the way and opened the front door. On the doorstep Emma turned and looked up at him with an awkward smile. 'You'll have to explain to me some time how my coming round to apologise turned into a date.'

'Excuse me,' said Declan in his poshest royal jokey voice. 'A date? Whatever gave you that idea. We're two friends going for drinkies. I don't want you trying any funny stuff.'

Emma laughed. 'I was trying to catch you out.'

'How does next week sound? Friday or Saturday?'

'It sounds good. I'll let you know nearer the time which day works best. You've got my address?'

'I'll figure it out.' He reached back inside the house and put on the outside light which lit up the front garden.

'Okay, so, I'd better go.' She wanted to leave but at the same time didn't want to, she also felt self-conscious walking away with his eyes on her.

'I'll let you go,' said Declan. 'It feels embarrassing standing here and waiting for you to walk next door.'

'Makes sense. See you soon.'

Declan nodded. He watched her for a moment and then

closed the door. Emma walked around to her garden and up the path to her front door. As she put her key in the lock she heard a noise next door. She paused, leaned towards the house and listened carefully. It sounded like Declan cheering followed by laughter and shushing noises. She chuckled to herself and went inside.

CHAPTER THIRTY-EIGHT

Ackland zipped up his jacket and was about to tell Tara he was popping out when she appeared behind him.

'Where the hell are you going at this time of night?'

'I'm off to the club. Work.' Ackland's hand was poised over the door latch.

'I heard you call in,' said Tara. 'You told them you wouldn't be there tonight.'

Ackland's face reddened. 'I won't be long.'

Tara's eyes burned into his like two blast furnaces.

Ackland put his arms around his wife. He knew what this was about. 'There's no one else. This is work. Everything I do is for you and the kids. I promise. I hate us living hand to mouth. I feel sick to my stomach every time a bill comes through that letterbox. I don't want to live like that any longer. I want you and the children to have more.'

'You're scaring me. You're not doing something illegal, are you? You said no more dodgy stuff. I need you here with me, not banged up.'

'It's a business transaction, pure and simple. I know a fella willing to pay good money for information I have.'

'You? What information?'

'It's better you don't know.'

'It is illegal. I knew it. You're not going.' She shoved him aside and stood in front of the door.

Ackland held Tara and kissed her forehead. 'I recorded someone doing something so bad he has no choice but to pay me off.'

'You're blackmailing him?' She looked disgusted.

'Sort of. Blackmail isn't the right word. It's not that simple.'

Tara frowned and folded her arms. 'What did he do?'

'I can't tell you.'

'If you can't tell me you're not going.' Tara pushed him back and put the chain on the front door.

'For Christ's sake, don't be silly.'

'I'm not. You either let me in on what you're doing or you're not leaving.' She spread out her arms and legs like a star.

'Tar, don't be silly.'

She didn't budge.

Ackland thought about it. This was his lottery win, an opportunity that came along once in a lifetime, he had to grasp it. 'The guy killed two kids,' he blurted. 'I saw it. I watched him do it and recorded him on my phone.'

'What?' Tara gasped and put her hand over her mouth. 'Who?'

'It was on the news. The family with twin boys.'

Tara shook her head. 'What family? I don't know anything about that.'

'You do. We talked about it, I'm sure we did.'

Tara shook her head.

'Anyway, from what I've learned the same bloke killed other families with twins. He deserves what's coming to him.'

'You've got to tell the police.'

'Shh! Keep your voice down.' Ackland looked upstairs to the children's bedroom. 'I will go to the police but not right away.'

'What? He might do it again. You can't let that happen. If he kills another family you'll never be able to live with yourself. You've got evidence. You're probably breaking the law.'

'This is an opportunity, Tar. I know what I'm doing. The recording's grainy as hell. It's not much good to the police.'

'They can make the recording clearer. They have special computers 'n' stuff, I've seen them do it on the telly, CSI Los Angeles. Really, think about it, what if he hurts another family and you could have helped the police?'

Ackland put his arms around Tara and lowered himself a little so he could look her in the eye. 'I will go to the police. But first I need to do this for us. He won't risk hurting another family, not now he knows I've got a recording. He has money, I know it. And if he doesn't he'll sure as hell find it. Trust me. This is for the children. We can move off this estate and live somewhere nice, in the country, like you always wanted. Your little picture-postcard chocolate-box cottage. I'll be able to quit the club and work proper hours. We'll be able to sit down at the table and have meals together. I'll be able to take the children to school and we'll be able to have holidays. Think about it. This is our golden ticket out of here. This landed in my lap for a reason. It's fate.'

Tara looked at Ackland. 'You're sure this is safe?'

'Yes.'

'The police will never know.'

'They'll never know.'

'No family is going to die because of what you're doing.'

'I promise.'

'Where are you meeting him?'

'The less you know the better. Plausible deniability, they call it.'

'What?'

'It doesn't matter. It means the less you know the better.'

'Bit bloody late for that.'

Ackland smiled. 'Just put it out of your mind. Let me do this for us. For the kids. I love you.' He kissed her on the forehead and squeezed her.

'I love you too. Be careful.'

Ackland gently moved Tara out of the way of the door and removed the chain. 'I'll see you in a few hours. Don't wait up. When I get back things will be different. I promise.'

CHAPTER THIRTY-NINE

A fox appeared from the Canford Magna churchyard and ran into the road. It stopped, stared at the van, then padded along before fading into the shadowy river bank. Ackland sat in his van drumming the steering wheel. He turned off the engine which he'd had running to keep warm. He flicked the stalk for the windscreen wiper to remove the mist that had formed. He checked the time again. 1.45 a.m. *He should have been here by now*, he thought.

The road leading down to the river was empty, except for his van. It was mainly used by those parking up before walking beside the river or going to church. About an hour earlier, a couple enjoying some intimacy in their small car had moved on when they realised the single man in the white van behind them wasn't going anywhere.

On the bank overlooking the river was a public bench. Ackland wondered whether he should have arranged for the money to have been left on the bench in an exchange, like the sort that happens in movies. An exchange where a hostage-taker collects the money then releases the hostage at a named location later. He'd dismissed the idea because in the movies those exchanges always seemed to go wrong.

Usually, the hostage-taker gets tricked or bad luck intervenes or the FBI foul things up. He'd seen all sorts, the bag of money taken by a random passer-by, usually a kid on a moped, or wet towels in the bag instead of money. There were all manner of ways the hostage-taker could be double-crossed.

He had a better idea. There would be an exchange, but for the plan to work he had decided both parties needed to feel trust to avoid the deal turning to crap. He felt sure he'd thought of everything. He'd removed his number plates so his van couldn't be traced. Having followed the guy home after the killings and having followed him for a few days after that, he knew a lot about him. He knew where he lived and worked and a lot about his life. Before tonight, he'd spoken to him in person on only one occasion, keeping contact to a minimum. The first time he'd spoken to him wearing a ski mask, he'd introduced himself and informed him he knew about the murders. He showed him proof, he played the recording and described what was taking place.

Ackland then told him he wanted one hundred thousand pounds in exchange for the recording and his silence. Before leaving, he handed him a cheap mobile phone which contained a single telephone number on which he could be contacted.

All subsequent contact was by text or phone call. After tonight he'd dispose of the phone and there would be no evidence he'd ever contacted the killer. He'd thought of everything. It had gone smoothly. His only regret was not asking for more money, he should have asked for double, at least.

In his wing mirror a car's lights caught his eye. Ackland grabbed his ski mask and pulled it over his round head. He couldn't make out the car model but the colour was dark. The headlights went out and the car overtook his van. As it passed the killer turned and looked him in the eye. Ackland's mouth felt dry, his tongue leathery. He gulped in air as he felt his body tense.

The vehicle continued a short distance, stopped then turned in the road until it faced the van. It pulled forward and finally came to a standstill about six or seven car lengths away. Ackland sat and watched. Inside the car was dark.

'What's he doing,' muttered Ackland. 'Just get out and bring my money?'

The driver stayed in the car and Ackland stared. He wondered what to do next.

CHAPTER FORTY

Ackland finally decided to take the initiative. He straightened his ski mask and got out of the van. Closing the door gently behind him he walked over to the dark saloon.

Taking a wide berth he approached and, as he did so, the driver lowered the window and stared directly at him.

'It's him! It's the killer!' thought Ackland as a burst of adrenaline flooded his body. He looked around nervously to ensure they were alone.

'Do you have the recording?'

Heart booming, Ackland stepped closer. 'Yes. Do you have the money?'

'I do. What now? This is your show.'

The two men stared at each other.

Ackland thought for a moment. 'Where is it?'

Tilting his head towards the rear of the car he said, 'The money's in the boot. One hundred thousand pounds. In a rucksack. Just as you asked.'

'Good. Open it.'

The driver turned towards his door.

'No, stay in the car. Unlock the boot from the inside.'

He smiled. He was about to press a button on the dashboard when he said, 'The recording. I need assurance this is the only one. It's a lot of money, a life-changing sum, to be handing over without any guarantees.'

'You have my word.' Ackland sounded annoyed. 'We've been over this in text messages.'

'I have your word? I don't know you. I don't mean to be disrespectful in any way but for all I know you could be someone who regularly breaks his word. I have no idea whether you're an honourable man or not. I hope you understand my predicament, when you hold all the cards. You know so much about me and I know so little about you.'

'That's how it's got to be,' insisted Ackland. 'We're not on a date. The less we know about each other the better and I certainly don't want to know about your fucked up life.'

'Okey-dokey. So that's how you're going to be.' He pressed the button to close his window, then sat back in his seat and crossed his arms.

Ackland scratched his head then stepped forward and tapped on the window. There was no reaction. Ackland tapped again. The window lowered a little.

'Are we doing this or not? If we're not, I'll just leave and give the recording to the police. It's up to you.'

The car door suddenly swung open and the driver got out. He nonchalantly extended his arms and stretched; slowly, he looked Ackland up and down.

Ackland's heart jumped up a gear; it felt like it was going to explode out of his chest.

'The ski mask is a good idea,' said the killer. 'Concealing your identity is a wise move. If I were in your position I'd do the same.'

Ackland held up a clear plastic sandwich bag; it held the recording from his phone. He pointed towards the back of the car. 'This is the only copy of what you did. It's yours. I just want the money.'

The killer dangled a key fob in his hand. He pressed a button and the car's boot sprang open.

'I see there's no changing your mind. I'll just have to assume you're a trustworthy fellow. What else can I do?'

Standing at a safe distance, Ackland stared inside the lighted boot. The spotless interior was lined with clear plastic sheeting and a black and blue rucksack sat in the middle.

'Pass it to me,' said Ackland. 'And the phone I gave you, put it in the bag.'

The driver unzipped the bag, put the mobile phone inside, and was about to pass it over when he said, 'You're not going to count the money?' He stepped away from the boot and looked at Ackland.

Ackland froze for a moment, wondering whether he should just grab the rucksack and run. Instead he said, 'Of course I'm going to count it. Do you take me for an idiot?' He tucked the clear bag containing the phone card in his trouser pocket and stepped forward.

The killer described the rucksack's contents. 'All twenty pound notes... fifty notes to a bundle... one thousand pounds per bundle... one hundred bundles... feel free to count the number of bundles... You'll find exactly one hundred thousand pounds.'

Ackland's eyes strained to see in the poor light as he flicked through a bundle of twenty pound notes and then counted the bundles. One hundred thousand pounds. This was for Tara and the kids, he'd done it for them. A fresh start. No more scrimping and scraping. He zipped up the rucksack, straightened and slung it over his shoulder. His hand moved towards his pocket for the phone card. He turned to where the figure had been standing. 'It's all there. Here's the card—'

The blow to the head came out of nowhere. Then

another. Ackland's legs buckled, he fell to his knees. The rucksack slipped from his shoulder. A sick feeling filled his stomach and chest. His head began to spin. A shove from behind sent him face down, hard, onto the surface of the road. Despite the numbness creeping through his body he felt his arms and legs being tied. His mind wanted to believe this wasn't really happening and it was nothing more than a nightmare. He desperately wanted to wake up. His head jolted as the ski mask was ripped off. A hand in his trouser pocket and then inside his jacket. Then a voice close to his ear.

'Paul Ackland, I have the recording, your wallet, your phone, your driving licence and bank cards. I'll soon know where you live. Is this a photo of your wife and children? Lovely family. Before I kill you I want you to know I might pay them a visit with my hammer and hacksaw, right now I'm undecided.'

Fear scorched Ackland's brain. He tried to fight back but he could barely open his eyes, let alone move his arms or legs. His face thumped and scraped against something solid as he felt himself being lifted, folded, bent and shoved. He was in the boot of the car. A face loomed close. 'I know a little place we can have a proper conversation. I need you to tell me everything you know. For starters, I'll need convincing there are no more recordings, and I want to be sure you've told nobody else about my... indiscretions. Have a little think about how long you want my questioning to last and how much pain you can endure.'

The boot closed. The lights went out. He heard footsteps then the car starting. Ackland prayed for help and wished he could turn back the clock.

CHAPTER FORTY-ONE

Alice and Faith weren't in school because it was a teacher training day. Having not seen them much due to my odd working hours over the last few days I decided to take the morning off and spend some quality time with them.

I parked the car in Poole Park, close to the miniature railway and children's play area. Monica and I walked and talked while Alice and Faith ran ahead. They enjoyed feeding the ducks and seeing if they could spot a fish jumping out of the water. I kept Sandy on a close lead as we made our way past the large number of Canada geese she was eyeing. The plan was to walk through the park until we reached Whitecliff where the girls and I would do battle on the monkey bars, seeing who could swing back and forth the most times. I didn't fancy my chances.

I waved my acknowledgement to Alice and Faith who were indicating they wanted to run ahead to a large lake on the other side of the road. They liked that particular lake because it had more swans.

I squeezed Monica's hand. 'Are you okay?'

'Yes. This is lovely. It's great to get out of the house and be together as a family.'

It had occurred to me that though it was on my mind constantly at the moment, I had no idea what Monica's current feelings were on the subject of marriage. I tried to sound casual. 'I was reading an article that stated the number of couples getting married has remained quite constant over the last few years. It seems to have only changed one way or the other by about one or two per cent. Though, the number has of course fallen dramatically since the peak in the nineteen-seventies, and even that's far lower than the peak in nineteen-forty.'

'Really?' Monica was distracted by the girls who were approaching a swan. 'They won't get too close, will they?'

'They know better than that.' I called out and waved to Alice to keep herself and Faith a safe distance from a couple of swans that were waddling across the grass. 'What did surprise me was that the average age for marriage these days was around forty for a man and thirty-five for a woman.'

'What does that mean? Is that couples remarrying or leaving it later to tie the knot?' I could see from her expression I was boring her.

'I don't know. The article was stating facts, it didn't speculate at all.' *What was I wittering on about? Please someone shoot me, put me out my misery!*

'Why were you reading about that? Is it part of your investigation?'

'No. I'm not sure. Actually, it might have been on the radio. Yes, it was on Radio 4.' The conversation was dying an agonising death.

'I suppose whether or not to formalise the relationship through marriage is down to the individual couple, and has been for a long time now. People aren't bothered one way or another whether a couple with children share the same name. Perhaps that was why the number of marriages surprised me.'

Monica wasn't even listening to me, she'd switched off. She was smiling at Alice and Faith. We were approaching them and they were beckoning us over to see the large cygnets swimming behind their parents. Another family was throwing grain for them and a large number of the birds were gathering. I dropped the conversation and stood back with Sandy while Monica joined the girls.

I shook my head at my total ineptitude. It seemed I could interview killers and psychopaths and find the grain of truth behind their lies but simply establishing whether I was on the same page as Monica about our relationship was beyond me. I glanced down and Sandy looked back. I crouched and gave her a pat. 'You know I'm not completely useless at all this relationship stuff, don't you?'

Sandy looked away.

CHAPTER FORTY-TWO

After returning from the park, and having had a family lunch, I got a phone call from Cotton. She had decided she wanted to visit the Venus Moon Gentlemen's Club where Ackland worked. She had questions for him and had been trying to get hold of him on the number he'd given us but the phone was off. She'd been to his house as well but nobody was in.

'Nice motor. He's doing all right for himself,' said Cotton. She peered inside the vehicle that straddled two of only three parking spaces. 'I know the guy who owns this place, he's a real dirt-bag. He and I have had quite a few run-ins over the years. I'm happy to take the lead.'

I thumped on the back door of the club in Exeter Road, Bournemouth. 'Sounds good to me,' I said.

Cotton peered inside the vehicle. 'Range Rover Sport. Brand new. Sixty to seventy thousand pounds. Who says crime doesn't pay.'

I pressed the intercom button and put my mouth close to the microphone plate. 'Detective Chief Inspector Hardy and Detective Inspector Cotton, here to speak to Paul Ackland.'

A deep male voice came through. 'He's not here. Tell her to keep her sticky fingers away from the car. Unless you have a warrant.'

I looked at Cotton and shook my head in exasperation.

Cotton pointed to CCTV cameras either side of the large Venus Moon Gentlemen's Club sign above our heads.

'In that case I'd like to speak to someone about your employee Paul Ackland. Open the door... please. Alternatively, I can come back later with a warrant and the drug squad.'

We stood by the door and waited. And waited. I was just about to press the button again when I heard a *clunk-click*. The intercom voice spoke again. 'Come upstairs.'

I pulled open the door and held it for Cotton. At the top of the narrow concrete staircase a fire door opened into the main floor of the club. It was late morning, almost lunchtime, and the lights were on. There were no girls in sight and the club looked run-down and unwelcoming under the bright lights.

Behind the bar a barman was unloading a dishwasher, checking and drying glasses. A strip of deep red carpet leading from the front of the club to the room we had entered was being vacuumed by a small lady of Asian descent. She looked up and scowled at us before tugging at the vacuum's long black power cable and continuing her work.

'Oi! Over here,' came a voice from inside a booth.

Cotton and I made our way over to where two men sat watching us. A big man in a tight black t-shirt put his hand over his mouth and whispered something I couldn't hear. The other well-dressed man listened and nodded. His narrow eyes looked Cotton up and down before his deeply lined face broke into a broad smile. He straightened his collar, adjusted his cuff-links and ran a hand over the sides of his neatly styled short grey hair.

'I remember when you were just a wet-behind-the-ears little street copper. Look at you all grown up.' He leaned over so he could get a better look. 'Still a hot cop. Emma, isn't it? WPC Emma Cotton.'

Jimbo laughed. 'A hot cop,' he repeated. Sweating profusely he dabbed his soft face with a napkin.

'You've got a good memory, Tinsnip,' said Cotton. She sounded forthright.

'Call me Stuart, Stu or Mr Daniels. Times have changed.' He opened his arms like a king welcoming his people. 'All this belongs to me now. Which means it's more important than ever to remember names and faces; you never know when you might need a favour. I mean, you need to know who you can rely on or who's up to something they shouldn't be. Secrets make good currency.' After holding Emma's gaze for an uncomfortably long time he turned his attention to me. 'Who's your friend, Emma?'

Cotton introduced me. 'This is my boss DCI Hardy. Sir, this is Stuart Daniels also known as Tinsnip. And this is Jimbo or James Blair.'

Jimbo emptied a packet of smoky bacon crisps into his mouth, then dropped the empty packet on the table between us. He stared at me while he crunched. The fingers of one hand played with a pint glass about a quarter full of fizzy orange, its red and white paper straw drooped. The other hand fiddled with a packet of salted peanuts for a moment before wiping crumbs from his mouth and t-shirt. His flabby chest shook.

'Have a seat,' said Tinsnip. 'Tell me how I can help.'

We remained standing. 'We have some questions for Paul Ackland. They're to do with a case he's helping us with. A murder investigation.'

'If you're here about Ackers you're out of luck. As I told you a moment ago, he ain't here.' On the table sat a portable wireless intercom and an iPhone. 'I haven't been able to reach him for a day or so. His wife doesn't know where he is either. He used to be reliable. I'd ask him to jump and he'd say, how high, Mr Daniels? I don't know what's got into him lately.' He kept his eyes fixed on Cotton as he spoke, clearly intending to intimidate. 'Trouble with his missus, perhaps? I say that because I know for a fact she doesn't like him surrounded by so much pussy here at the club. It must drive her crazy at night. Her at home with the kids, him here surrounded by tits and...'

'We get the idea,' interrupted Cotton. 'When did you last see him?'

'What am I, his mother?' said Tinsnip.

As he laughed Jimbo's body shook like a bouncy castle full of kids.

Tinsnip clenched his fists and leaned forward. 'I saw him two nights ago. As of this moment, I don't know where he is. What I do know is his not being here is inconvenient. Now if there is nothing else, I have a business to run.'

'How long have you known Ackland?' said Cotton.

Neither man replied.

'How many nights a week does he work here?' she said.

Both men stared back at her and said nothing.

'How long has he worked at the club?'

Jimbo picked up his drink and sipped noisily while Tinsnip stared at Cotton.

'A wall of silence?' I said. Tinsnip and Jimbo turned to me as though they'd forgotten I existed. 'Two tough guys, wannabe gangsters, who won't speak to the police? That's new.'

I looked at Cotton and she nodded. 'Very new,' she agreed.

'I've met enough killers and proper criminals to know you two clowns don't make the grade. You've done well for yourselves, but with this new club of yours it won't be long before some bigger fish come knocking on that door. And they will. Organised crime won't be able to resist. You boys are in the big league now. I hope you've got the balls you make out you do. Because if you don't it won't be long before we see you down at the morgue.'

I turned to Cotton.

'Which gang do you think will come after this club first? British, Irish, Scottish, Kosovan, Serbian, Italian?'

Cotton shrugged. 'This area? Hard to say. Though somewhere Eastern European, most likely.'

'You know why we're here? Of course you do. A little man like you has his ear to the ground. If for a second you thought Ackland was speaking to us about anything to do with your activities then you know we'd be here investigating you. Instead, we're here about the murder of children and their parents. Young boys butchered by a sick individual who cuts them into pieces. But don't let that bother you, go about your business, while you can.'

I turned to Cotton. 'Come on, let's go, we'll leave this pair to revel in their riches. When we find Ackland we'll let him know you're looking for him.'

We turned to leave. I looked back at Tinsnip. 'If he doesn't turn up soon I want you to know you'll be top of my list of suspects.'

Tinsnip snarled as he spoke. 'I don't ever want to see you two again. If you think Ackers has anything to do with the murder of them families then you're more stupid than you look. Take my word for it. He isn't smart enough to kill that many people and not leave a pile of evidence. You've met him. He's more Jack-in-the-box than Jack the Ripper. And as far as I am aware he is safe and sound, he certainly was the last time I saw him. He probably went home with one of the girls and thinks he's in love. And as for anyone taking over my club, you've got it all wrong. I've got connections. I'm going to do just fine.'

Cotton and I looked at each other. 'We'll show ourselves out,' I said.

Tinsnip jumped to his feet and yelled after us. 'You do that. Don't come around here again.' Despite his bravado, I must have touched a nerve. 'Hurting kids is wrong. When I see Ackland I'll send him your way. Now fuck off out of here.'

Cotton and I kept walking. I raised a hand in acknowledgement. I didn't anticipate any help from Tinsnip and Jimbo.

Tinsnip couldn't let his status in front of staff fall any lower. He called out, 'Emma, if you get tired of playing cops and robbers you can come and dance here. I'd bet good money under that suit is an amazing body. Think about it. It's easy money. All you've gotta do is wiggle that sensational arse of yours.'

Emma let the door slam on our way out.

CHAPTER FORTY-THREE

Cotton and I went straight from the club to Ackland's home where we hoped we'd either find him or catch up with his wife, Tara.

Tara peered around a crack in the door. She looked exhausted and upset. Her eyes were red and the part of her face I could see was blotchy. We showed her our warrant cards. Her face dropped some more. She opened the door further.

She called up to her children. 'Boys, wanna go and play in the park?'

I heard thumping as her two sons came running. They started pushing each other as they passed her. The eldest boy looked up at her in amazement and then at us, as though we were magicians.

'Really?' said the eldest boy.

She nodded.

They didn't need telling twice. They started running down the road towards the traffic lights and the playing fields.

She called after them. 'Stick together. Jacob, look after your little brother. Ethan, stay with Jacob. Don't get into any fights. And look after your school clothes. You put holes in those trousers I won't be buying new ones. You hear me? No stains on the knees.'

The boys were out of earshot.

'I'm wasting my breath with those two,' said Tara.

The youngest boy put out his hand for his big brother to hold as they crossed the road. We watched as they headed towards a large group of children playing soccer.

'They never listen. They're always putting holes in the knees of their trousers, or the elbows. They're good boys. But bloody hard work, and expensive,' said Tara. She spoke and watched the boys, stalling, refusing to look at us directly. I got the impression she knew something was amiss and whatever the news might be she didn't want to hear it.

Eventually, Tara showed us through to the kitchen. There were shopping bags on the floor in front of the fridge freezer which she began unpacking.

'So what's he done?' said Tara. 'I'd guessed he was locked up. I even told me mum as much. Had to be the reason he's not been home. Too ashamed to call me. He's a bloody idiot. God only knows why I married him.' Her voice began to break as she fought back tears. She wiped her nose on some kitchen towel. She put the chilled items in the fridge then opened the freezer door and put away pizza, fish fingers and frozen vegetables. 'What am I going to tell the boys? Oh, Christ.'

I tried to speak but she continued. Cotton looked at me and raised her eyebrows so we let her carry on.

'If he's been with another woman I don't want to know. One of those tarts at the club. He promised me he never would. He swore on the boys' lives he'd never look at another woman. "Just a job," he said, "I don't want nobody else." I'm a fool. So what's the story? Come on spit it out.'

'We're actually here to see if you can help us locate him.

Paul has been assisting us in our enquiries and we have a few further questions.'

'What enquiries? I don't know where he is. Where is he?' Tara's face went ghostly white. She stopped what she was doing. 'Have you tried the club?'

'We've just come from there. Nobody has seen him,' said Cotton. 'When did you see him last?'

'Two nights ago. He went out late.'

'And you didn't think to call the police?'

'It wouldn't be the first time he's been away for a couple of nights without telling me. He has to take work where he can get it.'

'Has he called you?'

She chewed her nail and stared at the shopping bags on the floor. 'No.'

'Was he going to the Venus Moon Gentlemen's Club?'

'Gentlemen's club,' she spat. 'He didn't tell me where he was going. He might have been going to the club. I don't know.' Her hands trembled as she moved from biting a fingernail to a thumbnail. She looked to me like someone who was lying or only telling us half the truth.

I cursed to myself as my mobile phone started ringing. I stepped into the hallway. 'Excuse me,' I said.

Cotton took over until I returned a few moments later.

'We have to go,' I said to Cotton. 'If we have any news we'll be in touch.'

The concern in Tara's voice suddenly became real and urgent. She reached out and grabbed my arm. 'Is that it? Are you going to try and find him? I need him here with me. His boys need him. I need him home.'

She thought she saw something in my eyes and her voice became panicked. 'If it's him you have to tell me. Is he dead? Did it go wrong? I warned him it would.'

'A body has been found,' I said. 'A male. I don't have

any further information. Don't concern yourself; I'm sure Paul is fine.' I wasn't telling the whole truth. Though the body had been badly mutilated, and no formal identification had taken place, there was evidence to suggest it was very likely the body of Paul Ackland.

I looked at her quizzically. 'What did you mean? Did what go wrong?'

Tara sat down, pretty much collapsing into a seat at the kitchen table. We joined her. Her head bowed, she stared at her pale trembling hands, her bony fingers clasped. Her short dark hair fell over her face. She took a piece of kitchen towel from her sleeve and wiped her nose. She looked up, her dark eyes filled with anguish. 'He's got himself killed. I know he has.'

'What do you mean?' I asked. 'You should tell us what you know.'

'I'll be straight with you because I need to know he's safe. But I don't want to get him in any trouble. Paul thought he might know who the killer was that killed those families. The night he went out he was going to make sure of it. That's all I know.'

'Make sure how?' said Cotton.

'I think he said he'd followed the man and was going to confront him.'

'What aren't you telling us?' I said. 'We can't help if you don't tell us the truth.'

Tara dabbed her nose with the tissue and sniffed loudly. 'I'm not saying any more until I know he's safe.'

The front door opened and the two boys came flying into the house. 'Mum! Jacob's hurt his arm,' shouted Ethan. 'I think he broked it.'

Jacob came into the kitchen. 'It's not broken. Just twisted. I was doing an overhead flying kick and landed funny. Scored a goal though, just like Cristiano Ronaldo, it was a classic.'

'Are you all right, Mum?' The two boys hugged their mother and looked angrily at us.

'The police officers are leaving,' said Tara. 'They're going to find Daddy.'

That was our cue to leave. 'As soon as we have some news, we'll be in touch,' I said.

Tara put her arms around her sons and nodded. She couldn't speak.

CHAPTER FORTY-FOUR

Twenty-four hours later I waited outside the mortuary for Tara Ackland who had arrived to formally identify her husband's body. She looked like a different woman, unkempt, slouched and shuffling along. I didn't want to intrude at such a difficult time and so kept my distance. It occurred to me she might have questions about her husband's death and though I had no real answers I felt it important for me to be there for her to talk to if she wished.

All I knew was that council workers collecting rubbish dumped by fly-tippers discovered the body wrapped in black plastic bin bags in amongst the discarded items. I was also aware her husband appeared to have been tortured. My assumption at this stage was his association with Tinsnip and Jimbo had somehow resulted in his death.

As she was about to leave she glanced up and saw me seated by the doors. I gave my condolences and offered to walk with her, which she accepted.

'It feels like the blackest, coldest shadow has been cast over our lives. Yet, somehow I keep imagining I hear his voice. I'm sure this is a nightmare that I'm going to jolt awake from, like it's not really happening. It's going to hit me like a tsunami at some point, I know it is,' she said.

'Do you have family who can be with you?' I asked. I knew from personal experience how important it is to have the right people around you at a time like this.

'My sister is staying with me. She's looking after the boys right now.'

'That's good. It'll help having someone with you. Someone you can talk to, if you want to.'

'Have you ever lost anyone?'

I thought about how family helped when I lost Helena. 'My wife. A few years ago. I wish I could give you some sage words of advice but truth be told I was a wreck. I fell apart. I dealt with it wrongly. I felt like my soul had been ripped from my body, so I buried my head in the sand and threw myself into my work. I realise now I prolonged the grief by pushing it away.'

Tara chuckled at my candour. She sniffed and dabbed her eyes with a tissue. 'At least you're honest. Everyone else has told me I'll be fine. That it's important I keep going for the boys. All I really want to do is curl up into a ball and hide away. I don't want it to get easier; that would mean I've distanced myself from him and our love has faded.'

'They mean well, and they are right to a certain extent. Everyone deals with grief in their own way. What works for one person might not work for another. Your boys need you, just like my daughters needed me. You're going to hurt like hell but your boys are what will get you through this. You'll live each day for them.'

We walked out into the car park. Tara rooted around in her bag for her mobile phone. 'My sister is picking me up. My car's battery is flat, I left the bloody lights on. I'm not thinking straight at the moment.'

I smiled understandingly and waited while Tara made

her call. When her sister didn't pick up, she looked annoyed.

'I can give you a lift,' I said. 'It's no trouble.'

'You know what. That would be useful. I need to get back to the boys and I don't want to be here a second longer than is necessary.'

We walked to my car and Tara sent a text letting her sister know she was getting a lift. 'I'm being extra cautious,' said Tara as she took a photo of the car registration and one of me and sent it to her sister. 'Right now I don't trust anyone.'

'I understand,' I said. 'It's perfectly natural.'

As I drove, Tara stared out of her side window. Her breathing was heavy. Her knuckles were white as she clasped the tissue in her fist. 'Did you see Paul? What was done to him?'

'I did. I'm sorry.'

'Who would do something like that?'

'A very sick individual,' I suggested.

'When he died he must have been in agony. He didn't deserve that.'

Paul had been tortured. The post-mortem would conclude actual cause of death but it was clear his body had been cut and beaten multiple times and acid poured into the wounds. All his fingers and toes appeared to have been broken.

'You said you thought he'd got himself killed. What did you mean by that?'

Tara didn't say anything for quite some time; she continued to stare out of the window. Then without looking at me she said, 'Paul was going to blackmail the killer.'

I wasn't sure I'd heard her correctly. 'I don't understand. Who do you mean? What killer?'

'The one who murdered the families, the ones on the news, with twin boys.'

I almost slammed on the brakes. I tried to stay calm and encouraged her to keep going. I spoke calmly. 'How was he planning on doing that, Tara?'

'The last time I saw him, that's where he was going. To meet the killer.' She sobbed. 'He had a recording, so he said. I told him not to do it. He wouldn't listen to me. I should have stopped him.' She looked at me. 'It's on his phone. Not clear, apparently. But enough to worry the killer. Enough to make him pay for the recording. At least that was his plan. I told him to go to the police but he refused. He was going to show the police after he'd been paid. He was, I swear.'

'We don't have his phone,' I said. 'It wasn't on him when the body was recovered. Do you know if he made a back-up of the recording?'

'I don't know. He might have done.'

'It might help us catch the person responsible for his death. Do you have a computer he could have copied the recording to?'

'No. We do everything on our phones.' We arrived at Tara's home and I stopped the car. 'Paul does have a second phone. Might be something on that one.' She shrugged.

'It's worth taking a look. Could I borrow the phone for a few hours? We have a wizard IT officer who could run some checks on it.'

Tara stared at me for a moment while she thought about it. 'If you think it'll help find who hurt him I'll let you have it. You must promise to return it. There are photos on it I want to keep.'

'I promise,' I said.

My hands trembled as I waited for Tara to bring me the phone. I couldn't help but hope it would give us access to the recording.

Tara returned with the phone. As she passed it to me I said, 'Do you have anywhere else you can stay? It occurred to me Paul might have told the killer about this phone.'

Tara looked like she couldn't take any more. 'My sister's place, perhaps,' she said breathlessly. 'Yes, we'll go there for a little while.'

'For safety's sake, I'd recommend going away if you can. I'll arrange for an officer to watch the house in the meantime.'

En route back to the office I called Becky Wang and asked her if she would analyse the mobile phone. I didn't hold out much hope of there being anything of use on it but it was worth a shot and I couldn't help feeling hopeful.

With Paul Ackland's murder it felt like one line of enquiry had been severed and another established. It was now time to reassess the evidence and decide in which direction to go next.

CHAPTER FORTY-FIVE

'A penny for your thoughts,' said Monica as she joined me. I stood in the back garden looking up at the stars. It had been a roller coaster of a day.

Monica handed me a mug of tea and sipped her own herbal brew.

I hadn't heard back from Becky Wang and my mind had briefly drifted to what might be if Ackland's phone came up trumps. I'd also been thinking about what I was missing and why I couldn't see the investigation clearly. My mind had flashed back to the bloody remains of the twin boys; their limbs hacked from their bodies. I turned to Monica and pretended my thoughts were less gruesome. 'I was just thinking how crazy-exciting our lives are right now. About everything we've been through. Mostly, I was thinking how lucky I am.' I leaned over and kissed her, I put my arm around her and gave her a squeeze.

'You sweet-talker you.' She grinned and put her warm hand on top of mine. We stared at a particularly bright star. 'That's the planet Venus,' said Monica. 'Named after the Roman goddess of love and beauty. It's the second largest natural object in the night sky, after the moon.'

'Sexy and smart, that's what I love about you.'

She leaned over and pretended to sniff me. 'Have you been drinking? You and Rayner abstaining from drink in solidarity during our pregnancies lasted all of five minutes.'

I was about to protest that I hadn't been drinking when she continued.

'How is the investigation going?'

I sipped my tea and thought about how to answer. 'Not good. Between you and me, I think it was a mistake to have agreed to get involved. I've started to wonder what we can truly contribute. We don't have the resources and we're being run ragged. I've got Heidi driving back and forth from London or I'm on the phone to her every five minutes. I feel guilty having got Rayner involved; he has enough on his plate looking after Jenny. And Emma; I thought I had her figured out but she's complicated. She's a great detective, don't get me wrong, I can't fault her work ethic. But she seems distracted. It's like she's got something more important she needs to be dealing with. Not all the time, just occasionally.'

'Wow,' said Monica. 'I'm glad I asked. I had no idea, I knew you were stressed but you can't believe you've made a mistake by investigating, can you?'

I didn't know what I thought. Were we really making any difference? I was about to explain further when Mum appeared behind us.

'Mind if I join you two love birds?' said Mum.

I put out a welcome hand. She pulled a throw over her shoulders and came out onto the patio. She must have felt the tension in the air. 'I'm sorry, did I interrupt?'

'Not at all,' I said. I was glad to change the topic. 'We were counting stars.' Monica and I looked up again. Mum followed our eyes. 'I remember nights like this when we lived close to London, you could hardly see any stars. Now look, it's incredible. And see how bright the moon is.'

Monica squeezed my hand. 'You know it takes around three days to travel the two hundred and forty thousand miles to the moon. An astronaut will spend years acquiring the experience needed to be selected for a space mission. It makes you wonder why they do it? I mean, there isn't a lot when you get there. The journey must be seat-of-your-pants scary as well as arduous and boring. It's not that picturesque when you arrive and apparently space dirt smells like the air after a firework show.' Monica looked at me to ensure she had my attention. 'Yes, it's exciting. After all, they're pushing the limits of human ingenuity and they're seen as heroes, but surely just as important are the heroic, but often mundane deeds of ordinary people every day. Like the unsung heroes who put the well-being of others before their own. They're heroes too. Even if those efforts don't make newspaper headlines. Those contributions are what *really* make this big old world a place worth living in. And something us ordinary beings are thankful for.'

Monica raised an eyebrow at me and I realised I was being schooled.

'Well that was heavy,' said Mum. 'I think I missed something and I'm not going to ask what. I'm just going to keep on looking at those twinkly stars.'

I realised what Monica was saying and I knew I was simply feeling exhausted and emotional. That my contribution *was* worthwhile. After a good night's sleep I felt sure I'd be ready and raring to get back to the case. But right now, I put my arms around Mum and Monica and looked up at the stars.

Did space dirt really smell like the air after a firework show?

CHAPTER FORTY-SIX

Alex's previous partner, Louise Greenslade, had changed her hair style and colour since the court hearing. Emma watched her from the car and as she entered the park for her early morning fitness boot camp she got out and followed her.

After Louise had almost killed Alex with a kitchen knife Emma had made sure his solicitor pushed for attempted murder, but at the hearing the judge had decided there was strong evidence she'd acted in self-defence and was granted bail.

A lot had happened in the intervening months and despite being sure Louise was guilty at the time of the attack, Emma was now not so sure.

'Louise,' called Emma as she approached. 'Louise.'

She turned, and on seeing Emma looked worried. 'What do you want? I can't talk to you. Leave me alone.' She began walking quickly towards the centre of the small group limbering up at the centre of the playing field.

'I need to speak to you,' called Emma.

'You've done enough.' Louise put up a hand in protest and kept walking away.

'I need two minutes, then I'm gone.'

'No.'

Emma jogged to get nearer. 'I believe you,' said Emma.

Louise stopped and spun around, her face confused and curious. 'What do you mean?'

Emma was puffing as she reached Louise. 'Alex wasn't the man I thought he was. Certain things he said and did worried me. I ended our relationship.'

Louise looked concerned. 'You've ended it.'

'Yes.'

'But he hasn't, has he?'

Emma nodded. 'Something like that.'

Louise raised an eyebrow.

'No. He hasn't ended it. Despite my telling him more than once that we're over.'

Louise looked behind her at the exercise class then back at Emma. 'Screw the class. Let's go get an almond croissant and cappuccino.'

* * *

The two women sat in the corner of the coffee shop away from the large windows and the eyes of the steady stream of passers-by on their way to work. They sipped coffee in plush armchairs either side of a low table; their breakfast pastries now nothing more than a few flakes on their plates.

'Being a police inspector you'd think I'd be smarter when it came to men,' said Emma. She noticed the chewed-down fingernails as Louise pulled on a sweater.

'You're a woman first and foremost. You're human. None of us like to be defined by our jobs. The job we do isn't who we are on the inside.'

'He was charming. Then he changed. Just the way you warned me he would.'

'I tried.'

'I couldn't see his flaws until it was too late.'

'Just like I did, you fell in love. He's a master at manipulation.'

'I was only with him a few months and it's taken its toll. You were with him, how long was it, four years?'

'Yes,' she nodded. 'I used to be confident and outgoing. Before I met Alex I loved nothing more than going out of an evening, drinking with friends and having a good time. I was the life and soul of any party. Now, it's a major challenge to summon the courage to meet my girlfriends at my early morning exercise class. I usually can't sleep the night before. I don't go out unless I have to. Certainly not on dates. The truth is most of the time I'm a wreck.'

Emma reached out and squeezed Louise's hand. 'I'm sorry I didn't believe you. So very sorry.'

'Do you think it'll help my trial? I mean, now you know what he's like. I swear to God I never stabbed him. It was just like I told you at the time. He took the knife from my drawer and stabbed himself. He knew exactly what he was doing. He aimed the knife where he knew he wouldn't catch a vital organ. He wants me to go to prison. He's punishing me.'

'I'll make sure that doesn't happen. I've already called your solicitor and left a message for him to call me. He'll get the charges thrown out if he can. If it does go to trial I'll give evidence myself, if necessary.'

Louise suddenly looked ten years younger, colour returning to her face as the anxiety she'd carried for so long lifted. 'You don't know what that means to me. Thank you.' Her mobile phone started to ring. She picked it up and looked at it. 'It's my friends from the exercise class, they'll be checking I'm okay. We usually go for coffee and cake after class. I'm not sure I can manage more to eat but I had better go.'

'You should go. And have that cake. You deserve it,' said Emma with a grin.

'I might. To celebrate.'

Emma watched Louise leave and felt relieved. She'd done the right thing and felt good about it.

CHAPTER FORTY-SEVEN

I'd woken early and unable to sleep, I'd opened up the office. Sitting in the doorway, perched on the doorstep, sipping decaffeinated coffee, I felt the cool of the morning on my skin and listened to bird song. Too soon, questions lured me back to my desk where I thumbed through witness statements and crime scene photos.

Leaning back in my chair I chewed the end of my pen. I tapped my nose with it while mulling over everything we had.

It turned out Andrew Yates, the institute's data guy, had been charged with affray outside a casino in Bournemouth three years earlier. He was found not guilty when the jury accepted the defence's argument that one of the casino's doormen had used unreasonable force when demanding he leave. What was clear from reading a transcript of the case was that Yates had a gambling addiction, and on the night in question he'd lost a lot of money. In the judge's summing-up he recommended Yates take steps to seek help with it.

I returned to chewing my pen. I wasn't sure how any of it fitted within our investigation but I decided I should pay Yates a visit. I had no idea where it might lead but it wouldn't be the first time someone with a gambling habit had found themselves doing something they later came to regret. It had to be worth giving Yates a shake to see whether anything fell.

I decided to give it an hour before setting off so I went and grabbed a toasted Philly bacon sandwich and coffee from Patisserie Mark Bennett on Sandbanks Road. The patisserie is a few hundred metres from Evening Hill, one of my favourite stops with views overlooking Poole Harbour, Brownsea Island and the Purbeck Hills. I sat watching windsurfers, kite-surfers and passing boats while eating breakfast and reading a newspaper. After an hour or so I set off, believing now was a reasonable time of day to pay Yates a visit. Though I knew either Rayner or Cotton would have come with me had I asked, I decided to go alone.

Yates's house was in the affluent area of Lower Parkstone in a quiet cul de sac. On the large block paved driveway sat two new cars, one of which was a top of the range BMW. Inside, the home was tastefully decorated and well appointed, the gardens front and back professionally planted and landscaped. The rattan furniture we sat on looked new and I noted there was another set of matching furniture on the garden patio. Yates appeared to be someone without any obvious financial difficulties. He'd come into some money from somewhere though I doubted it was down to his luck changing at the casino.

'It a beautiful home,' I said. 'Have you lived here long?'

'Thank you. We haven't lived here long. Our previous house was a little snug, what with the boys growing up so fast. Boys their age need their space. We've gradually been doing the place up, little by little.' His voice trailed off. Yates placed two mugs down on the glass-topped table that stood between us. He closed the conservatory door before sitting down opposite me.

I noticed Yates's brown eyes look past me. I glanced around and through the glass of the conservatory doors I saw his wife, Brianna, chewing her thumb nail and staring at us. She looked concerned. With difficulty, she smiled at me before turning her attention to the boys. When I arrived, the children had been complaining about having to go out to the shops to buy new school shoes. Perhaps she was exhausted.

'I have girls,' I said. 'They present their own challenges. Your two look similar in age.'

'They're thirteen. Twins. Non-identical. They're from my wife's first marriage. The ironic thing is she and Dave, her first husband, spent a fortune on fertility treatment. By the time she finally fell pregnant they'd fallen out of love with each other. The stress and heartache had driven them apart. We don't have any of our own. We decided Oliver and Dylan were enough.' A smile spread weakly across his long face. He ran a hand over his wild wavy hair.

'Is that the reason for your interest in working at the institute? Oliver and Dylan, I mean.'

'Not at all. That's just a coincidence. I've always worked as a data analyst; I joined the institute on a promise of something special and significant financial rewards, although it never worked out that way. It was meant to be a step up, a pay rise and promise of promotion. The guy who worked for me at the company I left when I joined the institute, he's now earning double my salary.' He shook his head. 'I suppose hindsight makes fools of us all, sooner or later.'

I sipped my coffee and watched Yates fiddle with a piece of cotton hanging from one of the seat cushions. I guessed he felt uneasy around police. 'As I mentioned when we spoke on the phone earlier I'm here to discuss any potential connection between the murdered families and the institute, and in particular your own access to all the records held there. It's all very routine. Boring really.'

'I'm simply an analyst. I'm given questionnaires and surveys that I set up online. I then use the results to find interesting similarities and trends. Nothing more than that. I'm not sure how I can help?'

'I understand. During an investigation like this we look at all sorts of things, including personal records.'

Yates sniffed and tugged his ear nervously. 'I see.'

I tried to choose my words carefully. 'It's come to light, and there is no delicate way to put this, that in the past you've struggled with a gambling addiction.' The colour appeared to drain from Yates's face; he seemed to age before my eyes.

'I knew that's why you were here, somehow, I just knew. I'll admit, I had a problem, it took me a long time to get over it but I've kept it under control for years now. I'm not sure it was ever a real addiction anyway, I just got carried away for a while.'

'I'm sorry, I had to ask.'

'How is it relevant?'

'There have been cases in the past when someone who'd prefer to hide their problem is put in a position where they are blackmailed. Or they've gone to extreme measures to hide an addiction.'

'I know what you're saying and nobody is forcing me to do anything. I don't shout about the issues I've had but I don't hide them either. It is what it is. I'm an open book. You're barking up the wrong tree.'

I kept my eyes fixed on his until he looked away. He was lying about something and he knew I knew it. I just wasn't sure where this conversation would end up. I pressed on. 'We have a theory that the killer has gained access to the list of families on the database you manage. Our investigations have confirmed all the families are on the institute's database. That is not a coincidence. The killer is picking families with boys similar in age to your own boys, Oliver and Dylan.'

'What are you saying? You think I'm somehow involved? Hang on, you don't think I'm the killer, do you?'

'Are you?'

'Don't be absurd. Me a killer? You've got to be joking. Seriously, you'd have to be crazy to think I'm involved.'

'I hear that a lot. It wouldn't be the first time I'd been called crazy only later to be proved right.' I took a sheet of paper from my inside jacket pocket and placed it in front of me. Yates stared at it. 'My team and I are thorough. It's the only way we're able to catch those who like to hide in the shadows. I know how much the institute pays you. I know how much you have in savings, your pension, how much you inherited when your father passed away. I know how much your wife earns, her savings, and how much child maintenance she gets each month from her ex-husband.'

'They don't pay me nearly enough,' said Yates angrily. He tried to laugh but he knew he was on the hook, he was now wondering how hard to fight. I began reeling him in.

'In the last six months four payments totalling sixteen thousand pounds have been deposited to an account in your name from a research centre in Barcelona, Spain.'

'You must be mistaken,' insisted Yates. 'I'm not sure what money you're referring to. It's probably a banking mistake. Banks are always depositing funds into wrong accounts.'

'Another payment of twelve thousand pounds was made from a research university in Maine, United States. Six thousand pounds from a private company in Dublin, Ireland. Do I need to go on?'

Yates shifted in his seat. 'I... I,' he gabbled. 'I can probably explain it. I'll need to look into it. Give me a few days.'

'It's important you're honest with me because I have a theory.'

'Really?'

'My theory is that you're dissatisfied with your lot and have been selling the data yourself. If so I urgently need to know who you've sold the data to. The killer's behavioural pattern suggests he is likely to kill again within the next few days or weeks. Scotland Yard have a team following up with every company the institute has sold data to. And we'd been led to believe nobody outside the institute had access to those files. So I'll ask you again. Have you been selling information privately?'

Yates looked like he was going to cry but he held himself together. He leaned forward and placed his hands flat on the table while he fought to control his breathing. His chest rose up and down like a nodding donkey as he calmed himself.

'You've got it all wrong. I haven't sold any data from the institute. That money is for something else entirely.'

CHAPTER FORTY-EIGHT

Andrew Yates made us both fresh coffee. He seemed relieved as he reclined in his seat. It was as though a weight had been lifted from his shoulders.

'I couldn't betray the institute,' he began. 'I helped build it from the ground up. It was Janek Bonne's brainchild but he needed me to find a way to see the value in the information we gathered. Just like he needed Robert Valentine to find buyers. Why would I put the institute's future in jeopardy by breaching data laws?'

'I don't know, Andrew, why don't you tell me?' I pushed the printouts of his financial records towards him to underline my scepticism. 'If it's established that you breached confidentiality laws by illegally selling data that eventually fell into the hands of a killer I think it's highly unlikely any court in this land is going to be very sympathetic. If you have a different story of how considerable payments from universities and privately owned companies came to be in your personal account then I'm all ears.'

Yates looked me in the eye. 'I licensed software I created at the institute to those other institutions.' He looked ashamed, uncomfortable.

'Let me get this straight. The money is for the software you were paid to create at the institute?'

He nodded. 'They lied to me. It was implied I would see wealth beyond my wildest dreams. Analysing the behaviour of the twins was just the start. Imagine if we could predict how each one of us would likely behave given a set of choices. Understanding our trigger points and what can influence decision making is the Holy Grail for commerce, government and industry.'

'So you thought you would be the next Steve Jobs, Bill Gates or Mark Zuckerberg.'

'Bigger. What we had planned at the outset was huge. But Janek Bonne lost interest. He'd banked on one of those big companies buying his start-up. When they showed little interest he stopped coming to meetings, went back to travelling the world. He was already a millionaire, he'd already accumulated a vast personal wealth from other enterprises.'

'Why didn't you start out on your own?'

'I signed a contract. My work belongs to Janek Bonne, everything I've done belongs to him. I still had the passion to create something huge but could see no way out of the restrictions he put me under. When the financial rewards I was promised never materialised I took matters into my own hands. The software I developed to analyse enormous amounts of data was something I could replicate and license to others. What I've done is unethical, perhaps. Unlawful, maybe. But what I haven't done is sell the data itself, just the software used to see trends and patterns. The killer did not get the families he chose from me, he couldn't have.'

I had no way of knowing at this point whether Yates was telling the truth. We'd need to contact the organisations themselves to establish what they'd bought. 'I want the name of everyone you sold to.'

'Of course. I can do that.' Without hesitation he took his

mobile phone from the pocket of his sweater. He looked relieved. 'Everyone is stored on here, I'll give you access to it.' Head down, he continued talking as he searched his phone. 'I expect I'll face prison-time, once Valentine finds out what I've done? He probably won't know what to do so he'll ask himself "What would Janek do?" Janek was stubborn, once his mind was set there was no budging it. The only good thing about that was you knew where you stood with him and that meant you did what you had to do to get the job done. He taught me that.'

I looked at him quizzically.

Yates opened his mouth and closed it. 'I'm sorry I shouldn't speak that way about a dead man.'

'I didn't think you knew him that well?'

'I didn't' Yates looked genuinely shocked. 'I didn't know him well at all. All I'm saying is, he made a lasting impression on the few occasions I met him or worked with him. Ask anyone. He was a special guy.'

I kept my face neutral.

Yates swallowed hard. 'So what happens now? Look, I understand I, um, did something I shouldn't have, but really, who's been hurt? No one. My contract was with Janek, and he's well, he's dead. And there is no reason for Robert to know. You'll have to check out my story, I understand that, but if it can be done discreetly you'll see I'm telling the truth and who at the institute needs to know? I mean, all I've done is share software I created to aid other research facilities. Really, no harm done.'

'Mister Valentine will need to be informed. I'm sorry.'

'Why? He abuses his position. All those conferences he goes on, raising awareness and doing deals, wining and dining, that's all bullshit. It's utter bullshit.'

'I understand. But I'm investigating a serial killer who's

targeting children. Delicacy isn't my priority right now. I'm sorry.'

'For Christ's sake, Valentine is a waste of space. He's supposed to be finding buyers on his little trips to Rome, Geneva, New York, Edinburgh and The Hague, or any number of cities, yet half the time he leaves early, I'm sure of it. No wonder the institute's growth has been slow, we don't have enough cash coming in to finance expansion. He's supposed to be the face of the company but he couldn't sell water to a thirsty man.'

I heard the front door open and close as Brianna and the boys returned. I looked at my watch. 'I should make a move.' I got up and made my way to the front door. Brianna ushered the boys upstairs. She looked between her husband and myself, her eyes searching for answers.

'I'll be in touch,' I said. 'I'll do what I can. I'll certainly take into account your co-operation this morning. But I'm not making any promises.'

CHAPTER FORTY-NINE

Rayner slung his jacket on the coat hook and went straight into the kitchen where he put down the shopping. He called out to Jenny as he went to the sitting room where he could hear the TV playing. 'I've got a baguette and some pickle and ham and cheeses and coleslaw for lunch and some "horrible tea", I mean herbal tea for you.'

'Sounds lovely. The baby and I are starving. I'll come and help you make it.' Jenny scooted forward in her seat. She muted the quiz show she'd been half watching and gingerly pushed herself up.

As soon as she turned to look at him he could see the cut over her eye.

'What happened?' He rushed over to take a closer look. 'Ouch.'

'Don't fuss, it's nothing.'

'What do you mean? You've got a cut. Let me take a look.' He stood in front of her so she couldn't brush him off. 'That looks deep. Your eye is swollen too. Let me get you a cold compress.'

'I don't need a sodding cold compress. Just forget it.'

'What? I don't understand.'

'Just don't fuss, okay? It was my own fault. It tripped and fell. I don't know what happened. My foot caught the carpet somehow and I went down on my knees and fell forward. I caught my face on the corner of the coffee table. It hurt at the time and now it's fine. Just forget it. Okay? It's nothing.'

'Jen, I'm sorry. That's it. I'm calling James; I'm taking time off. I need to be here with you.'

'You are not. You hear me. I fell. It happens. I knew you would over-react, that's just like you. My bloody legs let me down for a second, that's all. I got burned. I'm scarred for life. If I'm lucky I'll get most of my mobility back but who the fuck knows. The last I need is you here day and night with all your fussing and hovering over me like I'm some helpless fucking invalid.'

Rayner took a step back. He'd never seen her like this. He waited until he was sure it was all out. He wanted to throw his arms around her and tell her it would be okay. But was that the right thing to do? Was that what she needed or wanted?

'I'm sorry. I... I over-reacted. It scared me. You're right. Let's go and get some lunch ready. Or, I can do it?'

'No. We'll do it together.'

'Okay. Sorry.'

'That's fine. I just don't need anyone making a fuss. I know you mean well but it's grating. I need to do this on my own.'

'I understand.' Rayner led the way. He didn't look back to see if she was okay. He listened, watched out of the corner of his eye, and was ready to catch her should she stumble but he didn't look back. Hard as it was he gave her the space she needed.

CHAPTER FIFTY

Except for Sandy who lay at my feet, sleeping after a long walk, I was alone in the house. Mum had gone to one of her all-women poker evenings. She loved those evenings, I think for companionship of people her own age. I'm pretty sure they talked more than played cards. Monica had taken Alice and Faith to a school friend's birthday party, roller-skating followed by pizza.

I leaned back in my father's favourite chair. At times like these I missed him. With his years of experience on the force he was my go-to guy when I needed pearls of wisdom, be that on an investigation or in my personal life. He went too soon, far too soon.

Around the edges the chair's arms were worn, the cushions had collapsed and were threadbare, I was sure the frame was cracked where the seat sank in the corner. Each time I'd thought about getting it repaired and reupholstered I'd changed my mind. I worried repairs would mean it wouldn't have the same associated memories.

I remembered as a boy taking it in turns with my brother to sit on my father's lap while he read to us. The chair was relatively new then. After he had finished reading

I would try to delay going up to bed by asking him about his day and the cases under investigation at Scotland Yard. He'd lower his voice, so Mum wouldn't hear, before giving us just enough information not to scare us but to satisfy our morbid boyish curiosity. I knew back then I wanted to be a police inspector like him, working big cases, following the evidence, hoping for a lucky break, catching the criminal.

In recent months all our lives had been turned upside down. Even after so many weeks living here Mum's house still felt strange to me. Worse still for Mum after Dad's unexpected death. My house was gone, burned to the ground by Edward Fischer and his crazy girlfriend Faye Moon. My mind wandered as I looked around. Despite furniture and ornaments I recognised from my childhood this wasn't the house I grew up in; that now belonged to a new family after my parents moved to Dorset to be close to us. A lot had changed in such a short space of time, life felt in a constant state of flux where what stretched ahead seemed constantly uncharted and often beyond my control. I wondered what it must be like for families where life was consistent. Where you could draw comfort in knowing each day, and the one that followed, would be the same as yesterday and the day before that. Did a life like that even exist or was it a myth? In reality does each and every one of us close our eyes at night with the worry that just around the corner an imminent crisis lurks? I'd heard of people who describe their life as blessed but did those people simply see life through rose tinted spectacles? Do they possess some sort of super power where for them the struggles of life seem less painful?

I jumped as a knock at the front door snapped me out of my somewhat morbid contemplation. Sandy looked at me as I moved to get up. 'Some guard dog you are. It's fine, you just stay there, I'll check it's not a burglar at the door.' Sandy got up, stretched and lolloped after me. 'I'm sure you must be deaf. Until it comes to the sound of food packets being opened.'

The knock at the door came again. More insistent this time.

Rayner's face peered through a window beside the door. He didn't wait to be asked, he came straight into the house as I opened the door.

'Is everything okay? Is Jenny all right?'

'Yeah. Well, kind of. She's okay. I just came from there. We had lunch together. She's sleeping now. That's not why I'm here,' said Rayner. I followed him through to the sitting room where he paced around before coming to rest in an armchair which he dwarfed. I sat down on the sofa opposite him.

'Do you want to keep me guessing or...?'

I tried to make sense of the excited flow of words as they poured out. 'I've been working at home. Making calls and stuff. As you know I've been working on getting further background information on Janek Bonne. I started contacting family members in Denmark. During one of those conversations I was asked about funeral arrangements. I called Robert Valentine at his office because he's assisting with the repatriation of the body to Denmark. When I called he wasn't there. So I called his home and got through to Angie his wife. She informed me he was on one of his trips. I told her it could probably wait but she insisted Valentine wouldn't mind being called over a matter like that, so I took the telephone number of his hotel in Munich, Germany.'

I began thinking about my conversation with Andrew Yates and how annoyed he was at the way Valentine abused his position to take trips abroad. He clearly believed Valentine had a lover and used the trips as an excuse to spend time with her. 'He does a lot of travelling,' I said.

'You're right he does. I checked. I'd already looked at his movements at the time the families were murdered. He was out of the country on each occasion. He had an ironclad alibi for each date.'

'I remember, I saw the flights and hotel bookings myself?' I said.

A big smile crossed Rayner's face. 'They're the flights and hotel bookings he wanted us to see. He did get on those flights to each country and he did stay at the hotels. It wasn't until I spoke to the receptionist at the hotel in Munich that I learned something. The receptionist told me that it appeared Valentine had left the hotel without checking out. His room was empty and all his belongings were gone.'

'What do you mean, gone?'

'That's what I thought. Where is he? At first I began to worry something might have happened to him. You know, like Bonne. But people abducted from hotels don't take their suitcase and belongings with them.'

'So where is he?'

'Exactly. Everyone believes he's in Munich but he could be anywhere.'

Rayner was right. Everyone he knows thinks he's in Munich attending a conference, promoting the institute's work and eating alone in the hotel restaurant.

'Did you track him down?'

'Nope. Not yet.'

'Perhaps the hotel made a mistake.'

'I called his wife back and double-checked the hotel's details she'd given me were correct. I then called the institute and spoke to his personal assistant who also confirmed the hotel details. I then called the hotel again and got through to a different receptionist. He checked and confirmed Valentine appeared to have left the hotel without checking out. He told me travellers regularly forget to do that.'

Rayner stared at me. Waiting for me to process what he was telling me, hoping I'd come to the same conclusion and validate his theory.

'You think he leaves the hotel early and checks out later over the phone from a different location.'

'I went back over other trips he'd made and several hotels told me he appeared to check in and not use the room at all. They would have his credit card details from when he checked in so simply charge his card whether he uses the room or not.'

'Why would he do that unless he was looking for an alibi?'

'Exactly.' Rayner bounced in his seat like an excited child. 'As I said, I phoned other hotels he'd stayed at and he'd done the same thing on other dates.'

'The dates of the murders.'

Rayner's eyes widened as he nodded. 'Uh huh. Yes. Every date except one. That hotel was in Lyon and they couldn't be sure he'd left early. The receptionist said she'd have to check with the manager, who wasn't available at the time of my call. I'm waiting for her to ring me back. It's him, Valentine's our killer.'

'Let's slow down. What about Bonne?'

'It's not Janek Bonne, it never was. Deep down neither of us believed it was him. None of the pieces ever completely fitted. He didn't fit the profile.'

'What about the conference organisers? Can any of them confirm he was at the event at the time of the murders?'

'That needs looking into. Let's be honest, some of these

conferences are huge, who would know whether an attendee left early?'

My heart was racing as I thought about the possibilities of what Rayner was suggesting. There were of course any number of reasons why Valentine would leave a hotel or conference early. But I had to admit it suggested he was a man with something to hide. I couldn't help thinking about what Andrew Yates had said about Valentine's attendance at the conferences 'half the time he leaves early, I'm sure of it'. My concern right now was where he was.

I went along with Rayner's theory. 'He must have booked two return flights. One flight being earlier than the date he was supposed to return on. One flight was bought by the institute, the other he paid for himself personally, to hide his movements from the institute.'

'I was about to start calling the airlines but decided to come to you with the information first.'

'Okay. We need to find him. We're going to need help, there's too much work for just us. We have to know for sure whether or not he has an alibi for the time of each murder. He's done well covering his tracks. I'm going to call the chief super and see if we can get some resources to trace his flights, all of them. They can also call event organisers to see if anyone remembers whether he stayed for the duration of the event at the time of each murder. We need to search his office but first we should go to his home; we might find credit card statements.'

'What'll we tell his wife?'

'At this stage we have no proof it's him or any motive, just a man going out of his way to cover his tracks. He could be doing that for any number of reasons. As far as we are aware, at this stage, her husband is missing. I'm sure she'll be all too willing to help.'

CHAPTER FIFTY-ONE

Angie Valentine looked flustered as she opened the door. She put on her best smile when she saw who it was. I introduced Rayner and she welcomed us in.

'Nice to see you again. Please come in,' said Angie. 'Daddy's away so our darling teenage daughter is pushing her luck. You just entered a war zone.'

I chuckled. 'I know the feeling.'

We followed her through to the kitchen.

'Can I get you anything? Tea or coffee. As you know Robert isn't here right now. He seems to be on more trips than usual lately. It certainly feels like he's away more than he's at home sometimes. I lose track of where he is most of the time. I should start keeping a journal.' She looked at Rayner. 'Was it you I spoke to on the phone?'

'That's correct, Mrs Valentine,' said Rayner. 'That's why we're here.'

Angie looked at us, her face turned to concern. 'Is Rob okay? Is he hurt?'

'As far as we know he's absolutely fine,' I said reassuringly. There's no need for concern.'

'Thank God, I thought perhaps he might have done something stupid.'

'In what way?' I asked.

'He's not been himself.'

'Really? Not himself?'

'Just down in the dumps.'

'Because of Janek's death?'

She lowered her voice as though we were fellow conspirators. 'No. It started before that. It must be his age, mid-life crisis perhaps. He's been introspective and morose lately. Talking about his late brother again. He hasn't done that for years. Not since we were first together. Talking about his brother gets him very down. I even made him an appointment at the doctor's but he didn't go. I've tried to make another appointment but there's no point if he won't turn up.'

'You say late brother?'

'Yes. Robert is a twin. His brother, Mark, died when he was young.'

'How young? An infant?' I asked.

'Gosh, no. Older than that. Maybe, eleven or twelve. I can't really remember. Like I said he hasn't talked about Mark for years. I'm not even sure why it's bothering him now. I still think it's his age. Men can get very funny about their age, especially once they're over forty. I'm sure it'll pass.' She smiled at us knowingly.

I looked at Rayner whose eyes were wide. We were both thinking the same thing. Robert Valentine suddenly fitted the profile. Here was a man dealing with the resurgence of tragic loss in later life. He was also a man who was going to great lengths to cover his tracks and no longer had an alibi for the time of most of the murders.

Angie closed the kitchen door behind us. 'I can see from

your demeanour something's not right. If Rob's okay then has this something to do with Janek's death?'

Rayner cleared his throat. 'Janek's death remains unexplained, most likely death by misadventure. We have no reason to believe your husband is in any danger. But, after we spoke I called the hotel and it seems he'd left the hotel without checking out. His room is empty. His suitcase and all his belongings are gone.'

'I'll call his mobile.' Angie pushed past us and fetched her mobile phone from another room before returning to the kitchen and closing the door again.

'When I called, his phone was off,' said Rayner.

Angie let it ring and waited. When it didn't go to voicemail she ended the call. 'It's still off. It says "the phone may be switched off, try again later". Robert does that sometimes. It doesn't mean there's a problem. He might have been feeling unwell and so left the conference and caught an earlier flight home.'

'Absolutely,' I said. 'We just want to be cautious. To your knowledge has he ever left a hotel early before?'

'No. Why would he?' Angie was annoyed at the question. She was wringing her small hands. 'I'm not sure why you'd ask that.'

'No specific reason. We're just trying to figure out where he might be or a pattern of behaviour. It often helps in situations like these.' I smiled reassuringly.

'I don't think he's ever left early before. As far as I know he loves the conferences. I got the impression he was one of the last to leave. I don't really ask. He usually comes home exhausted. And you know how it is. Day to day we're busy, we hardly get time to talk.'

'I understand. It's the same for everyone, that's one of the joys of parenthood,' I said. 'Children keep us on our toes.'

Rayner's phone rang. We were expecting an update on whether Valentine had boarded an early flight. He stepped outside.

'You've got me worried now. I spoke to him last night and he seemed fine. It was just a quick call. He was missing us.'

'Did he say where he was?'

'He told me the conference had been busy and he was about to get something to eat. I just assumed he was at the hotel and using the hotel restaurant like he always does. He doesn't like shop-bought sandwiches or takeaway food.'

'Do you have any credit card statements? We can then phone the card company and trace any recent transactions.'

'Of course. Do you think that's necessary? Might he be in danger?'

'No. As I said I'm sure he's fine. He'll probably walk back through the door any moment now and make us look really stupid.' I no longer believed that for a second but it was what Angie needed to hear.

She disappeared upstairs to find a credit card statement.

Rayner returned and spoke in a hushed voice. 'I just heard from Cotton. Valentine arrived in Munich as planned. The three day conference started yesterday, she spoke to the organisers and they confirmed he signed in. But no one recalls seeing him after that.'

'I'm not sure that means a lot. It depends on the size of the conference.'

'True, but get this. Cotton phoned the airlines and they confirmed Valentine caught a flight back to Southampton the same day he signed in at the conference.'

'He checked in at the conference and left immediately?'

'Yes. Same thing at the hotel.'

I checked my watch. 'That means he's already been

unaccounted for nearly thirty-six hours,' I said. My body went cold. Rayner and I both knew what that could mean.

'How are we going to handle this with his wife?' whispered Rayner.

'We'll stick to our story. Until he turns up he's a missing person.'

Angie returned with statements for the last three months. Her hand trembled as she held them out. I folded them away into my jacket pocket.

'Thank you. When you hear from Robert please give me a call.'

'You've heard news?'

'It seems he might have caught an earlier flight, to Southampton. We're hoping to get confirmation of that very shortly. I'm sure he'll be home before you know it,' said Rayner.

'He's all right?' said Angie. Relief on her face.

'As I say, we're awaiting confirmation but in reality I'm sure he's fine, and has a suitable explanation,' I said. 'We're sorry we alarmed you.' I patted the card statements in my pocket. 'I'll keep hold of these just in case. I can pop back with them once Robert is home.'

'Better to be safe than sorry,' said Angie. 'You wait until he gets home. There's not much point having a mobile phone if he's not going to keep it on... like I don't have enough to worry about.'

We left Angie on the doorstep trying her husband on his mobile phone once again.

By the time we reached the car Rayner was calling the number of Valentine's credit card company. 'I don't suppose they'll divulge details of recent transactions but it's worth a try. He might have rented a car and it could have a tracker.'

CHAPTER FIFTY-TWO

Robert Valentine's flight had pleasingly landed back in the UK fifteen minutes early. He'd rented a car and driven the few miles to where he now sat watching the house of the family that interested him. He would later return the rental and switch back to his own car.

He pushed his seat away from the steering wheel to give himself some room. Reaching across the passenger seat he took the small biscuit tin from the travel bag that rested in the footwell and placed it on the seat. Prising it open, he put the lid to one side. Inside was a piece of silk fabric the size of a handkerchief. It was embroidered with pink and gold edging with light blue flowers and butterflies. There were also two dice which he removed from the tin. He pulled out the blade of a small penknife which he had taken from his keyring. Working his way around he scratched at all the sides until only the six on each dice remained.

'I want double trouble,' he said. It was his Aunt Evelyn's voice he heard in his head. And by double trouble she meant two sixes.

He clasped the dice in his fist and blew on them. He

tossed the dice into the tin. With a clatter they bounced and scattered across the metal surface.

Her warm husky voice took him back to the small dining table he sat at with his brother. He could still smell the mugs of warm cocoa. 'Nope. Let's try again, shall we?' He scooped up the blood red dice and threw them again. He threw them over and over until he got the double six. 'There they are! Double trouble. Just like my beautiful little boys.' She always lovingly called him and his twin brother 'double trouble'. She would brush their hair and say things like 'Peas in a pod. The spitting image of each other. Trouble and twice and all things nice. Two sides of the same coin.'

'Two sides of the same coin', he knew what she meant by that. He wasn't like his brother. Aunt Evelyn knew Mark was better behaved, cleverer, more confident and handsome. He was a pale shadow of him. Mark knew it. He knew it. Everyone knew it. They didn't need to say anything, he could see it in the way they spoke and treated the pair of them. He was an afterthought. And of course when Mark died he knew what they'd all thought. 'How tragic, Robert relied on his brother. It sounds cruel but wouldn't it have been fairer if they'd both been taken.' And, 'Surely God took away the wrong twin.'

Valentine rubbed his fingerprints from the dice with the embroidered silk fabric and placed them in a zip pocket in his jacket. He folded the fabric into the tin and put the lid back on top.

He pictured her taking one of her menthol cigarettes from the packet. She'd smoke it on the back doorstep, never in the house. 'There we go, my darlings, that's all we've got time for today. I know, I know, we'll play again tomorrow. What's that? Yes, I promise. Tomorrow we'll play for longer.

Now run along and brush those toothy pegs. I'll be along to tuck you in and give you a kiss.'

Valentine turned his attention to the house. It was in an expensive part of town and looked impressive in the light of the moon. He checked his watch, 11.27 p.m., the lights inside were off. He had little doubt the boys would be sound asleep. They'd had a busy day, running around the country park, navigating the obstacle course and tearing around the wood like a couple of lunatics. The other houses in the cul de sac looked quiet. There was no sign of life.

In the rucksack he had everything he needed. The saw had a fresh blade and he'd invested in a heavier club hammer.

The parents were the hardest part. If disturbed there was always a chance one of them might put up a struggle. He shuddered at the thought of how one of the fathers had fought back. Desperation in his eyes.

He'd considered separating the children from the parents, some form of abduction, abducting one child was probably easy but two was risky; very hard to work out how to do it effectively.

He was tempted to do what had to be done tonight but he'd learned that the fuller the moon the easier the task. It would be safer to wait another day. Tomorrow it was at its fullest which would make the process more satisfying. He'd be patient.

His tummy rumbled. 'What was that?' he chuckled like Auntie used to. He'd been so absorbed speculating on what might be happening inside the house he'd forgotten to eat. He fired up the car and headed back towards the hotel. On the way back he'd stop for something to eat, somewhere with a drive-through would have to do. Christ, how he hated takeaway food. He'd make do. He needed to keep his energy levels up, it was going to be hard work. People would be surprised how much effort goes into dismembering a body. Even a child's body.

CHAPTER FIFTY-THREE

Cotton's finger hovered over the columns as her eyes scanned the credit card statements on the desk in front of her.

'Ring, damn it,' said Rayner. He was pacing the office like a bear with an itch it couldn't reach. To confirm whether Valentine had indeed left early he'd called the hotel in Lyon again and was waiting for a call back from the hotel manager. 'What's taking them so long? Surely you look it up on the computer, how hard can it be? Did he check out or did he not? That's the bloody French for you, never any rush, they're probably having one of their fancy lunches,' he spoke in a cockney-style mock French accent, 'Brie, baguette, le side order of pommes frites and a glass of "Chateau de vin bloody-rouge."'

Cotton shook her head at him without looking up. 'Xenophobe,' she said.

'No, I'm not. I'm just saying that I explained this was urgent, I'm questioning how it can take this long—' His phone buzzed and he snatched it up to his ear. 'Inspector Rayner speaking. Ah yes. Mademoiselle Brodeur, lovely to speak to you. How did you get on?'

Cotton looked up and caught his eye, raising an eyebrow at his remarkable change of tone. Suddenly he was all sweetness and light and butter wouldn't melt as he spoke to the manageress. Rayner couldn't help but crack a smile.

'You're sure. I see. That's very helpful. Thank you. Have a lovely afternoon, Mademoiselle Brodeur,' said Rayner. He clasped the phone in his enormous hands as he digested the new information. He turned to the pair of us. 'He left early. The porter at the hotel remembers him leaving and getting into a taxi. It appears the porter remembers everyone, especially those who don't tip.'

'He was using his trips away as his alibi and that's been blown out of the water,' said Cotton.

'It's tonight,' I said. I'd been only half listening to the conversation in the office. 'The sixth family will be murdered tonight unless we find him. He has his dice ready and the only side not defaced is the side of the six. The Hunter's moon is at its fullest tonight. It's what he's been waiting for, obsessing over. In his mind tonight will be perfect.'

Cotton pushed aside the statements in frustration. 'Where do we start? The best lead we have is the car rental company he used. We know he's rented the car, what they can't tell us is where the car is now or where it's been.'

'Can't or won't,' said Rayner.

'We're missing something, I can feel it,' I said. 'Let's assume for a moment Valentine killed Bonne. The likelihood of two killers is not out of the question but slim. The question then is why would he kill him?'

'To take over the institute?' said Rayner. 'He'd be financially better off perhaps.'

'Or maybe, Bonne discovered Valentine was the killer. That he was using the institute's records to choose families?' said Cotton.

'What other business interests did Bonne have?' I asked.

Rayner opened a file on his computer. He scrolled through a few pages. 'He invested in or had started businesses of all types: software, 3D printing, robotics, fertility, cosmetics, online gambling, clothing, charities, you name it this guy had an interest in it.'

'I'd say the only one on that list that has anything to do with the institute is fertility,' said Cotton. 'What if Bonne saw a correlation between murdered parents at his fertility clinic and those at the institute. No, wait, what if we're looking at this wrong? What if the list of families killed never came from the institute but the fertility clinic; Bonne saw the connection and it got him killed.'

'I'm ahead of you,' said Rayner. He was searching through his statements, notes and articles on his laptop. 'Here we go, yes. Valentine left his old job and worked at the fertility clinic for six weeks before they were ready to employ him at the institute. Andrew Yates worked there too.'

The room fell silent like we'd received word from on high.

'I know the next family Valentine will target,' I said. I went to my desk and found the number. 'I need to warn them.' The phone rang and rang but nobody answered.

CHAPTER FIFTY-FOUR

In just black socks and tartan boxer shorts Valentine pressed out thirty more push ups. Beads of perspiration covered his body. His wrists and shoulders ached but he pushed through the pain. He was determined to reach three hundred. He'd been at it for nearly an hour and forty-five minutes and wouldn't quit, not now he was so close. He reached two hundred and ninety and paused. With arms straight he held his body in position, focusing on his breathing before pressing out the final ten. He collapsed onto his front and rolled over. Uncontrollable hysterical laughter forced its way out. Tonight was the finale; after tonight he'd be free. No more blood on his hands. The deal he'd made with the voice inside had been six sets of twins. That was the price of freedom.

Looking back he'd started out so hesitantly, pathetic really. Now he could see the process had been transformative. The need to respond to what had grown inside him since losing Mark. Acting on the compulsion he felt wasn't something he ever had control over and as soon as he accepted that he could put aside any blame or remorse he might otherwise have felt. Doing what he must had been liberating from the very start. And he accepted he was as much a victim in all this as anyone.

Trying to explain it all was as pitiful as the parents who were unable to protect their children from him. After their ascension they would look down on him under a full moon as he dispatched what they failed to protect. Just like his Aunt Evelyn failed to protect his brother and as his own parents failed before her. It was the parents' job to protect their child and they'd all failed miserably.

The press seemed to believe the killings were about the boys. To some extent they were but equally this was about the parents. He'd come to realise what he did was to demonstrate how in the end no parent can truly protect their child. No matter how much they want to believe they can.

Valentine got up and showered. His lean muscular body ached as he moved. While singing and lathering his hair he heard a knocking. He stepped out of the shower, wrapped a towel around his waist and opened the door.

'Your room service.' The young woman's mouth wrinkled on seeing his undress. She wasn't much older than his eldest daughter. Unlike Kimberly who had a natural beauty and barely used make-up, this girl's face looked pale from foundation and her eyes were dark from eyeliner. A streak of purple was noticeable running through her jet black hair. As she scrunched her nose he noticed it was pierced but the ring had been removed.

'Lovely. Thank you. Just leave it on the top there,' he said. He pointed to the desk area.

She did as instructed and backed out of the room as quickly as possible.

'If you wait a moment I'll get you a tip,' said Valentine. 'My wallet is in my trousers on the bed.'

The girl curled her lip and looked at him disgusted. 'It's fine. Really, I'm good.' As she walked away he thought about his daughters, Kimberly and Milly. He'd miss them, Angie too. He wished things had been different. It must be nice to have a normal life, not to be carrying around the thing that had gnawed at him until he had surrendered to it. The thing that after the first family had grown exponentially, like a disease spreading through his body, until it was no longer something he controlled, but instead consumed his every waking moment.

He got back in the shower and finished rinsing off. Stepping out and towelling himself down he walked into the bedroom and stared at his mobile phone. It was tempting to switch it on. Instead he pinched out the SIM card and squeezed until it folded in half. He then took his phone and held it against the corner of the wall, pressing down on both ends until the screen gave way and the phone folded. It joined the SIM card in the waste bin.

He was free.

After what would happen tonight there could be no going back to his old life.

CHAPTER FIFTY-FIVE

Andrew Yates wobbled like his legs were made of jelly as he walked away from the roller coaster. He slung his arms around Brianna and held her playfully as though he could take no more and was about to collapse.

'Mercy, please, rescue me,' gasped Yates.

'Don't give me that, you're like a big kid,' said Brianna. 'You're loving it. More than the boys.'

Oliver and Dylan came running over, their faces red and sweaty, beaming with joy.

'Mum, that was amazing. Dylan nearly puked,' said Oliver.

'No, I didn't. You looked like *you* were going to wet your pants.'

'Well I don't know about you two but I thought I was going to vomit,' said Yates.

The boys grabbed him and tried dragging him away from Brianna and in the direction of the next ride. 'Come on, Andy,' said Oliver.

'Yeah, we got Colossus next. It's got ten inversions,' added Dylan. He flicked his brother's ear.

'And it's really fast.' Oliver tried to flick his brother back but was blocked by Dylan's quick arm movements.

'Bieber from school went on it and he nearly came off at the top.'

'Bieber?' said Brianna.

'Yeah, he looks just like Justin Bieber, everyone calls him Bieber.'

'Yeah, Bieber said he was hanging on when it was upside down and the guy beside him only just stopped him coming out of his seat.'

'That sounds a little made-up,' said Brianna. She pointed to Dylan's shoe.

He knelt down and did up his shoelace. 'No, Mum. He never lies.'

'No, never, Mum. Bieber's like really popular, he's in the year above us at school.'

'In that case that particular ride sounds too dangerous to go on,' said Brianna. She winked at Andy. 'What do you say?'

'Well... How about we take a quick break and get a drink and a bite to eat?' said Yates, taking the coward's way out and not wanting to put himself in the middle.

The boys grabbed hold of Yates and started pulling at his arm again. 'Come on, Mum's joking.'

He dug his heels in like a mule, but couldn't stop the boys dragging him away. They were strong despite their small stature. He found himself laughing hysterically as they yanked, shoved and cajoled him into moving. 'No more. What about a snack?' He looked at Brianna for help as the boys prised his arms off her.

She removed his fingers from her waist and pushed him towards the boys and shook her head. 'You're on your own, mister, today was your idea.'

'Take him, boys. Go on. You go ahead, join the queue, I'll meet you there.'

'Thanks, Mum. Can you take this?' Dylan peeled off his hoodie, ran back and dumped it in his mum's arms.

'You'll freeze.'

'Nah, we're fine.' Oliver copied his brother, tossing his sweater over her shoulder.

Yates took the opportunity when the boys released him to run back, lean in and plant a kiss on Brianna's lips. 'Love you,' he said. 'See you in a bit.'

'Love you too. Have fun.'

Yates's grin and the twinkle in his eyes told her he would.

CHAPTER FIFTY-SIX

Having stayed until the very end of the day they'd got to ride Colossus a second time before the park closed. It had been a long time since he'd done so much walking and his feet were aching and sore.

They were almost home and the drive had been a breeze, he'd been lost in thought. Yates tapped the steering wheel as he waited for the traffic lights to change. He looked over at Brianna who was asleep. Her head was at an awkward angle and her mouth gaped. The day out had also taken her mind, and his, off the potential problems at work and whether there would be an investigation.

Oliver and Dylan slept in the back, both sporting their new theme park hoodies. It had been a warm October day and their faces looked rosy from all the running around.

The theme park had been a good idea, even if going on so many roller coasters had made him more than a little nauseous. He'd wanted to keep up with the twins and go on every ride they asked him to.

Spending proper time together during a shared activity always brought them closer as a family, away from the TV, phones and games and gave them time to talk together, which was the key. They'd all already decided Tower of London, London Dungeons, London Eye and Madame Tussauds should be the next four on the list, and in that order. In his head he'd decided he'd need to book a hotel for the weekend.

They were good boys who had been through a lot. His own parents had divorced and he knew how hard it was. It was clear their father, when they saw him, was critical of Andrew and never had a kind word. That was okay, the boys seemed to have made their own minds up about him and today had been another example of how they'd bonded. He was proud of them. They were at a challenging age as boys, they still had a need for their mother and displayed the sensitivities of being a child, but were also looking forward and trying to understand how they should behave as men. He remembered the last time he cried at school and how the other boys teased him for being a baby. After that he hadn't cried again in front of anyone.

The car stopped on the driveway. A huge red-orange moon hung over the house. Andrew was staring at it when Brianna woke. 'Are we home already? I must have fallen asleep.'

'You did. I had to listen to your snoring all the way home.'

'Yeah. Right. It's not me who snores.' She turned to look at the boys and smiled. 'They enjoyed themselves.'

'They sure did. I had trouble keeping up with them. I think they'll sleep well tonight.'

Without waking the boys too much Brianna walked them to the bathroom where she gave their teeth a cursory brush, then removed their outer clothes and tucked them into bed.

Downstairs Andrew was making coffee in the kitchen.

Brianna crept up behind him and putting her arms around him kissed his neck. 'I'm so proud of you. You know that?'

He shrugged. He hoped talk didn't turn to the ins and outs of where the money was coming from – she knew some of the details but not all – or whether he thought the police had forgotten about him. Right now, he was too tired for that kind of conversation.

'I am, incredibly proud. I mean it. Everything you do for us. I know the boys can be challenging and you put up with their antics. But when I saw you today, and how they were with you, and how you were with them, my heart was singing. Today was how I'd hoped it would be for so long. We were a real family.'

'It was great. I can't deny I loved every minute of it. As I've always said I don't want to replace their father. Just be a dad, a friend, someone they can rely on and talk to.'

Brianna kissed him again. They rubbed noses. 'Why don't we have our coffees in bed? We could, you know... If you have enough energy, that is?'

'Hello. I'm liking this. Has my missus been replaced by a sex-crazed alien lookalike?'

Brianna giggled, 'In your dreams.' She unbuttoned her top and tossed it over her shoulder into the pile beside the washing machine. 'You'd better decide whether you want to take a chance this alien won't kill and eat its mate after sex. Because she's going to take a shower, climb into bed and will be asleep pronto if this human male isn't interested.' She turned and headed for the stairs.

Andrew picked up the coffees and followed her. 'Well, I suppose the football highlights can wait.'

'I'll pretend I didn't hear that.'

CHAPTER FIFTY-SEVEN

As the key turned in the lock and the front door opened and closed, the almost inaudible click, click, creak, was barely noticeable in the otherwise silent household. This followed a moment of listening before light footsteps moved around downstairs, checking rooms. Then a minute squeak as pressure was placed on the first step of the stairs. A pause. More silence. Imperceptible movement as Valentine navigated the stairs to where he knew the children and parents slept.

The back of his neck was clammy, his breathing rapid, adrenaline pumping; blood surged through his veins like rapids crashing between canyon walls. With a trembling hand he opened the bedroom door, his heart pounding as he approached the sleeping boys in their bunk beds. He crouched down to look on a twin with flushed cheeks from the warmth of the bedding. The boy mumbled in his dream. Retreating, Valentine moved to the next bedroom where he took a moment to pull himself together. He looked at the hammer in his hand. What came next required complete focus.

A light flashed across the landing. Valentine turned to the window. More streaks of light. He peeked between the blinds. In the distance, a few streets away, blue lights lit the night sky. Then from another direction more blue lights and sirens. Police squad cars were getting closer. *Were they coming for him? How could they be?*

His hand tightened around the hammer. He turned and looked at the bedroom door. There wouldn't be time. What if he didn't finish? That would be worse than not doing it all.

The sirens grew louder. He felt rooted to the spot. He had to make a decision.

The approaching squad cars sounded so close now.

He took a step back as a light came on beneath the parents' bedroom door. He recognised Andrew Yates's voice. He must have been woken by the approaching sirens.

On tiptoes Valentine moved swiftly down the stairs, keeping close to the wall where the steps were less likely to creak. At the foot of the stairs blue lights flashed through windows. He turned nimbly and went to the back door. The key was in the lock. He was quickly out in the cold night air and beneath the giant moon that watched him mockingly. He couldn't look at it.

At the front of the house, sirens echoed. Voices called and shouted.

As Valentine opened the back gate he saw the house lights come on. He moved through an alleyway at the rear of neighbouring houses. He climbed a fence, crossed a lawn, dashed through a side gate and found himself on a street one road away from where he'd parked.

With a mixture of frustration and relief he threw his rucksack onto the passenger seat and climbed in. He ripped off his gloves and thrashed the steering wheel with his fists before getting himself under control. He gripped the steering wheel and squeezed, his knuckles turning white. Exhilaration had turned to fury.

He stared down the road at all the activity. Uniformed officers racing around like fluorescent night-time bugs in their police jackets. Emerging through them a single figure he recognised. Tall and commanding, Chief Inspector Hardy briefly instructed officers before charging through the front door of the Yates's home.

Valentine pushed himself back in the seat. He slowed his breathing. Reined in his rage. Inspector Hardy had taken away the twins that tonight should have belonged to him. It should have all ended tonight. His sickness finally over.

Putting one hand down on the rucksack containing the hammer and hacksaw, he knew what he must do. He fired up the car and headed out into the night.

CHAPTER FIFTY-EIGHT

Sylvia Hardy had been to the supermarket and now entered the kitchen with two bags of groceries, which she put at the end of the kitchen table. Alice was at the other end and without looking up from her homework said, 'Do you have more, Nana? I can help.'

'Thank you, sweetheart, I'm fine, it's just these two bags. Only a small shop this time. Where's Monica? I have her magazine.'

'She's upstairs resting. She's not feeling too good.'

Faith came running in. She gave her nana a hug.

Sylvia chuckled. 'You don't fool me, young lady. I know your game.' She searched through the bags until she found a toffee apple. 'To this day I've never understood why you'd want to cover a perfectly good apple in all that hard sugar but if you've never had one I suppose it must be exciting.'

Faith's face was beaming. 'Thank you! I'm going to save it and show my friends at school tomorrow.'

'Are you sure you're supposed to take something like that into school?'

Faith was already gone. She'd raced back upstairs.

Alice shrugged. 'She's probably going to show her friends.'

'Are they here?' said Nana.

'No. On her phone.'

'My goodness. It's like you children are never apart. Miles away but just a few clicks and you're in each other's houses.' As she unpacked the shopping she passed Alice a nutty health bar. 'Brain food.'

'Aw, thank you.'

Sylvia stopped her unpacking and froze. Her jaw tightened as fear gripped her. She looked upstairs towards where Monica lay. Something wasn't right. Intuition, or sixth sense she didn't know which but she certainly felt something was amiss. She was about to head upstairs to check when there was a cry for help.

'Sylvia! Are you there? I need you.'

Alice looked up. 'It's Monica.'

Faith yelled, 'Come quick, Nana.'

By the time Alice and Nana had reached the bedroom Monica was on her knees holding onto the corner of the wardrobe.

Monica grabbed Nana's arm and whispered. 'I thought I was going to pass out. Everything was spinning. And my head, it's pounding.'

'You and the baby are going to be fine. Just relax, calm your breathing. Hold my hand. Are you going to be okay if I help you to your feet?'

Monica nodded.

'Alice, please call the midwife, her name's Sally,' said Nana. 'The number is on the pad next to the telephone in the hallway. Tell her Monica felt dizzy and collapsed, again. Tell her we're going to the hospital. Remind her she's at thirty weeks. Can you do that for me?'

Alice nodded. She didn't hesitate, she took her mobile phone from her back pocket and ran downstairs to make the call.

Faith hesitantly moved closer to stand beside Monica. She stared, gripping her toffee apple. She winced as Monica groaned and pressed the palm of her hand against the back of her head.

'Faith, honey,' said Nana, seeing her concern. 'Would you do me a huge favour? Would you go downstairs and get my car keys. They're on the kitchen table beside the two bags of shopping I just brought in. We're going to the hospital for a check-up, all of us, so could you also get your coat and shoes on and please get Monica's coat?'

Faith looked at Monica. She was reluctant to leave her.

Monica nodded and winked at her. 'That would be amazing. You can be my helper.'

Faith grinned and without saying a word did as she was asked.

'That's a first,' said Monica. 'Faith... speechless.' She moaned and held her head. 'I feel so dizzy.'

Alice reappeared. 'Sally's going to call the antenatal ward and let them know we're on our way. She said it'd be best we go directly to the hospital.'

'That's the plan,' said Nana. 'Alice, you lead the way. We're going to get in my car, so grab your sister and anything else you and your sister might need. We could be at the hospital for some time. I plan on finding out what's going on.'

'James?' said Monica. 'I need James.' She went to the bathroom with a change of clothes.

Sylvia stood in the doorway and kept an eye on her. 'I know you do, sweetheart. Once you're in the car, one of us will call him. Right now, my priority is you and the baby.'

Monica came out of the bathroom, pushed her feet into her slippers, wrapped her dressing gown over her shoulders and said quietly so the girls didn't hear, 'There's a pain right here,' she pointed just below her ribs. 'We should get to the hospital as quickly as possible.'

CHAPTER FIFTY-NINE

After the break-in I'd spent a few hours going over the scene at the Yates's home with the forensic team. I then started updating local and Scotland Yard investigators on our theory that the killer was Valentine. With no physical evidence Valentine was the killer and no proof it was him who had broken into the Yates's home, I could feel the others' opinions ranged from open minded to sceptical. But my gut told me he was the man.

I'd gone nearly forty-eight hours without sleep and was on my way home when I got the call from Monica. I could hear she was scared and that filled me with dread. Monica was tough, she's had to be, she's had a lot of setbacks in her life, including a husband who was a drunk and abusive towards her. She found the strength to leave that relationship with nothing, knowing she'd have to start over and all the uncertainty that brought. As she spoke to me now she sounded calm and collected as she tried not to unduly worry me, but I knew something wasn't right and I could hear the frightened girl behind her words.

I drove as fast as I could, weaving in and out of the

traffic whenever possible. I parked and ran to the antenatal ward.

'Monica Reilly. I'm her... partner.' The midwife at the desk looked up at me in surprise. I might be old fashioned but in that moment, more than any other, 'Reilly' and 'partner' sounded wrong. She was my wife in all but name.

The young midwife with dark red hair, blue eyes and lightly freckled skin didn't need to check for the name, she pointed down the hall. 'Your mother told me you were on your way. She's waiting for you.'

I heard Mum before I saw her. 'Listen to me. I'm no doctor but I had two boys of my own and I was at the birth of my two granddaughters. You might be an obstetrician, young man, but I know a damn sight better than you, from first-hand experience, how giving birth is supposed to be and this isn't it. So don't tell me to wait. My daughter-in-law in there has waited long enough. If there are complications like we've been told then are we really expected to sit and wait and see what happens?' She pointed into a ward. 'It's been nearly an hour and she still doesn't have an answer.'

The obstetrician had his mouth open and was about to speak when he saw me.

Mum, who had her back to me, turned and looked up. 'Thank God you're here.'

I couldn't get in the middle of anything right now, I had to see that Monica was okay. I walked past Mum and the doctor and went to her.

She looked ghostly, no colour in her skin and dark rings around her eyes, but to my relief she was sitting up in bed talking to Alice and Faith who were giggling at her story. She was holding their hands as she spoke. I knew she'd seen me out of the corner of her eye but the girls had their backs to me. I stood and listened. '... Perhaps your little brother or sister is tired of waiting and wants come out early and play with you both.'

'And Sandy,' said Faith. 'We'll get him or her some toys too. Bath toys, definitely. I think bath times are going to be the most fun. You can't use normal shampoo like we do, you have to use baby shampoo.'

'That's right,' said Monica.

'The baby's not coming yet though, is it? It's better if it stays in your tummy.'

Monica looked at me and the girls turned. They spoke over each other. 'Monica nearly had the baby. It nearly came out, Daddy,' said Faith.

Monica discretely shook her head. She mouthed 'no it didn't'.

'I called Sally the midwife. Sally popped in but she's gone now. She said an obstetrician will check to see if Monica has pre-eclampsia,' said Alice.

I put my arms around them and leaning over the bed kissed Monica. 'You okay?'

'Yes. I had a bit of a dizzy spell, and a pounding head, but I'm fine now.' She looked at the girls and I got the message she didn't want to talk in front of them.

Alice, who'd always been smarter than her years, took the initiative. 'Come on, Faithy, let's go back in the family room. I'll read to you.'

'I want to watch a movie,' said Faith. 'Will you plait my hair while we watch it?'

Alice nodded. 'Okay. I don't have a hair brush but I'll do the best I can.'

When we were alone I kissed Monica again, sat beside her and held her hand. I wanted to give her the chance to talk first. Love swelled my heart as I listened to her telling me what she knew. She sounded vulnerable. Like a scared little girl.

'The midwife said they'll need to monitor me more closely. The headaches, swollen ankles, blurred vision, all that, could be a sign of pre-eclampsia. It's not unusual in older mothers.'

I squeezed her hand. 'Everything is going to be okay.' I could tell from her eyes she was concerned.

'They want to keep me in until the bloods are back.' She dabbed her eyes.

'That's good,' I said. 'You're in safe hands here.'

'I'm scared. What if...' She dissolved into tears.

I got up and put my arms around her and held her. 'Everything is going to be okay. You and baby are going to be fine, I promise. Just you wait until it's here, it's going to be amazing. Before you know it you'll be run ragged trying to keep up. Alice was always so inquisitive, never missed a thing, always wanted to know what was going on and wanted to do everything herself. And I remember Faith had a habit of trying to escape every time we removed her nappy for changing. She'd chuckle to herself and scoot off. It was a game she played.'

Monica broke into a laugh. 'I can imagine her doing that. You really think the baby will be okay?'

'I know it. The doctors and midwives are used to this sort of thing. They see all sorts.' I hoped my conviction didn't sound false as I did my best to reassure her. Inside I was petrified.

Mum had finished raising merry hell and joined us. 'I spoke to an obstetrician, a different one this time. She was very young but seemed to know what she was talking about. She's going to come and see you in a little while. For now she said you need to rest and be patient. I told her your recent ultrasound showed the baby is fine. She assured me they are monitoring the situation. Later on, if it is indeed pre-eclampsia, they might induce. But that's not something we should even think about at this stage. It's a last resort. Right now we wait for the bloods to come back, then depending on the results you may be able to go home and come back for appointments, but for now you have to sit tight.'

'That's it then. I've just got sit here and watch TV until I go doolally. I'm officially a lady of leisure.' Monica leaned back into her pillows and crossed her legs at the ankle. She spoke in a posh voice. 'Peel me some grapes would you, James? Oh, and when you next return home, I'll require my nail polish, my toe nails are an absolute disaster.' She wiggled her toes and we all laughed.

I got to my feet, bowed and pretended to doff my hat. 'Yes, ma'am. Of course ma'am.'

CHAPTER SIXTY

Valentine kept his head down, turned his back on Inspector Hardy, and what he guessed were his two daughters, standing outside the coffee shop opposite waiting for the grandmother. Thumbing through a cookery magazine in the WHSmith store he watched them over the magazine rack as they chatted and buoyed each other up. *I have a remedy for that smugness*, he thought.

'We're closing, doctor,' said Fatima the sales assistant. It was the second time she'd tried to get his attention from behind the till. Her voice was soft and weak, child-like. She raised her thick drawn-on eyebrows in anticipation of a response. When none came she put her hand to her mouth and gently coughed apologetically. She tried again in her small tinkly voice 'Excuse me, d-doctor, I'm sorry, we do have to close.' She pursed her lips and wrinkled her nose in anticipation of him turning.

Still no response. She couldn't bear the thought of actually approaching him. She anxiously straightened her Bella bluebell faerie figurine which sat beside the cash register. She brought Bella to work every day for company. She'd made a travel case especially for her, it made leaving home each morning a little easier.

'Oh purple pixie dust,' she muttered under her breath. She dug deep and spoke still louder. 'Excuse me, d-doctor. I'm so very sorry to bother you, but we must close the shop.'

Valentine looked around. He realised she was addressing him. 'I left my wallet in my other jacket,' he said bluntly. Dumping the magazine beside a stack of Poorly Bears that were in a tower of bright eyed grinning furry faces he left the store without looking back.

Fatima shook her head and grumbled to herself. 'F-f-fluttering faerie wings. Doctors! No manners whatsoever. Rude, the lot of them! Just like pixies. Rude the lot of them.'

Valentine stood in the main hallway of the maternity unit and watched through a floor to ceiling window as Hardy crossed the car park to his car. The two girls went to a separate car with the grandmother. As soon as they turned out of the car park and onto the main road he straightened the fake name badge on the lapel of his blazer and adjusted the stethoscope draped around his neck. He took a silver pen from his pocket and began clicking it on and off as he walked towards the labour ward. Reaching into his trouser pocket he took out two red dice and rolled them over and over in the palm of his hand. *Time for me to do my rounds*, he thought.

A midwife coming off the ward held the door for him as he approached. 'Thank you—' he read her name badge, 'Aretta. I've been asked to look in on a patient, Monica,' he hesitated as he pretended to remember her last name. 'Sorry, it's been a long day.'

Aretta smiled and said, 'Reilly, Monica Reilly. We only have one Monica on the ward today. You might have to wait, she was showering as I left.'

Valentine saw the main reception through the door.

The midwife behind the desk was on the phone, head down writing. 'I'm in a real hurry, you know how it is – so many patients, so little time. Could you show me to her room?' said Valentine.

Aretta looked reluctant.

'I'm sorry. You've finished for the day. I'm sure you're exhausted.' He put on his best smile.

'It's fine. I can show you.'

Valentine kept Aretta between him and the midwife at the desk, who was deep in conversation on the phone. He kept walking and talking. They headed to the antenatal ward where Aretta pointed to a door. 'That's the room, through there. She's in with Mrs Spense.'

'Perfect,' said Valentine. 'Thank you.'

Further down the hallway a midwife sat at a desk absorbed in the day's notes. Beyond her two women in dressing gowns and slippers talked. The pair laughed loudly and the midwife looked up from her notes.

He shoved his hands into the pockets of his blazer and moved quickly into the room. There were four beds. Two were empty. In the bed nearest the door, a woman lay on her side with her knees up. She'd been sleeping but must have realised someone had entered the room.

'Everything okay, doctor?' she said. She started to sit up. She felt around on the bed for her glasses, then looked towards the bedside cabinet.

Valentine walked over to the bed and in a whisper said, 'Please, no need to move. Just ignore me. I'm just passing through. Checking a few things.'

'Everything's all right though, is it?'

'Absolutely fine. Mrs Spense, is it?' He really didn't have time to engage in conversation.

'Uh huh. That's right. Shelley Anne Spence. SAS. My dad was a military man.' She squinted to see the doctor better but he remained blurry. She rubbed her bump. 'Nearly nine months married. Honeymoon baby, he was. Conceived on the beach in California.'

'California? Wow.'

'Yeah, that's what everyone thinks, until I tell them it was California in Great Yarmouth, Norfolk, not the sunshine state in America.'

'Still, sounds romantic.'

'Hardly, we were both drunk on cheap vodka and I froze my arse off. Sex on a British beach at night isn't the same as a beach in the USA; I was picking sand and shingle out of my knees for days.' She laughed raucously and slapped the bed.

Delightful, thought Valentine.

Shelley had found her glasses and put them on. She saw he was looking at Monica's empty bed. He was reading her notes. 'Lovely lady. She told me she was going to have a shower and then phone her parents. Don't know how long she'll be.'

Valentine grimaced. He took her wrists and checked his watch as though he was taking her pulse. 'Everything appears to be in order. I'll wait a few minutes for Ms Reilly and if she's not back I'll be on my way.'

He turned his back on Shelley. He stared at Monica's empty bed. He'd have to change his plans or risk being exposed.

He shielded himself by pulling the curtain screen around Monica's bed. Unbuttoning his shirt from his chest to his waist he ripped a 250 ml bag of blood off his stomach. Taking his pen he punched a hole then squeezed. The blood squirted like it was spurting from an artery as he covered the bed. When he was done he hurled the blood bag against the wall where it splattered.

Hearing the slap of the bag Shelley asked, 'Everything all right, doc?'

'Nearly done,' said Valentine. He once again reached into his pocket and took out the dice which he placed in the centre of the pillow. Satisfied he stepped back through the curtain.

'You off, doc?' said Shelley.

'Best continue my rounds,' said Valentine, ensuring the curtains were closed. 'Lovely to meet you.'

'I'll let her know you came by.'

'Thank you. Tell her Doctor Valentine has reviewed her notes and has left a message for her and her family on the bed.'

'I will, doc. She'll be so disappointed she missed you.'

'I wouldn't be so sure about that,' muttered Valentine. He quick-marched out of the room and as he turned left out of the door Monica walked towards him. She wore a fluffy white dressing gown and her clothes were slung over her arm. Her hair was wet and combed back. She lifted her eyes away from her mobile phone. Her eyes fell first on his name badge and then on his face.

He breathed in and held his breath as she passed. Her face looked fresh. She smelled of shampoo and soap. A thrill ran from his toes across his feet, up the back of legs and up his spine causing him to shudder.

He nodded politely and smiled. 'Have a comfortable evening.'

'Thank you. You too.'

By the time she turned into the room Valentine had reached the doors of the ward. He waited there for a moment.

Even though he was expecting it, when it came, the scream was so loud it made him jump. As he pushed open the glass door he saw the midwife on reception leave her desk and run towards the commotion.

It had been a little disappointing she hadn't been in the bed when he sprayed the blood but the message was the same, Hardy would know he needed to watch his back.

CHAPTER SIXTY-ONE

Rayner leaned in and kissed Jenny. 'I've got to go. I just need to pop in for an hour or so. Are you going to be okay?'

She stood at the front door, leaning against the frame. She gave him a look that said she'd be fine. 'I'll call you if there's an emergency. Otherwise, I'll see you tonight. Love you. Go catch some bad guys, carefully.'

He went to the car, blew her a kiss and waved for her to go inside. He watched as she cautiously lifted her bandaged legs, taking tentative steps before giving one last wave and closing the door.

Pulling away he drove towards Hardy's house and their makeshift incident room. Before he reached the next road tears erupted, catching him off guard. 'No! Oh Christ, Jen! Why?' All the emotions lurking at the back of his mind that he'd bottled up for so long now rushed to the surface. 'Oh, Jen.' He thumped the steering wheel in an effort to gain control. With eyes full of tears and his crying intensifying he pulled over and sat for a few minutes letting it all out. He took deep breaths. When he was ready he reached into the glove box and pulled out some tissues. He wiped his eyes and blew his nose before carrying on his journey. By the time he reached the office he'd once again buried his emotions, driving them back down to the darkest pit of his stomach.

He was the only one there. As he got out his key he could hear the office phone ringing. Moving quickly he got to the phone before it rang off. 'Hullo? Inspector Rayner speaking.' His voice sounded odd after the tearful episode. He coughed and cleared his voice to give it depth.

Rayner heard breathing.

'Inspector Rayner,' he repeated. 'Who is this?'

Silence. Only breathing.

Rayner listened. Waited. 'This is either a bad connection or the worst Darth Vader impersonation I've ever heard.'

There was no response. The breathing continued. Rayner was about to hang up when he heard a movement, somebody walking. A car door. Then a whimpering voice. A child crying.

'Who is this? I'm a police officer. Tell me your name? Where are you? Can you speak to me? Are you injured? Cough if you are in danger.'

The whimpering and crying faded.

Then a muffled male voice spoke, it sounded cold and unemotional. 'I have a boy. I've taken him. I will kill him. I have to.'

'Stop. Listen to me. We can talk about this. Tell me where—'

The line went dead.

Rayner slammed down the phone and picked it up again. He called an old friend at Scotland Yard. 'It's me, Rayner. I need a number traced. I need the number and location of the last call to this number. I need it now. I believe a child has been taken. Probable kidnapping and threat to life.'

CHAPTER SIXTY-TWO

We were in a room used by midwives when they need a private word with a patient or their family. The walls were a bland beige. Monica and I sat on two of the three blue low-back armless chairs. Behind me the tap of a corner sink dripped every minute or so. A dark green paper towel hung precariously from the dispenser on the wall.

At the other end of the room a computer perched on a near empty desk with an ergonomic high-back black office chair pushed underneath. The uninspiring view from the window looked out onto a flat roof and industrial chimney-like chrome vents. Two seagulls fought over a crisp packet.

I was finding it hard to contain my fury. As I comforted her and stroked her back my emotions were exploding like rockets from a blazing firework factory. One part of my brain, the primitive male, was going through scenarios of what I'd do to Valentine when I caught up with him, all of which started with my fist and ended with my boot on his neck. The other part of my brain, the logical part, the part fighting to be heard, was planning his arrest and the look on his face when a judge passed down sentence after his trial. What sort of man would do something like that to a pregnant woman? Monica stopped crying and wiped her eyes with a tissue. 'It's my hormones. I know it is. I'm bursting into tears at the drop of a hat these days.'

'It's hardly that, honey. What that sick bastard did was intended to shock.'

'Well it worked.' Her voice faltered as her emotions welled up, and unable to contain them, tears returned to her eyes. She raised a trembling hand and wiped them away with a tissue. She was working hard to hold herself together. 'Sorry. Look at me. Pathetic.'

Cotton knocked at the door, opened it and poked her head around. 'Hi, Mon, I heard what happened, how are you doing?' She looked weary but still managed a comforting smile.

'Hi, Em, you know, I'm okay. Bit upset, that's all. I'm getting over it.' She pointed to a chair and Cotton came over and sat down.

I gave a Monica a kiss on the top of her head. 'I'm going to step outside for a minute. Will you be okay?'

'I'll be fine.' She squeezed my hand.

I mouthed *thank you* to Cotton before stepping into the hallway for a little space to think.

Cotton nodded.

I looked down the hall towards the room. A forensic officer had been and gone. She'd taken samples of the blood, collected the blood bag and the dice. The dice, Valentine's calling card.

A young male uniformed officer was at the midwife's desk. He leaned casually against the wall chatting to a midwife like he was some local Lothario in a night club and it was happy hour on a Friday night. I was ready to bend his ear when I realised that perhaps I was just feeling bad tempered. The likelihood of Valentine coming back now was remote.

I walked towards the bloodied room which was undergoing cleaning. The officer caught my eye and stepped away from the desk. He went back to standing by the entrance to the room where he should have been. He took out his notebook. As I approached, he stood a little straighter. I was about to speak to him when the midwife he had been talking to came over and spoke first.

Her dark red hair was plaited and wound into a bun fastened on top of her head. Her pale face forced a polite smile. 'Mr Hardy. We have found another bed for Ms Reilly. It's a private room. We think she'll be more comfortable in a room of her own. Is that all right?'

By comfortable I assumed she meant safe. Her tone was frosty which was no doubt due to an earlier conversation I'd had with her and her colleague about the unit's distinct lack of security. The fact that it appeared to me just about anyone could breeze in and out and do whatever the hell they wanted. I'd lost it and now felt more than a little embarrassed at my outburst. After I'd calmed down it was also made clear to me that though the antenatal ward was busy twenty-four-seven, wards are secure, and security is of paramount importance. But sadly Valentine had slipped in, passing himself off as an obstetrician.

'Perfect, thank you. She'll be really pleased, I'm sure. About earlier, I'm sorry, I overreacted.' *Buzz! Buzz!* In my inside jacket pocket my mobile phone sounded the arrival of a text message. I ignored it.

The midwife shook her head and waved it away. 'No need. We were all shocked. You were understandably upset.'

Buzz! Buzz!

I was about to retrieve my phone when over the midwife's shoulder Rayner appeared. He looked flustered and was panting heavily. When a second officer, one I hadn't seen, questioned him at the door, he flashed his warrant card.

Buzz! Buzz!

Rayner came striding over and took me to one side. Still panting he said, 'I've just heard... Valentine... He's abducted a child... A ten-year-old boy.'

'What?' When what he'd said had sunk in I realised I was shaking my head and my fists were clenched so tight my nails dug into the palm of my hands. 'Are we sure it's Valentine?'

'Yeah. He snatched the boy off the street in broad daylight. The boy's been named locally as Luke Evans. He was on his way home after playing football in a park with friends.'

'A single child? Not a twin?'

'I went to the scene and spoke to the parents. He has an older sister. The boy is not a twin.'

My mind was racing. 'Has the street been sealed off?'

'And officers are patrolling the area.'

'It's definitely Valentine?' I repeated. 'It doesn't make sense.'

'He matches the description given by witnesses.'

Buzz! Buzz!

'We stopped him killing the twins. But he can't stop. He's found a new outlet. This has now gone way beyond what first triggered his need to kill twins. It's simply about the act of violence itself. If we don't find him first that boy is as good as dead.'

Buzz! Buzz!

Rayner looked at my buzzing jacket. I took out my phone. I'd received more than a dozen messages. 'What the hell is this?' I mumbled. I read one of the messages and opened some pictures. A young boy stared back at me. His eyes wide and red-rimmed. His face crumpled and contorted with fear. Tear streaks ran down his dirty face. I showed the picture to Rayner.

'That's him, no doubt about it. It's Luke Evans. I saw photos on the mother's phone when she was talking to detectives at the scene.'

I read a message that had come through. 'Valentine wants to meet with me. Alone. If I don't go, he'll kill the boy. If he sees anyone else he'll decapitate the boy and hide his head where no one will ever find it.'

'Where does he want to meet?'

'He's sending me the time and place. Let's go.'

CHAPTER SIXTY-THREE

I zipped my coat up tight and walked briskly around the lake. Aside from the occasional fisherman tucked in amongst the shrubs and reeds hoping for a bite I saw no one. I checked my watch again, it was 5.54 p.m. I glanced to my right where the offices and manufacturing units on the other side of the road were closed. The sun lingered but I was aware it would soon go down and it would be dark.

'You still there?' I said into the microphone under my collar.

'I'm here, mate,' said Rayner reassuringly. 'We're right there with you, every step of the way.'

'You can still see what I'm seeing?'

'We can see,' said Cotton.

'How much further?'

'Hardy this is John Unwin. The boathouse is the other side of the trees on your right.'

Parked behind a block of offices was a surveillance van and inside sat Cotton, Rayner and Unwin. Unwin was a member of the crisis and hostage negotiation unit. They were in contact with lead investigators from Scotland Yard who were still a good hour away; even with blues and twos fighting through the evening traffic was proving to be a challenge for them. We were unable to wait; we were on Valentine's schedule. With Dorset Police's assistance we had put our own team together. Valentine had been specific. I should be in front of the boathouse at 6 p.m. precisely.

John Unwin was an experienced negotiator. Having started at New Scotland Yard he now freelanced around the world with NGOs and charities who work in many dangerous situations. I'd met Unwin many years ago when he successfully talked a father out of killing himself and his wife and baby daughter after he'd learned the wife was leaving him and taking the baby.

'Remember what we talked about,' continued Unwin, his voice deep, gravelly and reassuring with a hint of a soft southern Irish accent. 'We know what we want out of this. We want the boy alive. The way we achieve that outcome is to encourage Valentine to see things our way and we won't get him to see things our way until he first believes we see things his way. The way we do that is to shut up and listen. The last thing you're going to want to be is sympathetic to his concerns and objectives. But that's what I need you to do.'

'Okay. Got it,' I said. I rounded several trees, navigated a wooden gate and arrived at the boathouse. I couldn't see any lights on inside. As I stepped closer I could feel my breathing speed up. I cast a long shadow as I stood in front of the building.

'Breathe calmly and slowly,' said Unwin. 'We need him to remain calm. If he sees you're stressed his own adrenaline will go into overdrive. Worse than it already is.'

In my mind's eye I could see Unwin's piercing blue eyes reading my body language to make sure I understood. I shrugged back my shoulders and tried to relax. I exercised my face in an effort to relieve the tension. It was difficult when all I could think about was how Valentine had butchered so many families. And caused Monica such distress at a difficult time. Yet had managed to lead what appeared to be a normal and successful life.

The boathouse was a long narrow building, part brick, part green cladding with a red tiled roof. Along each side were four large square windows. Unwin and I had been over the plans. Two-thirds given over to boat and equipment storage. The other third was separated into rooms including a workshop, office, toilet and kitchen. I looked up at the security cameras over the doors and on the corners of the roof. I waited in front of two green shutters.

The left-hand shutter door creaked and began to rise. I stepped forward. Once it was around a metre off the floor it stopped. I waited for it to continue up but it went no further. I stood back to see if anyone came out but I saw no movement. 'He must be watching the outside of the building. I think he wants me to go in,' I said.

'I think you're right,' said Unwin in my ear. 'I don't like the look of this; he wants you to crawl inside. It's up to you.'

Rayner sounded worried. 'Hold on. We might lose signal inside. You go in like that you're at his mercy. If he decides to come at you while you're down on the ground you won't stand a chance.'

I looked at the small space under the shutter door. Fearing what might be on the other side I couldn't help but picture the parents Valentine had clubbed to death with a hammer. 'I know what you're saying but I don't have a choice. If Luke is in there I need to go in and get him out.'

'Just hold on,' insisted Cotton.

I stepped closer, got down on my hands and knees and looked underneath the shutter. The room was dark and it took a moment for my eyes to adjust. A light at the end of the room meant I could make out the shape of wide rowing boats loaded onto racks, the kind used for pleasure by families on hot summer days. 'I'm going inside,' I said. I got onto my back and wriggled head first under the shutter. I had no illusions as to how vulnerable I was as I inched my way under the shutter door.

CHAPTER SIXTY-FOUR

Rayner moaned to himself and shook his head. He fastened a stab vest over his shirt.

'What the hell are you doing?' said Unwin.

Rolling up his sleeves Rayner said, 'This is bloody ridiculous. He's gone in there alone. We can barely see what's going on inside that boathouse. If we lose communication with him he won't be able to call for back-up if he needs it. If Hardy gets in trouble we're too far away to help. I'm getting closer, that's what I'm doing.'

'That isn't the plan.'

'Screw the plan, that's my partner out there, we're figuring this out as we go.'

Unwin could see Rayner wasn't about to back down, and the size of him, it would be futile to stand in his way. 'If Valentine sees you it could trigger something in him and if that happens then God only knows what he'll do to the boy.'

'Listen, that psychopath in there has needed no help from me in the past to kill. I'll keep myself out of sight; you stay in contact with Hardy until I get close. Don't tell Hardy what I'm doing until I get there, it might distract him and he needs his wits about him.'

'Okay. Keep your mic and receiver on. Once you're in position let me know.' Unwin checked Rayner's equipment and patted him on the back.

Rayner had the door of the surveillance van open and was about to step out. 'If I get the slightest inkling Hardy or the boy is at risk I'm going in, I'll tear Valentine in two if I have to. Continue with your approach, I hope for all our sakes it works, but if it doesn't...'

'I get it,' said Unwin. 'Do you want to take another officer or two with you? Strength in numbers and all that.'

'Nope. Look at the size of me, I'm visible enough as it is, we don't need a bunch of us increasing the chances of getting seen. Let me get into position. Once I am, I'll be able to coordinate and can get other officers moving in at the right time.'

CHAPTER SIXTY-FIVE

Inside the boathouse the air was icy. I felt around on the cold stone wall for a light switch but failed to find it.

'I'm in,' I whispered into the microphone.

'I hear you,' said Rayner. He sounded like he was running. I pushed all the reasons he might be on the move out of my mind.

'I can barely see anything,' added Unwin. 'You're breaking up. There's a lot of static.'

'Almost pitch black in here. I see a light ahead. Looks like it's coming from one of the back rooms. I'm going to be silent from here on in.' I placed my hand against the hull of a boat to steady myself as I moved gingerly in the darkness. I looked from left to right, peering over and under the boats, looking for Valentine, expecting the worst at any second.

Behind me the shutter suddenly creaked and squealed as it closed. It was apparent that though I could see no one, I myself was being observed.

As I got closer to the room with the light I made out a doorway. Inside I heard a whispering voice and the sobs of a child. I quickened as I moved towards the sound.

'Luke?' I said in a whisper that came out louder than I'd anticipated. 'Luke. I'm Chief Inspector Hardy, I'm a police officer. Can you hear me?'

The room was cut in half by a wall of plastic sheeting hung from floor to ceiling posts. I looked around and saw boxes of sportswear, shoes, and life jackets. On a wall hung oars, and ropes. A silhouette beyond the wall of plastic sheeting caught my eye. On the other side I could make out the blurred shape of someone standing. As I approached, the shape moved from view. 'Robert Valentine, is that you? Robert, I have come alone as you asked. Let's talk.'

I pushed apart the plastic sheeting and stepped through into the boat repair workshop. The smell of cut wood and varnish filled my nostrils.

Under a spotlight, on a workbench with each slim arm and leg clamped was the small figure of Luke Evans. The upper half of his young body was bare. His shirt, which had been ripped or cut away, draped over the waist of his jeans. The jeans around the crotch and inside legs were dark where he'd wet himself. On his chest rested a hacksaw.

In my earpiece I heard Unwin say, 'My God.'

'Are you seeing this?' I asked.

'Is the boy okay? Where's Valentine?'

'He may have run.' On hearing me, the boy attempted to lift his head, our eyes met but he struggled to keep his open. The way his head swayed he appeared drugged. His mouth was stuffed with a rag and held in place with tape. He mumbled incoherently. He winced and whined as he jerked his body away from the clamps that held him. His small fingers contorted as he tried pathetically to break free.

'Luke, I'm a police officer, you're going to be okay. The man who did this, do you know where he is?' I removed the gag from his mouth.

Luke began sobbing and shaking his head but he was so drugged he couldn't speak.

There was no sign of Valentine so I ran to the bench, looking for a way to release the boy. Using the hacksaw I struggled to make any impact on the metal clasps. Feeling frantic, my fingers fumbling and my hands clumsy, I went from clasp to clasp sawing at each metal clasp desperately sawing at them and their securing bolts.

'Are you seeing this?' I repeated to Unwin.

'We can just m-m-make it out. But you're b-b-breaking u-up. W-w-where's Valentine?'

'There's no sign of him. Maybe he got spooked and left,' I said. I looked around to be sure. Unwin was speaking but I couldn't make out what he was saying. All I could hear was static.

I ran to shelves on the wall looking for something that might prise the clasps off but found nothing. Under the bench Luke was on I noticed a wooden box. I dragged it forward and began pulling out files, screwdrivers, chisels; at the bottom I could see a selection of spanners.

I was focused on getting all the tools out to get to the spanners, thinking I could release the bolt holding each clasp. It wasn't until too late that I heard footsteps behind me. As I turned there was a solid thump across the back of my head and shoulders. Lights sparkled behind my eyes then my world turned black.

* * *

When I awoke my head was pounding and my neck throbbed. As my eyes came into focus and my recollection of recent events returned I tried to move. I struggled but my body felt useless.

I jerked and tried to thrust myself forward, but I'd been

restrained. I was strapped against a floor-to-ceiling post. My legs were taped together at the ankle, my arms were pulled behind the post and taped at the wrist. My head was held in place with more wrapped around my throat and the post. I could do little more than look straight ahead at the workbench where Luke lay and where Valentine now hovered over the him like an evil shadow.

'You're back with us, Inspector? I'm so glad you could join us.' Valentine rolled two dice around in his hand, he blew on them before tossing them across the workbench. 'Time is ticking and we have so much to do. Let's not waste any more time, let's play a little game.'

'Let the boy go. You've got me. You don't need the boy.'

'I'm not interested in you,' said Valentine. He shrugged and pulled a face as though what I'd said was ridiculous. 'I would like you to watch, however. The boy reminds me of myself at his age. Alone. Mind and body effectively decapitated. Isolated from the rest of the world. A lost twin separated from all he knew and all he understood.'

'But he's not you. Whatever happened to you has nothing to do with this child. The demons you harbour can be dealt with without harming anyone else. I know people who can help you. Whatever anger or hatred or resentment you feel, it shouldn't be brought to bear on this child. His name is Luke. His parents desperately want him home. He has a sister who is heartbroken. Look at me. They love him.'

Valentine looked like a different man to the one I'd known. His demeanour had changed. With one hand on the workbench his stooping shoulders loomed over the boy. His eyes grey, his skin wrinkled, his complexion pallid.

'Look at me,' I repeated. 'This doesn't have to be you. You don't have to do this. Let Luke go. I want to hear your story. Talk to me. But release the boy first.'

I heard nothing in my ear, no advice from Unwin, and

realised Valentine had removed the earpiece and the camera from the collar. Luke and I were alone with this madman. Rayner and the rest of the team could have no idea what was happening.

CHAPTER SIXTY-SIX

Despite his huge muscular frame Rayner moved with surprising speed. He kept to the main path most of the way, only hugging the grass, shrubs and trees once he got close to the boathouse. He hunkered down on one knee once the boathouse was in view. What he really wanted to do was get around the rear side. He'd heard through his earpiece that Hardy had gone in under the shutter and made his way through the building to a workshop at the other end of the building. As close to that room as possible was where he wanted to be.

Ahead he could see a four-rail wooden fence with access through a gate. It ran from the water's edge around the building. Beyond the fence on the right hand side was a private gravel road where vehicles could approach when coming from the other side of the boathouse. The problem was the cameras. Approaching from the right side of either end would no doubt trigger the camera. That only left the side of the boathouse which was beside the lake. Rayner looked at the cold dark water. A swan moved gracefully past, hardly giving him a second glance. Behind him there was a break in the foliage, access to the water. *'You've got to be kidding, am I really going to do this?'* he said to himself.

Rayner checked his pockets. He removed his heavy stab vest and tucked everything he didn't need behind a bush. Arms out and moving like a circus bear on tiptoes he entered the water. He couldn't help cursing under his breath as the needle-like icy water sucked the heat from his feet, then legs, then waist and stomach. He sank down until it reached his armpits. 'F-f-f me this is cold and it stinks!'

'You okay?' asked Unwin in his ear.

'Yeah. I'm in the bloody lake. It's cold, it stinks and the bottom is muddy, my feet keep sinking in and tripping over roots.'

'I'm not even going to ask why you're in the water. Just come back to me when you're in position.'

'If I don't catch a life-threatening disease or get eaten by piranha or pecked to death by ducks I'll be in position in a few minutes.'

'Pretty sure the ducks won't attack. Not so sure about the disease or piranha.'

'Good to know,' said Rayner. He tried laughing but was concentrating too hard on his footing.

Staying close to the bank he walked and stumbled and swam towards the rear of the building. He kept on a short distance until he arrived in front of a startled angler.

The angler sat-up open mouthed as Rayner approached. His narrow pointy face was both curious and confused. 'I've seen it all now, mate. You're one big ugly duck.' He put his flask of coffee down, stepped over his fishing rod, and put out a long thin hand. After a couple of false attempts and with Rayner hanging on to some tree roots he yanked him out onto the bank.

'You must be freezing. What sort of idiot are you? What did you do, fall in?' The angler reached into his fishing shelter and retrieved a fleece and thermal hat. 'I don't want you dying of pneumonia. Here, have this. I don't have any spare trousers but you're welcome to this. The fleece might be all right, I wear it over the top of a couple of thick jumpers. It'll certainly keep you warm.'

Rayner removed his shirt and pulled on the fleece which he just about managed to zip up. 'Thank you. There's an incident at the boathouse. I'm part of the police surveillance team.'

'Yeah, right, of course you are. Don't they have frogmen or boats for that sort of thing? I'm supposed to believe they're making the police swim across lakes now due to cutbacks?' He looked around for more officers. 'All I know is I won't be catching much this evening after you've been thrashing about in the water like a herd of hippos.'

Rayner didn't hang around to debate. He thanked the angler again then followed the path back towards the boathouse.

CHAPTER SIXTY-SEVEN

Using trees and shrubs as cover Rayner moved close to the boathouse. His eyes scanned the building for cameras. On the apex of the roof there was one camera covering the approach but as far as he could see there were no others.

He heard the crunching of someone walking on the other side of the shrubs. As he looked around a Dalmatian dog came up to him and began to playfully bounce, as though it had found something interesting hiding in the hedgerow. The dog excitedly began barking at him. Rayner got to his feet and taking the dog by the collar began walking towards the owner. He realised that as he approached the boathouse with the dog in tow he looked like nothing more than a dog walker, wearing what felt like a child's fleece top, attempting to keep his dog under control.

He kept his body and face turned away from the camera on the roof. Walking swiftly Rayner kept a firm grip on the dog's collar while the dog bounced and barked and twisted to get away. On seeing the owner, a small round man in a flat cap and Wellington boots, Rayner gestured warmly and spoke loudly, pretending they were friends in case the camera picked up sound. 'Here she is. I'm thinking we should put her back on the lead. She seems excitable today, chasing anything that moves. Worse than yesterday.' Once close he let the dog go and it ran back to its owner's side.

'Who the hell are you, and what are you doing with my dog?'

Rayner walked up close. 'I'm a police officer. Just keep walking. Act like we know each other.'

'What are you talking about? Bugger off before I call the police. Get away from me and my dog, you nutter.' He picked up speed and Rayner matched him step for step. Keeping an eye on the side of the building Rayner prepared himself for making a dash. Once they were just past the corner he turned and sprinted over, placing himself flat against the wall. He looked up at where the camera must be; he knew it was there somewhere but he couldn't see it.

The dog walker looked back at the strange man running around like a secret agent. He straightened his cap before sinking his hands deep into his waxed jacket. He looked at his dog. She looked at him. 'I think that fella is probably off his medication, Dodie. Best you stay close.'

Rayner moved along the wall, past the back door until he came to a window. He peered in and though his vision was obstructed he saw Valentine. He appeared to be talking to someone he couldn't see. Valentine was close, no more than a few metres away. Rayner crouched down out of sight.

'Unwin, I see Valentine. I'm behind the boathouse.'

'I hear you. We've lost visual and audio on Hardy. Do you have eyes on him?'

'Negative. I can't make out Hardy or the boy.' Rayner went back to the window to get a better look. 'This is extremely bad, Unwin. We have no idea what's happening in there.'

'I need you to be ready to go in on my command,' said Unwin.

Rayner moved towards the back door. He could see it was locked. He'd have to kick it in; the door didn't look much and would open easily. Rayner's muscles tensed as he prepared himself. 'We need to move now. I'm ready to go. I'm not waiting much longer.'

CHAPTER SIXTY-EIGHT

Valentine's fingernails clawed at his face as years of frustration and torment seeped to the surface of his deluded mind. 'People think they understand, but they have no idea. Not about real loss.'

'Tell me. I want to hear.'

Valentine's eyes narrowed as though he was deciding whether I was being genuine. 'I was a twin,' he said. 'I shared our mother's womb with my brother. When my brother died it was like losing a limb, literally. He and I were two parts of the whole. We were one. We used to stand in the sun and cast our shadows so they merged. I was his shadow, and he was mine. For a short while we would be one. Only a twin understands that. Are you a twin, Inspector?'

'No. I'm not.'

'Then you can never know real loss. Losing a parent or wife or child could never match the loss. It could never even come close. I was physically and mentally left in pieces.'

Valentine moved around the bench tapping Luke's body; his head, and each arm and leg as he walked and talked. 'The body separates neatly into six pieces. Six like on the side of a dice. I used to play a game of chance with two dice. My Auntie Evelyn invented the game.'

'The auntie who raised you and your brother? The auntie you showed me in the photograph at your home?'

His eyes shone as though he were pleased with the attention. He put the dice down on the bench and pushed them around with the tip of a finger. 'My brother loved to roll the dice. We both did. The game is important. Life is like the roll of a dice. It demonstrates that no matter how unlikely the outcome, and how cautious you might be, the course of life is completely beyond our control. Two dice, two sixes, you'd be surprised how often you get a double six.'

'You're playing with lives. That's not a game. Release me, there's still an opportunity to make amends.' I spoke as loud as I could in case the microphone was able to pick up our voices.

He snickered and ignored me. 'I'll explain the rules. If the dice lands on a double six during any of the throws then we must separate a limb. This continues until we have six pieces. As my Aunt Evelyn told me when my brother died "For no apparent reason life is sometimes cruel. There are few certainties, that's for sure. One of life's certainties is that we're all going to die. So play the game of life while you can, because life as you know it can end when you least expect it. You can't predict what's around the corner any more than you can predict the roll of a dice." It's time to roll the dice, Inspector.'

Before I could stop him Valentine swept up the dice, rattled them in the palm of his hand and dropped them back down on the workbench. They bounced and skidded, turned and spun until they settled. Valentine read the dice then looked at me. Three. Five.

He moved around the bench and this time rested the

hacksaw blade on Luke's left calf. He scooped up the dice. He had a sickening smile carved across his face. 'It's nice to have this time together. Before, when I went to the homes I felt rushed. I waited until I rolled two sixes then went to work. But now we're finally able to take our time. We roll a double six for each limb. I feel sure this will come close to the separation I felt as a child.'

I fought and struggled against my restraints, desperately trying to pull my wrists apart but the tape was too strong and tightly wound. Valentine rolled the dice again. I stopped struggling for a moment as though I were hypnotised by the dice dancing across the bench. Six. Two.

Thank God, I thought. *I've got to get loose.*

Valentine kept on going. Round and round the bench. He was back to Luke's right thigh, he rolled the dice; again he was unsuccessful. He moved back to Luke's right arm and rested the hacksaw on the boy's shoulder while he tossed the dice. I could see the blade pressing down on his soft skin. Valentine kept rolling the dice and moving round the body as if he were on a macabre merry-go-round. Rolling and moving. Rolling and moving. Eventually he was back in front of me; the blade poised over Luke's right thigh.

Valentine had his back to me. He rolled the dice between Luke's legs. I struggled to see what was going on. I felt very afraid. From the way Valentine gasped and held his breath I knew something wasn't right. His demeanour had changed. He turned slowly to reveal the dice. 'It was only a matter of time. Look what we have here.'

With a showman's flourish Valentine pointed.

My heart stopped.

On the bench both dice showed a six. I began to yell at Valentine and go crazy, my body thrashing as I tried to break free.

'For Christ's sake, Valentine, he's just a boy. Don't you

fucking touch him. Release me, I'll do everything I can for you, I promise. Don't harm the boy.' He wasn't listening; his mind was elsewhere, in the place that had driven him to kill and destroy so many lives.

He pressed the blade against the boy's thigh and began to saw. As he drew the blade across the skin and tissue the drugged boy moaned. For a split second Valentine looked up, paused momentarily then stepped back to get a better angle.

I took my chance and did the only thing I could. I pressed my body back against the post and at the same time pushed down with my arms. It meant I was able to raise my legs. To gain momentum I did it again, and again. I raised them as high as possible and with every ounce of strength I could muster kicked out hard and fast. My feet hit Valentine squarely in the lower back and hip causing him to lurch forward over the bench. I kicked out time and again, stomping and pounding his back. As he collapsed my feet came down hard on his head and shoulders. He sunk to the floor groaning and writhing, attempting to drag himself away.

At that moment a door in the back of the room thumped several times before crashing open. Through shelves I saw Rayner's shape as it filled the doorway. 'Hardy!' he shouted. He began to clamber over boxes and push his way past shelves.

'Over here.'

Valentine got onto his knees, then his feet. I tried to kick out and slow him down but he stumbled out of range.

'Rayner! Over here. Quick.'

Before Rayner could reach us Valentine had staggered away, disappearing through the wall of plastic sheeting.

Using the hacksaw, Rayner cut away the tape that held

my wrists and neck. He then turned to Luke's blood-soaked thigh.

I cut away the tape binding my ankles. 'Make a tourniquet, stop the bleeding,' I said.

Rayner was on the same page, he'd taken off his belt and was tightening it around Luke's leg. 'I'll stop the bleeding and call for a medical team. He's losing a lot of blood.'

I looked Rayner in the eye with gratitude and said, 'I'm going after Valentine.'

CHAPTER SIXTY-NINE

I had to catch up with Valentine before he got too far. I couldn't risk him slipping away. I sprinted as fast as possible, my arms and legs pumping like engine pistons. I guessed by now Unwin was coordinating a search and had sent in all available officers to set up a perimeter but it would be impossible to ensure he didn't slip through.

Up ahead I heard voices, it sounded like an argument. As I rounded the corner I almost ran straight into a young couple pushing an infant in a buggy; the rosy-faced child was asleep under a thick quilt.

'Have you seen a man running this way?' I suggested he might be limping.

The young woman, in her early twenties with dyed blonde hair began waving her arms about as she described what happened. 'The flamin' idiot wasn't looking where he was going. He came flying round the corner, and fell arse over tit, nearly knocking the babe out of her pushchair. You got any idea how long it took to get Beyoncé off to sleep? Can't get her to sleep at the best of times. She's not much of a sleeper.'

The young man piped up. He nervously flattened his

greasy looking hair as he spoke. 'Little Beyoncé's always hungry too—'

'Which way did he go?' I interrupted.

The pair pointed to an overgrown gap in the hedge which I would have missed.

I thanked them and carried on running. I charged through the shrubs and onto a path bordered with a run-down wood and wire fence. The path immediately started going uphill until it eventually turned into steps leading to the top of a steep bank. My thighs burned and my lungs were raw as I raced up the steps, my heart and chest pleading for me to stop.

The steps came to an end, levelled off and I arrived at a railway line. To my right I could see Valentine. He was limping and out of breath. I felt reinvigorated as I realised I was in with a chance of catching up with him. As I got closer Valentine stopped running and simply walked. He turned and looked at me, began shouting something which at first I couldn't make out.

'You're not arresting me. Could you imagine the humiliation! My family would be devastated. Think of my wife and daughters. I love them, I can't do that to them. There's no point you coming after me, the killing is over. I'm ending it. I can't carry on like this.' Valentine turned and looked towards the bridge up ahead. He picked up his limping pace with a struggle; putting in extra effort to stay ahead of me.

'Valentine, stay where you are,' I shouted. 'Listen to me.'

'There's nothing to talk about, it's over. I'm ending it.'

I sprinted now. But by the time I got to him he had already reached the bridge. He'd climbed over the railings and looked down at the road below. 'It's better this way. I'm a monster. Somebody should've stopped me sooner. You should have stopped me. There was nothing I could do. It was always there. It grew and spread like a disease inside me the day my brother left me behind.'

I stepped closer, my arms out wide, non-threatening. Behind me, in the distance and out of sight I heard a train approaching. I stepped off the railway line and closer to the bridge railings, keeping a safe distance from Valentine, not wanting to spook him, not wanting him to jump.

'Step back over the railing,' I said. 'You need help. Let me help you.'

'No. It's over.' He shook his head and lurched forward.

I jumped and grabbed his wrist, wrapped my arm around his chest and, despite his flailing, dragged him kicking and screaming back over the railing. I threw him to the ground, grabbed his hair and an arm, and rolled him over onto his face. I kept him down with my knee on his back.

'Get off me. What the hell are you doing? Let me jump.' He began sobbing. It was as though at that moment, having reached rock bottom, the enormity of his actions and realisation of his vile acts had finally registered. He continued wailing uncontrollably.

While he thrashed I cautioned him. '...it may harm your defence if you do not mention when questioned something which you later rely on in court. Anything you do say may be given in evidence.' He bucked and squirmed. 'Stay down. You're going to face up to what you've done. The families of your victims deserve their day in court.' I thought about Elizabeth Poulson's father and the promise I'd made him. A broken man who would now see justice done.

Over my shoulder the train squealed against the tracks as it approached. I could see it now, still a little way off but coming fast. I turned to make sure we were at a safe distance. I lifted my knee from Valentine's back and raised his arms to keep him prostrated. Valentine submitted. His complaining ceased. He quit struggling and lay perfectly still.

'Need these?' Rayner appeared behind me. Doubled over and panting he held out a pair of handcuffs. Cotton stood beside him, red-faced and staring at Valentine.

A short distance behind them two uniformed police officers appeared at the top of the bank. Huffing and puffing they followed the railway line towards us.

The killings were finally over. It felt like a war we'd been fighting had ended and the atrocities Valentine had inflicted had come to an end.

I cuffed him and got him to his feet. I held him tight until the two officers arrived. 'Take him,' I said.

'Yes, sir,' said the young officer taking his arm. The second officer was about to grab hold of Valentine's other arm when he shrugged his way out of their grip. Cotton stepped aside and Rayner pushed through the two officers and tried to grab Valentine but it was too late.

Valentine ran as fast he could back up the line. We ran after him. There was no way he was getting away again.

Before we could reach him Valentine stopped running. Instead he took a sidestep onto the tracks and into the path of the oncoming train.

As the train bore down on him he turned his head and looked at us. I saw sorrow filling his eyes. A second later his shattered body vanished beneath the thundering wheels.

CHAPTER SEVENTY

I was alone in my home office on the phone with Chief Superintendent Webster.

A calmness had descended over the room since closing the case. The huge whiteboard was completely full of the notes, leads and reminders. Names circled with lines and arrows going this way and that.

Every desk, surface and available chair seat was covered with files, sticky notes and papers.

The sick feeling I had carried in my stomach for so long had been replaced with a chest full of pride.

'How's the young lad doing?' said Webster.

'Luke's doing surprisingly well; doctors worked on his leg and the prognosis is good. He might need another operation, but physically he's good. He's home from hospital now, and the whole family are doing well. I visited with Cotton and they couldn't stop thanking us. Lovely family.'

'Well, it's a big win all round. Your whole team are to be congratulated, excellent work, Hardy. And the business with Janek Bonne's death?'

'That's all in hand. The trap has been set. It's just a matter of waiting now.'

'Good. I wish I could be there to see his face when you cuff him.' Webster paused before continuing. 'What are you thinking of doing after that? I know you've got a baby on the way, that being said, I have a mountain of unsolved murders as soon as you're ready to get back to it One or two are right up your street.'

I thought about Monica, Alice, Faith and the baby.

'Give me a few days. I need to be around for Monica at the moment.' I laughed. 'I say that, she'll probably want me out from under her feet. Send over some case files and I'll take a look. I think the team we've put together is a winning combination. A good way to keep their spirits up is to consider a new case.'

'That's what I like to hear. My love to the family. And once again, congratulations to you and your team, sterling work.'

I put down the phone and stared at the pile of letters on my desk. The top one, with its handwritten address, pricked my curiosity. I slipped it open, pulled out the note and a cheque fell out. I read the sum then read it again. In my hand was a cheque for two-hundred-thousand pounds. It was signed by Patrick Simpson, Elizabeth Poulson's father. The note attached simply read *Thank You.*

My name wasn't on the cheque, the pay section had been left blank. Simpson realised I couldn't accept money and knew I'd either return it or donate it to a charity of my choice. I put it down and pondered. The decision wasn't mine alone, it had to be a group decision. The team would decide whether we return it or which charity or charities we should donate the money to. I locked it away in the safe and went for a walk around the block. If Monica was up to it I was planning on getting Rayner, Cotton and few others over to the house for a celebratory drink. The trouble was, everyone had such busy lives, pinning them down to a date was proving tricky. I decided to make some calls while I walked.

CHAPTER SEVENTY-ONE

Sunlight was beginning to creep through the bedroom curtains. Watson stood beside the bed and meowed. He looked up at Emma and rubbed himself along the side of the bed. He meowed again.

Emma opened first one eye and then the other. 'What? Go out if you want to go out.' She lifted her head to make sure the bedroom door was still open before letting her head flop back on the pillow. She rolled over onto her back and reached for the bedside clock. 'It's nine-fifteen. It's too early. You know I was up late. I'll get your breakfast soon. Give me a few more minutes.'

Watson clawed at the bed and meowed more insistently. He jumped up and stood looking at her.

'What's got into you? I need my sleep.' She grabbed a pillow and put it over her head. 'Bad cat. Let me sleep. And stop staring at me. I know you're staring at me. Stop it.'

She tried to relax and slow her breathing but it was too late. She was awake and that meant her brain had begun processing everything going on in her life. And that included Declan. She smiled beneath the pillow.

A creaking came from downstairs.

She ignored it. Probably the wind rattling the cat flap.

Watson meowed.

Thump. Scrape.

No longer unable to ignore the noise she lifted the pillow off her face. She looked at Watson. 'Did you hear something?' He was looking at the bedroom door. He'd heard it too. He was circling at the end of the bed.

Her heart thumped. Quickly and quietly she climbed out of bed. Putting on her slippers and dressing gown she went and stood by the bedroom door, listening.

Nothing.

She looked at Watson. 'You got me all spooked for nothing.' Watson stared at her from the end of the bed.

She went out onto the landing and looked over. Still no sound. Probably just the bloody postman putting letters through the door. In the back of her mind she knew it was too early.

She went to the bathroom. When she came out Watson was standing at the top of the stairs looking down. 'I'm up now. I hope you're happy. I'm getting a tea. If you want breakfast you'd better follow me.' He stayed where he was. 'For the love of...'

There were no letters by the front door. She passed the sitting room, peered in, then went straight to the kitchen. She grabbed the kettle, filled it up and put it on to boil. She looked at the pile of dirty clothes in front of the washing machine and decided they could wait another day. Unplugging her mobile phone from the charger she checked for messages before reading the news then scrolling through Facebook.

Watson appeared at the kitchen door.

Emma tore open a sachet and filled his bowl. 'There you go. Hopefully it'll taste better than it smells.'

Watson padded over, took a sniff and walked away.

'You're acting peculiar today. I've never known you leave your food.'

He brushed himself against her leg, then jumped up on the worktop. She put her arm around him and gently stroked. The pair of them looked out of the kitchen window and into the garden. Next door, Declan was power-washing the patio. Probably removing beer and wine stains from after the party. She watched him through the blinds. Though he was the other side of the fence she could make out he was moving the barbecue out of the way so he could clean beneath it. She kissed Watson and spoke to him quietly. 'What do you think, am I making a mistake with him? There's no denying he's a hunk but if it all goes wrong it could be very awkward living next door.'

Declan looked up and caught Emma watching. 'Shit!' she gasped.

She crouched down below the kitchen worktop and began to giggle. Watson pulled himself away from her embrace and ran across the kitchen and out through the cat flap.

Emma got to her feet and keeping low went to the kettle. With her back to the window she reached up and took a cup from the cupboard. As she did, out of the corner of her eye she saw movement. She leaned back and looked down the hallway. For a split second she couldn't comprehend what she was seeing. Then she let out a shriek of shock. Alex was stood in front of the closed front door. He began walking towards her.

'What the fuck? What are you doing here? Get out. Get the fuck out of my house.' She stormed towards him and stopped him in his tracks. She tried to turn him around and began pushing him back towards the front door. 'How did you get in?'

'I've got a key, remember?'

'No you don't. I took the key back. You must have made a copy.' She began screaming at him. 'I want you out. Out!' Her eyes flicked towards the front door where she saw the security chain was cut.

Alex dug his heels in and pushed back. 'I'm not going anywhere. Not until you listen to me.'

'I'm not listening to anything. Out. Get out.'

He tried to grab Emma by the hair. She seized his wrist, twisted his arm up behind his back and forced him against the hallway wall. Alex began to struggle. She lifted his arm up and up in an attempt to make him submit. Instead, he raised his free arm and thrusting his elbow back he hit Emma in the face. He hit her again and again with his elbow. She fell backwards, smashing her head against the staircase spindles. She slumped to floor but immediately jumped back up and made a run for the kitchen. As she reached it she slammed the door shut behind her, pressing her weight against it to hold it closed. Alex kicked it. She could see him through the frosted glass window panels. Over and over he kicked and threw himself at the frame.

Emma peered over her shoulder at the back door. It was unlikely she could reach it and get it open before he got to her. 'Alex. Calm down. We'll talk. Just stop.'

His face looked distorted and grotesque as he pressed it to the glass of the kitchen door. His grunting and laboured breathing sounded like some monstrous primeval beast. 'Why? You think I don't know about you and him? You'd make a fool of me. Embarrass me. You expect me to take it? Expect me to just slope off. Fade away like some pathetic nobody.'

Emma looked around for something she could use to defend herself. 'It's not like that. You're overreacting. Let's talk. I need you to get yourself under control.'

'Overreacting?' he spat. 'You didn't want to talk, remember. When I wanted to talk you weren't interested. Now it's too late. I know whores like you. I've met them my whole life. Treat men like they're insignificant. You know what, I won't stand for it. Never have, never will. A bitch like you deserves what's coming to her. I'm going to fucking show you. Teach you a lesson you'll never forget. Right here. Right now. You hear me? I'm going to show you.'

'I'm a police officer. You'd better not try anything.' Hearing the panic in her voice as she spoke heightened her fear.

'Because you're police makes you untouchable? Above the rest of us, are you? I don't give a fuck what you are. You think you can demean me in front of your friends? Well I'll show you what that feels like.' The door rattled, shuddered, glass cracked and wood groaned as he pushed and kicked harder than ever. Head down, she pushed back. She could barely keep it shut. It opened and slammed over and over. Eventually, a whole pane of glass broke. Then as quickly as it started everything went quiet. Panting and trembling Emma leaned against the door to keep it shut. She blinked through the broken pane of frosted glass. Alex had vanished.

She ran to the kitchen table and shoved it. It screeched as she pushed it across the floor and in front of the door. It wouldn't keep him out but it would slow him down. Emma ran to the kitchen window and banged on the glass, she hollered and yelled, waving like a mad woman hoping to get Declan's attention. She went to the back door and turned the key. Through the glass she could see she had caught Declan's attention but wasn't sure he understood. Emma was about to open the door when behind her there was a loud crash as Alex gave the kitchen door an almighty kick sending it flying open and upturning the table. He barged his way into the room.

CHAPTER SEVENTY-TWO

Alex's eyes were lost in rage, his face full of loathing. In the small kitchen Emma had nowhere to go as he stormed towards her. She stumbled backwards. She slammed the pedal bin in front of him, which he stepped over like it wasn't even there. She grabbed a chair and thrust it towards him, he brushed it aside. Grabbing whatever she could from the worktop she pelted him with it, but he kept bearing down on her. Finally cornered, the only thing she could lay her hands on was washing detergent on top of the washing machine. She grabbed the bottle, leaned towards him, and squirted it in his face. As his hands shot up to protect his eyes she threw the bottle at his head and attempted to rush past him. As she did he grabbed her and slammed her to the floor. She rolled over and kicked out. It was no use, like a man possessed with every hate from hell he towered over her. Straddling her body, his hands pressing down on her neck, squeezing. She could smell his stale breath and sweat as he loomed over her, tightening his grip.

'Humiliate me, would you?' said Alex, his face staring and contorted.

She rasped and choked. The pressure in her throat became unbearable. She punched and clawed at him.

'You think I don't know you went to see Louise? I'll kill that bitch next. The pair of you, conspiring against me!'

Emma reached around for something, anything, to use against him. Her fingers like tiny tentacles feeling around, hit upon what felt like a can; the sharp edge of a tuna can from the pedal bin. She was about to thrust it up towards his face when the pressure on her throat suddenly eased. Alex slumped over her then rolled off. When she looked up, Declan was standing there with a small terracotta pot in his hand. He tossed the pot back onto the patio and knelt down beside her. She threw her arms around his neck as he pulled her to him.

Alex lay slumped on his side, blood seeping from a cut over his ear, wetting his hair.

'He was going to kill me,' gasped Emma. She held him tight as he helped her to her feet. She was shaking and unsteady as they went outside. He walked her to a garden seat.

'Sit. Breathe. You're okay. He's not going to hurt you.'

'What the devil's going on,' called Sue over the fence.

'Call the police, Mum. A fella just attacked Emma. She's all right, but we need the police.'

Declan got to his feet and looked at Alex who was beginning to stir.

'Don't,' said Emma.

'We can't just let him come round, he might try something,' said Declan.

'I don't intend to.' Emma slowly got to her feet. She went back to the kitchen. Declan followed. 'Watch him,' she said. She went out into the hallway where her coat and handbag hung. She found her mobile phone and handcuffs before returning. She held out the handcuffs. 'Roll him over. We'll put these on him. Be firm about it, he might resist.'

'Happy to oblige,' said Declan. He grabbed Alex and yanked his arms behind his back. He leaned close to his ear. 'Attempting to murder an off duty police officer, sounds like a lengthy prison sentence to me, you worthless piece of shit. I wouldn't want to be in your shoes, mate. I hear blokes who hurt women get a tough time on the inside.'

CHAPTER SEVENTY-THREE

A week had passed since Valentine had thrown himself under the train and it was time to finish the final piece of the puzzle. Rayner and I stood behind the check-in desk at Gatwick airport.

'He's not going to show,' said Rayner. 'You're going to owe me a tenner. Should have made it twenty.'

'He'll be here. The deal on the table is too juicy, he won't be able to resist.' My eyes scanned the faces of holidaymakers and business people looking to catch their flights. Rayner and I had cooked up a plan to lure out of hiding the man who no longer wanted to be found. Finally realising the game was up, he'd abandoned his family and gone on the run. We knew he needed money and so hatched a plan where the deal on the table would create enough wealth for him to disappear. Enough so he could relocate his family once the dust settled. After sending numerous emails to an address we hoped he'd still monitor, he eventually replied and after a bit of back and forth he took the bait.

'That's him,' said Rayner. He pointed to a man pulling a small suitcase towards a table at a coffee shop.

I waved and pointed to airport security staff and we watched as they swooped in and headed him off. Before he could put his butt in the seat he was escorted away to a secure room on the pretext they wanted to do a random stop and search.

I gave Rayner a nudge. 'You owe me a tenner. Let's go.'

'If you insist,' he said with a broad grin.

We followed the officers to a secure room where we observed him for a while. We wanted him to sweat. Then when we were ready we entered the interrogation room and watched as every ounce of colour drained from his face.

'Andrew Yates, it's great to see you again,' I said. Rayner and I sat down opposite him.

'We've had trouble reaching you,' said Rayner. 'You're a hard man to track down. Your wife put on a good performance. If we didn't know better we'd think she was genuinely dismayed you'd left her.'

'What is this, what's going on?' His mouth gaped open. He knew what was happening and it was beginning to sink in. He was like a fly helplessly trapped in a spider's web. I could see his mind whirring as he made a futile attempt to free himself. He stammered as he tried to get the words out. 'I-Inspector? Thank goodness you're here. Hopefully you can sort this nonsense out. There's been some sort of mistake. I'm going on a business trip. My flight leaves very soon. I need to be making my way to the departure lounge. Airport security took my passport and haven't returned it.'

'Where you're going you don't need a passport, buddy,' said Rayner with a wry smile.

'W-what are you talking about?' He swallowed hard.

'Things have come to light since Valentine's attempt on your family.'

'And to every officer involved in stopping him my family and I will be eternally grateful. I still cannot believe how very different that outcome might have been without the incredible work of your team.'

Rayner and I looked at each other in a 'are you going to tell him or shall I?' kind of way.

'We know it was you who killed Janek Bonne,' I said.

Yates looked dismissive. He shook his head. 'What? Absolute rubbish. Is this some sort of joke? Are there hidden cameras?' He looked around the room for cameras.

'The cameras are not hidden. We know he was going to have you fired from your job for copying and selling the institute's proprietary software. He was going to press charges. We've spoken to his legal team.'

'Ridiculous. What is this?'

'We know he spoke to Valentine and instructed him to terminate your employment.'

'You're crazy. You're barking up the wrong tree.' He shook his head vigorously.

'My guess is that you thought with Bonne out of the way you'd be able to persuade Valentine that you should stay on – before you knew he was a killer, that is. You decided that you and he could make a go of it. That you'd make a fortune and you'd eventually push him out of the company, leaving you as sole owner.'

'What utter nonsense. You've had your fun. I really must be going.' He got up to leave.

'Sit down,' barked Rayner. The big man glared at him.

Yates looked terrified. He sat back down.

I continued, speaking calmly. 'My only question is why someone with your obvious talents didn't simply start your own business? You could have walked away and set up some other project of your own.'

Rayner leaned forward, and almost growled when Yates didn't answer. 'We know it was you. We have fingerprint and DNA evidence you were on the boat. We know you weren't at home the night of the murder and you have motive. We also have a witness who saw a man fitting your description arriving and leaving the boat around the time Bonne was murdered. And that's just for starters. It's going to go a lot better for you if you confess.'

Yates sat back in his chair and rolled up his sleeves. His once perplexed face turned stony. 'Who did he think he was to fire me? It was more my company than anybody else's, my computing and software know-how built it. The software is my baby. Who the hell did he think he was? He was never there. Swanning around like some international movie star. He'd made his fortune, and now he was standing in the way of me making mine. It wasn't right. You have no idea what he was like. He was an arrogant tosser through and through.'

'Plenty of those in the world. Why kill him?' said Rayner.

'I had no intention of killing him. I went to his boat to talk. What happened was his fault. His death was an accident.'

'Go on, we're listening,' I said.

'I heard Bonne was leaving the country and he'd delegated the task of getting rid of me to that useless prick Valentine. I couldn't have that; I'd borrowed heavily against the new house, so I went to his boat to talk to him. Bonne tried to turn me away but I convinced him that we needed to talk. At first things were cordial, but he wouldn't listen to reason. He kept banging on about trust and loyalty and theft.'

'That's when things got out of hand?' I said.

Yates scoffed. 'More than a little heated. He tried to throw me off the frigging boat. It was him that got physical. He got angry, really angry. He tried to manhandle me out of the cabin. He was pushing and shoving, trying to force me to get out. I was defending myself. I grabbed him and we fought. I ended up with my hands around his throat. I wanted him to pay attention to what I had to say, to stop talking and listen.'

'You strangled him to death?' said Rayner.

'I didn't mean to. I swear.'

'You then stole his laptop. You were trying to hide any trace that he wanted you fired, including emails he'd sent to Valentine.'

Yates closed his eyes and thought long and hard before he spoke again. 'I didn't know it was that easy to kill someone. I knew how it would look once the police were involved. I needed to make it look like an accident.'

'That's when you made it look like auto-erotic asphyxiation gone wrong.'

Yates nodded. 'He wouldn't be the first to accidentally die while choking himself for sexual pleasure.'

'Fingerprints were found on the trouser belt you put around his neck. Your fingerprints,' I explained.

'I was both angry with him for not listening to reason and scared of getting caught. At the time I wanted him humiliated, and to be discovered dead in that way was perfect.'

'You should have gone to the police,' I said.

'I know. Like I said, it was all an accident, unintentional. It all escalated so quickly. If he'd been reasonable, we could have all carried on making money.'

'Instead, Bonne is dead, and you'll probably spend several years locked up.'

'We'll see. I'll get myself a good lawyer. Off the top of my head, a plea of temporary insanity might be an option. With involuntary manslaughter I might get a couple of years. A good lawyer will work out a deal.'

I left the room leaving Rayner to formally arrest Yates. I

was exhausted and ready to get home to my family. They were the ones who grounded me. Reminded me there is so much good in the world and that it's still only a tiny proportion of people who ever encounter the worst side of human nature.

CHAPTER SEVENTY-FOUR

Declan lifted a Szechuan salt and pepper prawn with his chopstick and held it out for Emma to taste. 'You've got to try this, it's amazing.'

Emma took the prawn and popped it in her mouth. 'Mm, that is good. This is a great restaurant, I've never noticed it before.' She wore a silk scarf around her neck to cover bruising. Her lipstick and make-up did a good job of concealing the cuts and bruises on her face.

'It only opened about six months ago. It was recommended by someone at work. I asked if anyone knew anywhere local that would be good for a special occasion but not too expensive.'

'I like your style. I also like the way you sneakily upgraded what was meant to only be a drink to a meal in a restaurant.'

'After what you've been through you deserve it. As your friend, I wanted to do something special for you.' He raised his small glass of beer. 'To happier times.'

'Happier times,' said Emma. The pair of them clinked glasses and laughed. She was quiet for a moment and then said, 'If we do, you know, do this again, which I think could be a possibility, I want to take things slowly.'

Declan's face refused to hide his pleasure. 'I one-hundred percent agree. We take our time. Yes, definitely. Baby steps.'

'I'm serious,' said Emma. 'When I'm around you I feel I can be myself. That's important. I can't be something I'm not. The same goes for you. We need to be open and honest with each other. I want you to tell me if things aren't working out the way you imagined. I'm not as young as you; I can't waste years on something that's going nowhere. I want you to promise.'

'Wow. Heavy stuff.' He took a long sip of his beer. 'If you want me to be honest, I will. First off, forget the age thing, it's nothing. Secondly, I've been attracted to you for as long as I can remember. Everything about you. You're intelligent, confident and kind. And did I mention gorgeous? I love the way you talk, laugh, walk, the way you tuck your hair behind your ear when you're nervous, even when it doesn't need tucking. The way you bite your lip when you're thinking, like you're doing now.'

She stopped biting her lip and tucked her hair behind her ear.

'See, you just did it.' He put out his hand and held Emma's. With a finger he gently stroked a bruise on her wrist. 'I fell for you a long time ago. I tried dating other women but when I was with them I could only think about you. I agree we should take it slow. Not because I'm worried you and I might be a mistake, but because I want you to feel as happy as I am being here with you right now. Take as long as you need.'

Emma smiled with satisfaction. 'Excellent. With that out of the way, let's enjoy the evening. Another drink is in order. And more of those prawns?'

Declan got the waiter's attention and ordered more. 'You're smiling. Why are you smiling?'

'I'm just happy. Thank you for taking me out. It's just what I needed.'

They sat and talked until the restaurant closed, then walked the short distance home. It felt natural to share a first kiss before saying goodnight and going their separate ways.

CHAPTER SEVENTY-FIVE

I opened another bottle of wine, took a case of beer from the chiller and returned to the garden where I watched as Mum wagged a finger at Rayner. He put up his hands in mock surrender and with a booming laugh wrapped a giant arm around her tiny frame and gave her a hug. He swooped in to kiss her on the cheek but she shooed him away, almost knocking the bottle of beer out of his bear-like paws.

'You great idiot, get off,' she laughed. 'You're not too big for a clip around the ear, you know.'

Emma, Becky, Jenny and Monica were sitting on the garden chairs around a large glass-topped table. I glanced over at Monica who looked relaxed and happy. Her blood tests had come back looking good. She was to have regular check-up appointments and was under strict orders to take it easy.

Emma had arrived early and filled Monica and me in on the attack at her home. Mum was ready with her opinion on the sort of medieval punishment a man like that required. Despite what had clearly been a traumatic event she somehow seemed happier than I'd seen her in a while. She had the same twinkle in her eye that I recognised from the first time I met her.

The red wine I was opening was for Monica's parents, Frank and Gail, who had travelled up from their new home in Cornwall; they'd moved there recently to be closer to her.

Monica and Jenny were busy catching up while enjoying non-alcoholic grape juice.

Alice and Faith were in charge of the music and though I didn't recognise many of the tracks it was really adding to the celebratory vibe. They'd also made me put the fairy lights on in the garden even though it was only three o'clock in the afternoon.

I thought about Dad and how much he'd enjoyed our family gatherings. It was times like these that I most liked to remember him, he was such a great host, and put up with our ribbing him about his grilling skills. I had taken over the mantle of barbecue master and was doing my best to make sure I didn't let him down by burning the food – too much. Just a little, but not too much.

Though we hadn't mentioned work, some of us knew we were celebrating the end of the investigation. We had a result, and though it hadn't ended how any of us would have wanted, it was hard to complain.

I passed Rayner another bottle of beer and topped up Mum's red wine. I went to the dining table and poured Gail and Frank a glass of red, topped up Becky's and passed Emma a small glass of beer. I then raced back to the grill to turn the meat and veggie kebabs.

Rayner came over and joined me. He gave me a nudge that knocked me off balance. 'Whoops,' he said. He held up his beer and examined it. 'What's in these? It's gone straight to my head.'

'You're getting old, mate.'

'Rubbish!' He took a sausage straight from the grill and

began blowing on it to cool it down. I reached behind me and grabbed a hot dog roll.

'Here you go, you animal.'

He opened the bun, dropped in the sausage and put pretty much the whole thing in his mouth. Still chewing and barely able to speak he said, 'So?'

'So. What?'

'You can't pull the wool over my eyes. You're up to something.'

'What are you talking about?'

'I can see it. We've been mates since we were kids. I know when you're up to something, I just haven't figured out what it is. But you're *definitely* up to something.' He downed his bottle of beer and looked around for another. I pointed under the food table where I'd put the case of beer in the shade.

Mum came over and put her arm around me. 'Why don't we pop the food in the oven for a minute?'

'Good idea,' I said. 'Rayner senses something is afoot.'

Mum looked at Rayner who was down on his hands and knees pulling at the box of beer. Alice and Faith had spotted him and were attempting to climb on his back. 'Who is *that*?!' roared Rayner. The girls squealed and after hitting his head on the table while climbing out from under it he chased them.

'I'm surprised that boy can sense anything,' said Mum. We wrapped the food in foil and put it in the oven to keep warm.

We returned to the garden. Mum turned down the music then took Alice and Faith to one side and put her arms around them.

I helped Monica up, took Monica by the hand and led her onto the patio. I whispered to her, 'I'm just going to say a few words. Thank everyone for coming. That sort of thing.'

'That's a nice idea,' she said. She had no idea of my real motive.

I looked at the small group of family and friends, old and new, and felt excited and at peace. I started by thanking everyone for coming. I then moved on to the real reason I wanted everyone gathered. I called Alice and Faith over to be with me. Mum passed them cards we had prepared. We stood so everyone could see. Faith held onto her card and Alice passed me my two cards. Only we knew what was painted on them. The two girls were beaming.

'What's going on?' said Monica. She looked around at everyone and then back at me. Everyone shook their heads, even those who were in on it.

'Monica Reilly,' I said. 'At the darkest time of our lives you were there for us. A beacon of light, and of hope. You guided us back into the sunshine. You were by my side, by our side, to offer support, guidance, love, comfort and hope when I, we, needed it most. You have shown me how to love again. And I cannot imagine my life without you.'

Monica's teary eyes widened. She giggled along with Alice and Faith who were ready with their cards. 'What is this? Stop being so daft,' she said.

I nodded to Faith. She held up her card and read it out loud and clear, 'Will.'

Next was Alice, 'You.'

Then it was my turn. I got down on one knee and held up my cards and said, 'Marry me?' I put down the cards and held up the ring I had carried around for so long.

Monica gasped. I looked at her and she looked at me. For what felt like an eternity she was speechless. Then came her resounding, 'Yes!'

I jumped up and we kissed. Alice and Faith grabbed

hold of us and I crouched down and scooped them up to be with us.

I suddenly realised there was clapping and laughter and whooping.

Mum stood back and watched, her face full of joy, her hand on her heart.

Monica's parents came over and congratulated us. I shook Frank's hand and thanked him. Gail must have seen something pass between us. She looked at her husband and said, 'Did you know about all this?'

'I might have,' said Frank. There was pop of champagne as he opened a bottle he'd had stashed away.

* * *

That evening, after our guests had moved from the garden to the warmth of the sitting room, Monica cornered me in the kitchen. She held up her hand and admired her engagement ring. 'It's beautiful. You never cease to surprise me.'

'I do my best.' I took her hand and kissed it. 'You inspire me.'

I put my arm around her as she leaned against me and rested her head on my shoulder. 'We've come a long way, you and I. We've been through a lot.'

'We have. And it's made us stronger.' I looked down at Monica's tummy and our baby. 'I would also say we have plenty more adventures ahead of us.'

'Is the great Chief Inspector Hardy happy?'

I turned and looked at her to capture the moment. 'I've never been happier. I know I've said it many times but you saved me. I simply can't imagine my life without you.'

'You're such a softie. A little of a romantic too.'

'Sh! I have a tough guy image to maintain.' I turned my

head and pretended to look around as though someone might be eavesdropping.

She placed a hand on my chest. 'I won't tell a soul. So, what next?'

'Not a lot,' I quipped. 'We have a baby. Plan a wedding.'

'A wedding. That is a lot of work. You look excited by the prospect.'

'Are you kidding? I can't wait until you're Mrs Hardy.'

'I've been Mrs Hardy a long time. Just not in name.'

'You have, and it's time we made it official.'

We stood in the kitchen, held each other, and listened to our friends and family as they chatted and laughed in the next room. Without saying it we both knew this was a moment to cherish. I took her hand and the future Mrs Hardy led the way as we re-joined our loved ones.

Inspector Hardy will return in
Don't Go Home

If you would like to be kept up to date with new releases from Jay Gill, please complete an e-mail contact form on his Facebook page, @JayGillAuthor or website, www.jaygill.net

ABOUT THE AUTHOR

Born in Dorset, southern England, Jay Gill moved to Buckinghamshire where he worked in the printing industry, primarily producing leaflets and packaging for the pharmaceutical industry. After several years of the London commute, and with his first child about to start school, he realised it was high time for a change and moved back to the south coast of England. This change freed up time for him to write the detective stories he dreamed of one day publishing.

Safe to say, he's caught the writing bug in earnest now. With three Hardy novels and a novella under his belt, a growing "family" of characters both good and heinous, and a host of exciting new ideas bouncing around in his head, Jay busily juggles his writing and family life and is hard at work on the next instalment in the Chief Inspector James Hardy series of thrillers.

If you enjoyed *Killing Shadows*, please consider leaving a review online.

If you would like to be kept up to date with new releases from Jay Gill, please complete an e-mail contact form on his Facebook page, @JayGillAuthor or website, www.jay-gill.net

ACKNOWLEDGMENTS

I sincerely hope you enjoyed *Killing Shadows*. If this is the first time reading one of my books, thank you for giving me a try and if you're wondering which of my novels to read next, I would suggest *Knife & Death* which is the first DCI Hardy story. By going back to the beginning you'll understand Hardy better and realise just how far he and his family have come. If this isn't your first Hardy novel and you've followed the series, thank you for coming back, I promise there's much more to come.

With each novel I'm thinking about you, the reader, and how I can immerse you in the story, not just the twists and turns, but the way personalities behave and interact with one another. One of my greatest joys when writing is putting characters under pressure and seeing how they get on.

Each book is a collaboration.

Special thanks to my editor Loma, and my proofreader Linda, who knocked my manuscript into shape. Their hard work, knowledge and advice made this book far better than it might otherwise have been.

Thanks also to Yasemin Serpen for her advice on

midwifery and my many ante-natal questions. And, from a man who doesn't know his port from his poop deck, thanks to Dave Street, Jeremy Stephens, Joe Coleshill for their boating expertise.

A whopping thumbs-up 'Like' to my Facebook group (facebook.com/groups/JayGill) for your constant encouragement and enthusiasm. Hearing your love for Hardy and friends keeps me going — *you're all fantastic!*

My advance reader group grew substantially for this book and I'd like to thank each and every one of you for taking the time to read the un-proofread copy and (fortunately) reporting back that you loved the story. *Phew!*

I'd like to dedicate this book to one of my oldest readers, Rita Hopkins, a close family friend and champion of my writing, who recently sadly passed away at the age of ninety-one.

And finally, special thanks and love go to my family for putting up with my early mornings and late nights behind a laptop. I'm doing it all for you... no, really, I am.

THE INSPECTOR HARDY SERIES

Knife & Death

Walk in the Park

Angels

Hard Truth

Inferno

Killing Shadows

Don't Go Home

Printed in Great Britain
by Amazon

50869501R00201